THE LADY'S DANGEROUS LOVE

LANGLEY SISTERS

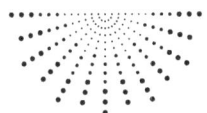

WENDY VELLA

The Lady's Dangerous Love is a work of fiction. Names, places, and incidents either are products of the author's imagination or are used fictitiously.

The Lady's Dangerous Love is published by Wendy Vella

Copyright © 2019 Wendy Vella

OTHER BOOKS BY WENDY VELLA

Historical Romances

Regency Rakes Series
Duchess By Chance
Rescued By A Viscount
Tempting Miss Allender

The Langley Sisters Series
Lady In Disguise
Lady In Demand
Lady In Distress
The Lady Plays Her Ace
The Lady Seals Her Fate
The Lady's Dangerous Love

The Raven & Sinclair Series
Sensing Danger
Seeing Danger
Touched By Danger
Scent Of Danger
Vision Of Danger

The Lords Of Night Street Series
Lord Gallant
Lord Valiant
Lord Valorous

Lord Noble

The Haddon Brothers
The Earl's Encounter

Stand-Alone Titles
The Reluctant Countess
Christmas Wishes
The Earl's Encounter

Contemporary Romances

The Lake Howling Series
A Promise Of Home
The Texan Meets His Match
How Sweet It Is
It Only Took You
Don't Look Back
A Long Way Home

The Ryker Falls Series
Somebody To Love
From This Moment
Love Me Tender

Larry

*"When I come to the end of the road
And the sun has set for me
I want no rites in a gloom filled room
Why cry for a soul set free?"
-Christina Rossetti*

CHAPTER ONE

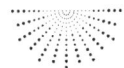

"Primrose Ainsley would make an ideal wife for you, Ben."

"I don't want a wife, Phoebe."

Benjamin Hetherington fought the urge to loosen his necktie at his sister-in-law's words, but as his arms were currently trapped by the women at his sides, he could do nothing but endure their lectures.

"But she is perfect, Ben. Sweet natured, and every inch a lady."

"How do you know she is perfect? The woman never says a word. I have yet to hear her conversing at length with anyone. She could be Russian or Egyptian for all I know."

"Don't be ridiculous, you know that is not true. She is a lovely young lady with a rich intellect," Hannah said. "She's humorous and speaks in melodious tones."

"Well there you go, then. I want a wife who barks like a bullfrog."

"Why are you fighting this? You have to wed, and she would be the perfect wife for you," Phoebe added.

"And I repeat, I have no wish for a wife."

He'd been foolish enough to accept the invitation delivered by his sisters-in-law to walk with them through the gardens at Rossetter House, where they were at present attending a house party.

Just a stroll, Ben, as dear Hannah needs the exercise. Her belly looks like an overripe melon now.

Phoebe certainly had a way with words.

To his right walked Phoebe, Lady Levermarch. Married to his eldest brother, Finn, she was something of a force a nature. A rare beauty who made men's heads turn and jaws drop. With her honey-blonde hair and curvaceous figure she could fool any man into thinking she was sweet and biddable —to their peril—should she wish it.

To his left walked his twin brother Alex's wife, Hannah. Hers was a different beauty to Phoebe's but equally as disturbing to men. With her porcelain skin and raven hair, she looked like a doll. What she actually was, was equally as opinionated and determined as Phoebe. However, she was also due to have her first child in four months, which had made her emotional and at times irrational... or so Alex had told him.

"But we wish for you to be as happy as us, Ben."

"I am happy, thank you, Hannah."

He thought about his brothers, who were likely playing billiards or reading somewhere in the huge mansion at their backs. He should have found them instead of agreeing to this walk.

Shooting Rossetter House a look, he noted the flags fluttering high up on the turrets. Ben liked to imagine those who had walked the great halls before him. Who had stomped the exact paths he had?

I bet they weren't being hounded as I am.

"Primrose Ainsley is lovely. I spoke at length with her and Lady Jane, who is sponsoring her this season, yesterday and she told me she is a capable young woman. She plays the piano and sings well, and I believe is something of an expert gardener."

"Another thing we do not have in common. I can't tell the difference between a rose and ragwort."

"She's a little older also, which would suit you as she has no silly ways."

"And I repeat, Phoebe, I have no wish for a wife, and definitely not one like Primrose Ainsley, who is as interesting to me as… as Lady Blain's latest gout-swollen toe. Plus there is her smile."

"What is wrong with her smile?"

"It's not genuine. Besides, were I to take a wife, I would wish for a young woman to mold to my every wish," he said bluntly, only to put them off. He really didn't care how old Primrose Ainsley was. He was also not that callous he would expect someone to change for him. "Now please, when and if the time comes, I shall find my own wife, *never*, so this matter is at an end, thank you." Ben hadn't meant to raise his voice, but there had been a definite snap to it. Not that it would deter these two women. Tenacity was etched in their souls.

"Oh dear."

"What?" He looked at Hannah, who had stopped. Her body was turned slightly as she stared at something over her shoulder. Ben turned, and his heart plummeted to his toes. There stood Primrose Ainsley. Pale-faced, her eyes seemed huge, and her bottom lip was trapped between her teeth.

Christ!

"Miss Ainsley." He released his sisters-in-law and started toward her. "Please allow me to—"

"I have no wish to be your wife, sir!"

Before he could reach her or speak in his defense, she'd hurried around him and was running down the path.

"Really, Ben!" Hannah scolded him. "Gout-swollen toe is all you could come up with… and in such a loud voice."

He felt suddenly ill.

"Well, go after her, you fool!" Phoebe's words were accompanied by a hard shove in the back.

"I can't go after her if she's alone!"

"We shall follow. Now make haste before you lose sight of her. Really, Ben, that was very shabby of you to speak that way." She pointed a finger to where Primrose Ainsley was disappearing.

"Bloody hell, all right. But may I point out that this is entirely your fault… both of you. Had you not been hounding me, then I would not have been forced to speak as I did."

"You could have done so in a more diplomatic manner," Hannah snapped.

He didn't wait to hear more, instead taking the shell path in pursuit of the fleeing Miss Ainsley.

Picking up the pace, he reached the end in time to watch her climb over a stile and disappear into the trees that bordered the gardens.

"If you will give me a moment, Miss Ainsley, I shall attempt to remove my foot from my mouth!" he called out to her.

She ignored him, picked up her skirts, and started running in earnest.

Ben was momentarily shocked. He'd never seen the woman do anything that wasn't considered correct. Picking up her skirts and flashing her ankles did not fall into that category. Most evenings, Primrose Ainsley was seen blending into the walls of any ballroom, about as enticing as bread pudding.

Cursing his sisters-in-law again, Ben climbed the stile and followed. Silly girl; he'd find her weeping piteously against the trunk of a tree, and have to apologize profusely for something he hadn't meant to do. Perhaps he'd thought it, but it had been unpardonably rude of him to say it out loud.

The problem was, Phoebe and Hannah had been at him for months now to marry, and he was heartily sick of it. He didn't like to think of himself as mean, but he had been to say such a thing out loud. Anyone could have been in hearing distance—and as it turned out, had been.

"Bloody bothering hell."

He didn't want to marry, and that was the fact of the matter, but they were determined.

He followed her into the trees and over another stile. Where the hell was she going? He'd probably find her with a turned ankle and have to carry her back to the house.

He'd just about made the decision to return to the house, when the trees overhead thinned, and he walked into a small sun-filled clearing. Before him was a pond, and it was there he found Miss Ainsley—well actually, he found her shoes and bonnet first.

Looking at the pale peach slippers, Ben thought they would be no bigger than the length of his hand. A straw bonnet sat beside them, and a pair of white gloves. The owner was standing ankle-deep in water with her back to him.

"Miss Ainsley, allow me to apologize."

"Go away, Mr. Hetherington."

"I should not have spoken as I did."

"I have no wish to hear what you have to say, and as my skirts are raised and my feet are bare, it is compromising for you to be out here with me alone. Especially considering your abhorrence for me."

Her hair was pale, a mixture of honey and ash-blonde blended to make a pretty head of hair pinned into a simple bun. She wore cream, and a row of buttons ran the length of her spine. Above that he saw her pale skin. A few freckles were dotted here and there, and Ben wasn't sure why the sight of her bent head and exposed neck made something clench inside him, but it did. He thought she looked lost and vulnerable standing out there in the water alone. His guilt magnified.

You're an ass, Benjamin.

"Come out of the water, Miss Ainsley, and allow me to walk you back to the house."

"I have no wish to spend time in your company, Mr. Hetherington, nor did I ask you to like me. You know nothing about me and yet felt it acceptable to say what you did in public. I do not want to spend time with such a man, so please leave."

It surprised him that she was speaking in such a forthright manner, because while all of what she said was true, he'd danced with her a handful of times and she'd barely uttered two words, and those usually about the weather.

"I rarely take the time to talk to young women, Miss Ainsley. If I did, their mothers would have me betrothed in a matter of days."

"Yes, I could see all that adoration must be taxing on you."

Was that sarcasm?

He couldn't tell, as her eyes were still on the water.

"Come out of the water, Miss Ainsley."

"It would take me a positive age to do so, considering my advanced years, so I shall just stay where I am, thank you."

"Look, if you will just let me explain—"

"What I want is for you to leave."

"Come out of the water, please."

"No."

"Then I shall come in."

"What?" Shock had her turning to face him. He caught a glimpse of pink cheeks and wide blue eyes. He'd never thought her pretty; actually, he'd never really thought about her at all, because… well, because she was just there, like any number of pink-cheeked, eager young ladies every night he walked into a society function.

"If you do not come out, then I will be forced to come in and get you."

"Why, for pity's sake? We loathe each other, and I am harming no one standing here ankle-deep in water. Go and flirt with someone, Mr. Hetherington, or at the very least find someone who does not remind you of a gout-swollen toe!"

"I do not loathe you, and I am not having this conversation or begging your forgiveness while you are standing ankle-deep in water. Come out here, Miss Ainsley, and allow me to explain my behavior."

"No. Now go away before someone sees us together."

"Very well, you leave me no choice." He began to wrestle off his boots, no easy task. His valet usually did this, and he was forced to hop about the place.

"Oh, for pity's sake, Mr. Hetherington, I said stop!"

"No." More hopping and some grunting as he tugged on the boot.

"Then I shall leave."

Ben managed to pull off one boot before looking at her. To his horror, she'd walked deeper into the water; it was now past her knees. She had given up holding her skirts and they now puffed out in the water around her.

"What are you doing?"

"Leaving."

"How? You are facing the wrong way!" His voice had risen to a roar as fear gripped him.

"Good day to you, Mr. Hetherington."

Ben watched her move deeper into the water; it was at her waist now. "It's too deep. Stop at once, or you'll drown!"

He stepped into the water, but as he did, she disappeared under it.

"Christ!" She'd drown if he didn't get to her soon. Ignoring the boot, he ran in, heart pounding. Taking a large breath, he dived under and struck out. Opening his eyes, he looked for her but saw nothing. Rising to take a breath, he prepared to go under once more, but a glimpse of cream had him stopping. Miss Ainsley was now on the opposite side of the pond.

"You fool!" he bellowed, treading water. "What the bloody hell were you thinking!"

She climbed up the bank as agilely as a cat. He then watched as she shook herself. Her dress was now plastered to her, and if he hadn't been so bloody furious he would have taken a moment to acknowledge she had a surprisingly lovely body.

"Answer me, damn you!"

Long blonde hair had come free of its pins and trailed down her back in a sleek waterfall. She looked like a sea nymph… a luscious sea nymph, he thought, running his eyes over her.

"You're mad!" he shouted. "Crazed," he added so she understood he was furious. "Addled in the head!"

"Yet another reason for you to abhor me then! Good day to you, Mr. Hetherington, and just so we are clear, I have no wish to be your wife… ever! Good riddance." The last was muttered, but Benjamin had exceptional hearing.

She did not look at him again, instead simply walked away, leaving him in the middle of the pond with God knew what beneath him. He hoped there were no eels; Ben didn't like those.

Shaking his head when Miss Ainsley's retreating figure had disappeared, he swam back to the bank. He had no idea what had just happened, but one thing he did realize was that there was a great deal more to Miss Primrose Ainsley than he'd originally believed.

Squelching out of the water, he wrestled off his second boot, then emptied it and sat to replace them both. Regaining his feet, Ben picked up her shoes and bonnet, then skirted the pond and followed her back to the house.

Tonight, Ben thought. Tonight he would make sure he was seated beside Primrose Ainsley for their evening meal, and he would spend the entire event making her extremely uncomfortable, just as he now was.

CHAPTER TWO

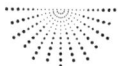

"*G*ood Lord, why are you all wet, Primrose?"

"I fell in the pond while trying to fish out a lily."

Virginia, Lady Jane tsked. "Of course there was some kind of flora or fauna involved. Well, I hope no one saw you."

"No, I ran back and slipped inside undetected through a side door."

"I shall call for a bath."

"Thank you."

Primrose began removing her sodden clothes while she thought about what she'd done. That loathsome Mr. Hetherington had started it all. Horrid man. How dared he say she was as interesting as Lady Blain's latest gout-swollen toe? He didn't even know her.

"Turn, and I shall undo the buttons. The dress is quite ruined, I fear."

Guilt thickened as Lady Jane proceeded to help her undress.

She was one of Primrose's mother's oldest friends. Widowed, she was still a formidable society matron, and had

THE LADY'S DANGEROUS LOVE

agreed when Primrose's mother had asked her to sponsor her daughter for a season. All of Primrose's protests had got her nowhere. She was having a season no matter how much she wished for the opposite.

"It is just as well we purchased more gowns for you upon your arrival in London, Primrose."

"Thank you for doing so."

Primrose knew she'd become a burden to her parents, and they certainly let her know often enough how the extra expenditure was unwelcome. They were botanists, along with her brother, John. All had vocations that drove them to spend months travelling to far-off places; any and all spare money was set aside for that. They had no wish to waste it on her.

Primrose had never quite been struck down with the same fever for exploration as her family. Yes, she loved flora and fauna, but she had no wish to write about them or travel to far-off places to dig up rare species. Thus, she and her family had nothing in common.

It had been a relief to them when Lady Jane had taken Primrose off their hands so they could focus all their time on what they really loved.

It was said that one never heard anything good about oneself by listening in on a conversation uninvited. She'd realized that much was true the day she'd listened to her mother and Lady Jane talk before they were due to leave for London.

"Yes, well, we shall hope to achieve a desired match for Primrose, Posie," Lady Jane had said to her mother. *"Of course, with very little by way of a dowry and considering she is twenty-five, it will be difficult, but I shall give it my best shot."*

Her mother had said she would be grateful, as they were due to leave for India in one month's time and would like

Primrose settled in a marriage before they came back, instead of lolling about the place.

She'd never lolled a day in her life.

She'd felt like an unwanted weed that had been ripped from the earth. But Primrose had not let on that she'd overheard. Instead she said goodbye to her family and left Hollyhock Cottage, the only home she had ever known, without a backward glance or tear in her eye.

"I want you to experience what I had, Primrose," her mother had told her before she left. She'd come to her room and sat on her bed, which had been a shock, as Posie Ainsley did not have a maternal bone in her body. *"Make the most of it, and don't give Lady Jane any trouble. This is your chance to secure a future for yourself. Enjoy it like I did."*

From where Primrose had been sitting at the time, directly beside her mother, she hadn't thought those years in society had been comfortable ones for her. Posie had run away with Primrose's father and been banished from her family. Primrose, however, had kept those thoughts to herself. One did not argue with Posie Ainsley and come out a winner.

"Don't bungle this," her father had said with a peck on her forehead.

"We need you to do this right, Primpy," her brother had said, using the nickname Primrose had always loathed. *"It will make life easier for everyone."*

But that was the rub, really. Money from a wealthy husband would indeed make their lives better. They could use anything she sent them in the pursuit of their quests, and Primrose leaving would be one mouth less to feed.

"Frowning is flattering on no one," Lady Jane said.

"Sorry," Primrose mumbled as she began to wash herself.

"Neither is mumbling."

"Sorry," she added in a louder voice.

The problem was, she didn't really like London. She was forced to be a lady there, which she loathed, and conform to any number of rules that society placed on their young ladies. Primrose lived in fear that at any moment she would commit a horrendous faux pas that would have her run out of town. At least here at Rossetter House she could breathe the country air and spend time outside exploring.

"Honestly, Primrose, how many times have we discussed this. You cannot grovel about in the dirt and dig up flowers now. You are not at home anymore. How can we hope to secure you a husband if your fingernails are continually dirty?"

"I shall wear my gloves."

"That's all very well, but you must try harder."

"I know, and I am sorry, Lady Jane."

A large woman with thick silver hair that was wrestled ruthlessly into an elegant creation daily, she was a stickler for living by the rules society set. Lady Jane had strong opinions on everything. Primrose had been terrified of her when first they met, but she'd soon realized that beneath that exterior was a gentle heart.

"Yes, well, enough said on that. Now we must hurry, as we are to walk into Two Oaks with a small party. We shall find you a new bonnet to replace the one you lost in the pond."

Primrose knew refusal was futile, so she sank lower in the water. It wasn't chilly, but still, she was cold from her impromptu swim.

"There are only four weeks left of the season, Primrose. Something must be done to secure you a husband, and I believe I have the solution to that problem up my sleeve."

Her heart sank. "Dare I ask what?"

Lady Jane tapped her nose but said nothing as she went to instruct the maid on which dress Primrose would be wearing for their walk.

WENDY VELLA

She did not know much about Mr. Hetherington, only that he had a twin brother and another who was a viscount. He was connected to many well-associated people with whom he spent time in the ballrooms of society most evenings. He was also a fiend... a vulgar, ill-mannered one.

"Lady Levermarch commented to me just this morning what a lovely young lady you are, Primrose."

"That's very nice of her."

"Indeed it is, and she is a powerful woman in society. I'm quite sure she thinks you will make a wonderful match for her brother-in-law, Mr. Hetherington."

Primrose choked on air. She started coughing so hard, the maid had to bring her a drink to stop it.

"I'm sure that cannot be right, Lady Jane," she managed to wheeze when she could speak again. "He is a highly sought-after man, and I am simply a—a nobody. Plus, as you have stated, there is the matter of my dowry—or lack thereof—and advanced years."

"You are also the granddaughter of an earl, Primrose, please do not forget that. Your mother turned her back on her family, marrying your father, but you can still use the connection."

Never, she vowed. Her mother's family had never spoken to their daughter again after she left.

"And Mr. Benjamin Hetherington has no need of marrying for money, Primrose. He is quite wealthy in his own right."

"How lucky for him," she said under her breath when Lady Jane walked away again.

Primrose let her eyes wander around the room she had slept in since arriving. Twice the size of the one she had in Hollyhock Cottage, it had windows facing the parklike grounds and a bed so large that she needed to roll several times to get from one side to the other. The furnishings were lavender and pale blue. The floor had a thick rug that she liked to walk over with no shoes on, as her feet sank into it.

"Now stop woolgathering, and let's get you dressed."

"Yes, Lady Jane."

Her hair was washed thoroughly by Melanie, the maid who had been tasked with looking after Primrose. About her age, they had got along from the start. Both were country girls, and both missed their homes. Melanie also missed her family, but Primrose didn't. She missed her family's staff, however.

Thirty minutes later she was dressed in a pale blue creation that Lady Jane said brought out the beauty of her eyes. Her hair was twisted and pinned, which to Primrose seemed a waste of time as she would be wearing a bonnet, but as she had no say in the matter she kept her mouth shut.

Of course, she understood that she was honored to have such an opportunity, and she always made sure Lady Jane understood she was grateful, even if in her heart all she wanted was to return home.

Maybe her home life was not filled with love, but that house was hers alone for so many months of the year when her family packed up and left to visit some rare species of something. Hers, and the two servants who looked after them. Mr. and Mrs. Putts were more like her parents than her actual ones.

At Hollyhock Cottage she could spend hours in her gardens, tending mundane plants like daisies and hocks.

There was also Herbert.

"Come along, Primrose."

Following Lady Jane through the halls of Rossetter House, Primrose had to admit that not all parts of her foray into society were bad. Indeed, some of them were more than tolerable.

There were the gardens, of course, and the small stash of

cuttings Lady Jane's gardener nurtured for her. The grand houses were also a wonder. She loved seeing all the things on display and the beautiful furnishings. Plus, somewhere in this house was *the* book. The last remaining copy of Lucian Clipper's renowned work published in 1532, simply titled *The History Of Plants.*

Oh, to see that book. To read the pages of the master. Her mother often quoted Lucian Clipper as the reason she loved botany. She'd attended many lectures during her time in London, and Clipper had been quoted often. This love, she had passed on to her daughter.

Primrose's reasons for wanting to see the book were entirely different from those of her family. She wanted to see the pictures, see the lilies and poppies that he'd painted.

"Primrose, I have asked you the same question twice!"

"Forgive me, Lady Jane, I must have water in my ears."

This was her first house party, and Rossetter was spectacular, and so old that she wanted to spend time exploring. She hoped to do that when Lady Jane napped in the afternoons.

"Good day." The Duke of Rossetter walked toward them.

"Duke." The older lady sank into a curtsey, and Primrose followed. Tall and distinguished, he gave the appearance of being a perfect fit for his title. He even had graying hair at the temples.

Primrose had spoken with him on her first night here. They had conversed briefly about the gardens, and she'd confessed her love of plants. He'd told her to walk where she wished, that the grounds were hers to explore. Primrose had liked him very much after that.

"Are you to walk into Two Oaks, ladies?"

"Indeed we are," Lady Jane said.

A shriek erupted from down the hallway.

"Sophie, do not run!" the duke roared.

Alas, his warning was not heeded, and the next moment a

little blonde-haired girl came barreling toward them with what looked to be a kite in her hands.

"Out of the three of them, this child will be the death of me," the duke muttered, striding away from them to reach her in two long paces. "I have told you not to run in here, sweetheart. I have no wish for you to break hundred-year-old antiques, as your mother will be displeased."

Primrose watched as he leaned down and scooped up his daughter, placing a loud kiss on her cheek. The gesture was genuine and spoke of his affection for the girl.

Never having been loved, Primrose often wondered what the feeling was like. It never really bothered her unless she saw displays like the one before her. Then she got a sharp pain under her ribs.

"Lady Jane, Miss Ainsley, may I introduce my daughter Sophie to you."

"She is beautiful." Primrose smiled at the little girl. Dressed in pink, she was like a bundle of sweetness. "Hello, Sophie." Leaning in, she took a tiny hand and shook it, making the child smile. "It is lovely to meet you."

"What's your name?"

"Primrose. Do you like it?"

The little girl nodded, then urged her father to lower her to the floor. The duke wrestled the kite from her first.

"Can I walk with you?"

"Please," the duke prompted.

"Please."

"Of course, if that is all right with your father?" Primrose replied.

"Of course." The duke's smile turned him into something different. No longer austere, he simply looked like a doting father.

They let Lady Jane and the duke go first, as they would be slower. Holding out a gloved hand, Primrose enjoyed the feeling of Sophia's fingers slipping into hers. She missed her time spent with the local children in her village, teaching them to read and write and the walks they'd taken together. This wasn't her world, but one she would endure, briefly. The lance of longing was constant inside her when she thought of home.

Sophie chattered the entire walk down the stairs and outside into the sunshine, talking about her dolls and her siblings.

A small group had gathered ready for the walk into Two Oaks, and Primrose was not pleased to see Mr. Hetherington was one of them. She stiffened as he detached from those he was speaking with and came to meet them.

"Hello, Sophie."

To her surprise, he dropped to his haunches and greeted the little girl first. The early afternoon sun bounced off his hair, turning it to bronze. His jacket was black this afternoon, and the waistcoat gray with black stripes. Gray breeches stretched to accommodate muscular thighs, and his large feet were in black boots polished to perfection. Primrose wondered if, like her gown, his clothes had been ruined after a dunking this morning.

"'Lo, Ben."

"Where are you taking Miss Ainsley, Sophie?"

"For a walk."

"It's a lovely day for a walk, just as it would be for a swim."

Primrose felt a dull flush of heat fill her cheeks at his words.

"I like to swim, but I can't if an adult is not with me."

"Yes, I can see that would be important, Sophie. Swimming is indeed a serious business, and one that you must not rush into without thought."

He was saying those words deliberately.

Mr. Hetherington then rose to his feet, and was now only a matter of a few feet from Primrose.

"Come along, daughter, we have a kite to fly, and your brother and sister are likely stomping from foot to foot with impatience." The duke once again picked up Sophie. "My wife will be accompanying you all. Please have a nice trip," he said to the group of milling people, and then he was striding off and disappeared around the house.

"Miss Ainsley." Mr. Hetherington bowed before her. "How has your stay at Rossetter been so far?"

Primrose came to a startling realization as she stood before him. She no longer had to have impeccable manners around this man, as he had made it clear he would never be interested in her, and after what he'd said about her earlier, there was no way she would be interested in him either. Of course, she couldn't be rude, Lady Jane would find out, but she didn't have to subdue her normal nature around him. It was a liberating thought.

"Well, as to that, sir, I had an unsavory encounter with a rodent earlier today. I was forced to take evasive measures and flee. It was quite terrifying."

Rather than be insulted, a genuine smile lit his brown eyes. Actually, they were more treacle than just plain brown. White teeth flashed, and she found a small indent on the right cheek. He was already handsome, just as Laura Tomley and several other young ladies had told her—repeatedly, and in detail, when they thought it not beneath them to converse with her—but that smile added a little something extra.

"Really?" He leaned his weight on one leg while he studied her, and Primrose was very aware of the fact that Lady Jane and some of the other guests were watching them closely. He did not appear overly concerned that she had just compared him to a rodent, but then surely, as he'd compared her to a gout-swollen toe, the insult was warranted.

"Yes. But never fear, I am sure it will not bother me again."

"You were forced to take evasive measures, Miss Ainsley. How drastic."

"In the extreme."

He leaned in to make sure no one else overheard them.

"What you did was reckless and foolhardy, Miss Ainsley, and you were lucky to escape unscathed."

She inhaled him, and the scent was crisp and sharp in her nostrils. She refused to admit it only added to the impact of this man up close. Big and solid of form, he carried his clothes well, and yet sometimes, like now, there was a slight malfunction to his wardrobe. She'd noticed them the few times she'd watched him.

Primrose spent a lot of time skulking in corners of society gatherings watching people.

"Your collar is turned in."

"What?" He blinked, and she thought how unfair it was that his eyelashes were longer than hers, and that his brows, although thick, had a lovely curve. Primrose's were straight.

"Your collar." Primrose pointed. "It's turned under on the edge."

He lifted a hand and flicked it out.

"Better?"

Primrose refused to match his smile.

"I would hate for you to suffer ridicule, Mr. Hetherington," Primrose lied with a false smile.

"How exceptionally kind of you, Miss Ainsley."

"We would not want your legion of admirers to see you looking less than perfect." I do not enjoy sparring verbally with this man, Primrose told herself.

"Let's go then, Ben." Mr. Hetherington's brother came to his side; Mr. Alexander Hetherington. She knew they were twins because Laura had told her that too. They shared a smile, and something around the eyes, but not a great deal else. Alexander Hetherington was blond and always dressed elegantly in the latest fashions. His hair was rarely out of place, and he even walked with a certain style. His wife was beautiful, and together they made an imposing picture.

"Alex, allow me to introduce you to Miss Ainsley."

"Hello." He bowed, and Primrose dipped into a curtsey. "How lovely to meet you. Surprisingly, I don't believe we have before?"

"No, this is the first time," Primrose said. She was not a person who moved in elevated circles in society, nor one who instigated conversation. In fact, most evenings she hid in a corner hoping no man would take an interest in her.

Looking at Lady Jane, she noted the woman was watching the encounter. Primrose needed to get away from these men before Lady Jane decided a match was in the making between her and Mr. Benjamin Hetherington, which it definitely was not!

"We are not walking into Two Oaks," Mr. Alexander Hetherington said, much to her relief. "So we will bid you good day. I hope your shopping trip is a pleasant one, Miss Ainsley."

"Watch out for rodents, Miss Ainsley," Benjamin Hetherington said with a wicked smile.

"Why does she need to watch out for them?" His brother frowned.

"She had an encounter with one this morning. A nasty experience, I believe."

"Really? I'm sorry to hear that."

Primrose wanted to smack the laughter off Benjamin Hetherington's face.

"It's quite all right, Mr. Hetherington," she said to his brother. "As it turns out, the rodent was somewhat dim-witted, and I outmaneuvered it."

"Excellent. Well, brother, we must be off." Alexander Hetherington shot her a look that suggested she was not quite right in the head, which suited her just fine.

Primrose exhaled slowly in relief as the brothers then bowed and walked away.

"Mr. Benjamin Hetherington seems quite taken with you, Primrose," Lady Jane said, moving to her side.

"No, he is just being polite. He found me searching for hellebore seeds and asked what I was doing." Primrose was congratulating herself silently for throwing Lady Jane off the scent.

Then she spoke.

"I thought hellebore grew in the winter months?"

"There are many different varieties," Primrose said quickly.

"Yes, well, I think you're wrong about the unattached Mr. Hetherington. In fact, I think he is quite interested in you," she added. "So stop grubbing about in the earth and focus on getting him to marry you."

Botheration!

CHAPTER THREE

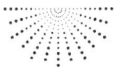

"She seems nice, if a little odd."

"Who?"

Alex made a noise in his throat.

"You know bloody well who. Miss Ainsley. That rodent comment was strange though, don't you think?"

"Hmm." Ben made the appropriate noise.

She had seemed nice actually, a great deal nicer than he'd thought her yesterday or this morning, but that was only because now that his temper had cooled, he could see there was a great deal of backbone to Miss Primrose Ainsley. A woman did not simply dive fully clothed into the water without a great deal of strength to their character... unless she was insane. Either way, she intrigued him, as prim and proper young ladies did not do such things—even if they were done to avoid him, which, while hardly flattering, had been understandable and taken courage.

He didn't think she was insane, as her lovely blue eyes were certainly clear enough and lit with an intelligence Benjamin had been guilty of not seeing earlier.

"She barely speaks," he said, which actually wasn't true, as she'd spoken quite clearly to him just then. In fact, she'd called him a rodent.

"Nerves, very likely. I believe Hannah told me Lady Jane is sponsoring her for a season. Can't be easy, leaving your family and entering society. Then there's the fact that young ladies can be ruthlessly vindictive to those they see as beneath them."

"What the hell does that mean?"

"She's here at the charity of Lady Jane, Ben. Surely you understand all the connotations that come with that? Plus, she's older than the other debutantes."

Ben thought about that and took a few seconds to come up with the right answer.

"Hannah made you understand that. There is no way you would be that aware," Ben said.

"Possibly. But the point is, life cannot have been a chocolate eclair for Miss Ainsley."

A chocolate eclair was the highest form of confectionery excellence as far as Alex was concerned.

"Perhaps."

They wandered along yet another path—Rossetter was littered with them—and around the house. Finn had several amazing estates, but this was something special. Age, Ben thought. The age of this place gave it so much character and strength. History was etched in the walls here.

"Ben, what are you not telling me?"

Having a twin was both a blessing and a curse. The blessing came in having someone who knew him as well as he knew himself. A person who was in his corner no matter the circumstance. Alex was his confidant, as he was Alex's. They were two halves of a whole and always had been. That hadn't changed with his brother's marriage to Hannah.

The curse was that he could hide nothing from him.

"Let's hear it." Alex waved a hand about and made that

clucking sound with his tongue that Ben loathed. In fact, he hated the noise so much he'd bloodied his twin's nose over it several times in their lifetime.

"Desist!" Ben snapped. Alex continued.

"It is hardly my fault that certain noises make you uncomfortable. I mean, who can't stand it when someone crunches their food, or achieves a certain pitch? They are not the actions of a well-balanced person."

Ben shrugged. It had always been thus for him. He hated certain noises, and crunching and rustling were two of them. As an adult he'd simply accepted the fact it was a foolish problem and dealt with it in his own way… often by surreptitiously sticking a finger in one ear.

"It's my only abnormality, unlike you," Ben said. "You have the thing with your toes."

"One toe sitting on top of another one is not an abnormality, it's originality."

"You're certainly original," Ben agreed. "And as we speak, another one of you is forming. The thought makes me shudder."

"Makes me shudder, too. Hannah is unreasonable most days, but now…."

Ben laughed.

"Now, tell me about Miss Ainsley before we reach the others," Alex added.

"Very well, and I do not need to tell you to keep this to yourself."

Alex hooked his little finger around Ben's as he raised it. They had completed this particular ritual many, many times since its conception when they were aged five years.

He told Alex what had transpired between him and Miss Ainsley earlier.

"And she just dove under the water with her dress on?"

"Yes."

"Good God, surely they are not the actions of a sane woman? But then, that does explain the rodent comment."

They were walking to where their eldest brother and some of the other male guests were assembling. Fencing was the activity of the day, which Ben was not bad at, but his brothers were annoyingly better.

"Are you telling me that Hannah or Phoebe would not have done the same given provocation?"

"You have a point there, but it is not something one expects a debutante to do."

"Yes, you can imagine what I thought when she went under the water. I had visions of her drowning and me having to carry her body out."

"But then in her defense, you had just likened her to a gout-swollen toe, and not just any toe but one that belongs to that tartar Lady Blain."

"There is that."

They walked in silence as they often did, not needing a constant flow of words to communicate.

"It was extremely bad of you to call her a gout-swollen toe, brother, but given that you were in the company of my wife and Finn's, I understand the provocation. Were they attempting to pressure you into marrying someone?"

"Not someone. Miss Ainsley."

Alex whistled. "Are you interested in her, Ben?"

The jolt that went through him was not pleasant. How could he be interested in someone he had rarely conversed with, and when he had it was about the weather? Plus, there was the small fact that he'd vowed never to marry.

The problem was, she'd shown him another side to her personality today. A window into her character. Spirit was not often something he saw in a debutante. He wasn't interested in her, but still she was intriguing.

"No."

"Not every woman is like our mother, Ben. Some can actually be trusted."

"I know that." Ben loathed his mother. "I have to admit that when you see a woman do what Miss Ainsley did, it is intriguing."

Alex grunted his agreement.

"Before today I thought her an insipid, timid creature."

"Which is beneath you, as we both know that what we see each evening is not necessarily the entire picture. Young women are molded into what we see in society; they are not often born that way."

Ben sighed. "You're thinking of both Phoebe and Hannah, aren't you?"

"Finn misjudged Phoebe, and I may have done the same with Hannah… a bit, but only briefly."

"You've always hated criticism, even if it's you giving it to… you."

"That's because the majority of the time I'm perfect."

"Says who?" Ben snorted. "Your wife tells me regularly that you have a great many flaws."

Alex smiled, that annoying, secretive smile that people in love sometimes wore.

"She is a truly exceptional, if slightly annoying, woman, my wife."

Alex stopped suddenly. His eyes were on the small gathering of men a short distance away.

"Christ, do you see Panchurch? Man's a blithering idiot."

Ben searched the milling men, and found Lord Panchurch. Dressed in snow-white breeches and shirt, his waistcoat was made up of black and lilac diamond shapes, and he was dashing forward and back like a headless chicken.

"What is he doing?"

"Practicing."

"For what?" Ben asked. "A new dance, perhaps?"

Their brother, Viscount Levermarch, Lord William Ryder, Mr. Oliver Dillinger, and Mr. Luke Fletcher were standing about, also looking at Lord Panchurch with varying degrees of disgust on their faces.

Ben and Alex joined them.

"Do you carry a pistol, Finn?" Ben asked.

His brother was big, like him, but older by quite a few years, a fact the twins never failed to use to their advantage when the opportunity presented itself. He was a man who handled responsibility with the ease some powerful men did, and as he'd raised his twin brothers when their mother had decided she wanted to follow her lover to France, he had a depth of character Ben was sure others lacked.

"No, it's in the house. Why?"

"I though perhaps you could shoot Panchurch to put him, and us, out of misery. There's no one here who would blame you, and between us we could bury the body."

"I could easily go back and get it," Finn said, contemplating the man still prancing. "Only take a matter of minutes."

"Fencing is for noblemen, and seeing as I am not one, you cannot make me do this," Oliver "Ace" Dillinger said.

He had been born a coal miner's son and run away to London where he became a bare knuckle fighter at a young age. He was a savvy businessman and had invested his earnings wisely, and now was one of the wealthiest industrialists in the United Kingdom. Big and dark, he was married to the Duke of Rossetter's sister, Althea.

"You've fenced," Ben said. "I know this, as I was there."

"I hated it, and if you were there you remember that I nearly skewered you."

"What I want to know is why the duke is exempt from such activities?" Alex looked to the rise in the distance, and there was the Duke of Rossetter with his children, running hither and yon with a kite.

"That does look like more fun," Will Ryder agreed. Brother to the duke, he was married to Olivia, who was Phoebe's sister. Tall, with a leaner build than his brother, he was a man who had left England to find himself and returned a better man. Beside him was his best friend, Luke Fletcher.

"Fletcher, do you wish to fence?"

"I do not," the man said. Quiet, Luke Fletcher was an observer. Starting life as a servant had no doubt played a hand in that.

"Shall we sneak away and see if the billiards room is free then?" Will said. "Or we could go and run about in reckless abandon like my brother."

"The former," Ben said. The agreement was universal.

"Help!"

CHAPTER FOUR

*T*urning toward the shriek, Ben watched Olivia Ryder wave her hands about and run toward them. Will took off at a sprint with the others on his heels.

"What has happened, love?" Will grabbed her hands.

"A carriage, it has overturned and fallen into the river! You must come quickly, I fear there are still several occupants inside."

"Dear God, tell me Phoebe isn't in that water," Finn said, the color leeching out of his face.

"She wasn't when I left," Livvy said.

"You!" Will bellowed at a servant in the distance. "Fetch the duke at once, tell him a carriage has overturned in the river!"

Ben sprinted round the house and found some more servants milling outside.

"Ropes and blankets at once, and have them brought down to the river; a carriage has overturned," he said. "Prepare rooms for people who have been in the accident."

"Send word for a doctor at once!" Finn added. "And bring carts."

They started running again, down the long driveway.

"A horse would be quicker," Alex said.

"No time!" Luke Fletcher sprinted ahead.

The run was not a long one, and soon they had reached the small rise. Below they saw the carriage; it was half submerged. It was a large, lumbering vehicle, and the luggage attached to the roof had come free and was bobbing about in the water. The road was not narrow, but if a driver got too close to the edge it would not take much to send the carriage into the water. The horses had been cut free and were shivering with fear on the bank.

They ran down to where the people were standing.

"Is everyone out, Lord Neil?" Finn asked a large, dripping wet man.

"Yes. I'm not sure what happened. One moment we were rolling along looking forward to joining you all, and the next, listing sideways."

"Are you sure everyone is accounted for?" Finn asked again.

"Yes, although the girl has gone to save that wretched dog."

"Girl?" Ben said. For some reason he was suddenly tense.

"My little Ebony," a young girl cried, rushing to Ben's side. "My baby is still in the water. I begged the lady to save her."

"Primrose!" He heard someone shriek.

"Good God, Miss Ainsley is in the water!" Alex roared.

Ben's eyes darted to the river, following the direction of his brother's hand. Primrose Ainsley was indeed in the water up to her shoulders.

"Get out, you bloody foolish woman!" Ben yelled, making his way down to the edge of the bank.

Ignoring him, she suddenly disappeared. He stripped of

his jacket. Holding out a foot, he ordered Ace, who had joined him, to pull his boot and its partner off.

"Save her!" Lady Jane yelled from behind him. "Please save Primrose!"

Ben waded into the water knowing the others would follow... those who could swim at least.

"Do you see her?" He looked to the bank. Ace shook his head. Taking a deep breath, he dived under the water, but it was murky, and he could see nothing. Surfacing, he climbed on top of the carriage and wrenched open a door.

"Ben!" He heard Finn's yell, but ignored it and lowered himself inside. Submerging himself, he waved his arms around but couldn't feel anyone or anything.

"There's no one in here!" he called up to Alex, who now stood above him. Climbing out he looked back to the bank where the people had gathered.

"Is Miss Ainsley there?" Heads were shaken. "Where is she?"

Getting back into the water, he and Alex swam around the carriage, and it was then he found her. She was struggling with a dog in her arms to the opposite bank.

"You go back, Alex. I'll get Miss Ainsley," he told his brother, and then followed her. By the time he reached the bank, she was lying on it with a small black scruffy dog clasped in her arms.

Ben waded out to her side. Her eyes were closed, and the breath rasping in and out of her throat told him she'd used up all her strength in rescuing the animal. Her dress was stuck to her like a second skin... again.

"I hope you pay your maid a great deal," he said, kneeling at her side. "Open your eyes for me now, Miss Ainsley."

She did, and this was the first time he'd really studied them. The color of the deepest ocean, almost black, they were big and took up half her face... a pale face.

"We need to get you dry… again, you bloody foolish woman."

"I-I had to rescue him, the little girl begged me."

"I'm sure you felt you did, but a more prudent action would have been to wait for one of us to assist you."

"He would have died."

Looking at the pup lying still and barely breathing in her arms, Ben thought that was still a possibility.

"Can you walk, Miss Ainsley? We need to get moving now and warm you up." Even though the sun shone, the day had a cool breeze.

"Of course," she said with a bit more strength. "I-I am wet, not sick."

"Yes, well, you will get sick if you do not get warm."

"Rubbish. One does not get s-sick from cold water on s-such a warm day."

"Your teeth are chattering," Ben felt he needed to point out. "Stop arguing with me and move."

One of her hands grabbed the front of his shirt as Ben went to rise.

"I'm not usually so much trouble, you know. In fact, I'm the sensible Ainsley."

"Really? One can only imagine what the others get up to, then."

Her lips had a blueish tinge to them now, and Ben didn't like to think of her sick, so he stood and lifted her into his arms.

"I can walk," she protested. "If you carry me, Lady Jane will see."

She pushed against his chest, so Ben lowered her feet to the ground.

"And this is a bad thing?"

She nodded. Her wet hair was in a long braid that he guessed had started out on top of her head. It would be beautiful loose, he thought. All those lovely, thick fair waves for him to run his fingers through.

Where the hell had that thought come from?

"V-very bad."

Ben held an arm around her back until she was steady. The little dog was still clasped to her chest.

"Why?"

She shot him a look that suggested he was a dimwit for not knowing; the effect was ruined slightly by the shivers rocking her body.

"No really, why?" He placed a hand at her spine and started her moving in the hopes that would warm her up a bit.

"You are a wealthy, t-tolerable-looking man. Surely that is enough to say on the matter."

"Tolerable-looking?" He wasn't sure why he thought that was an insult, but he did.

"At least it is not a gout-swollen t-toe."

"Come, you are shivering, we must get back to the others with some haste before you fall ill."

"I am r-rarely ill. My brother says I have the same constitution as Hilda."

"Hilda being?"

"F-Farmer Jessop's prized ox."

"Charming. Now hustle along. The blankets will have arrived, and Lady Jane will be worried. And just so you know, I don't think you resemble a gout-swollen toe. I said that for effect," Ben said gruffly. "If Lady Jane wishes you to marry, then my sisters-in-law wish it for me twice as much."

She didn't speak again, and Ben thought it due to the fact her teeth were now chattering, and not that she had nothing further to say on the matter.

"Allow me to take the dog."

"N-no."

"No, thank you," he added.

"I'm c-conserving my strength."

He snorted but said nothing further. Miss Ainsley, Ben realized, became a far more interesting prospect with every minute he spent in her company. He wondered how many other young women he'd put into the category of simpering debutant or marriage-hunting woman who had deserved more interest from him.

"Ebony!" the little girl cried from her position wrapped in a blanket beside her father.

"W-we shall bring her to you!" Primrose called back.

"Primrose!"

The shriek came from Lady Jane. She was hurrying to where they stood.

"Brace yourself, Miss Ainsley."

"I-I am d-doomed," Ben thought she uttered, but couldn't be sure as her teeth were chattering uncontrollably now.

"You foolish, foolish child!" The scolding began as she reached her. "What were you thinking to take such a risk? And let us not begin on how unsuitable your behavior was… and in front of so many ladies of birth and standing."

"I'm s-sorry, but the d-dog—"

"Dog!"

Ben winced at the piercing screech.

"Drop that creature at once!"

"I w-will not. He is unwell and n-needs tending."

"At once, I said!" Lady Jane had a look in her eyes that suggested it would be prudent to do as she asked. It did not bode well for Miss Ainsley, whose lips had turned blue, if she continued to disobey the woman.

"I'll take it to the little girl." He stepped in front of her and held out his hands. "I promise I will see it cared for," he said softly, so only Miss Ainsley could hear.

She was fighting not to cry, and the sight made his

stomach clench. He wanted to tell her it would be all right and not to listen to Lady Jane, but he couldn't, because… well, because she was nothing to him.

CHAPTER FIVE

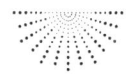

*P*rimrose stayed in bed that afternoon and the following day because Lady Jane had insisted, even though she felt no adverse effects from her impromptu swim. She had not uttered a word in her own defense as Lady Jane had scolded her, using words like propriety and reputation constantly. Who would want to marry a girl who behaved in such a hurly-burly manner? Primrose had apologized several more times, and then finally Lady Jane had finished and left her in peace.

She lay in the bed in blissful peace for an entire day and read. Primrose had been tempted to say she was unwell just so she could stay in there longer, but she did not like to lie, and especially not to the woman who had given her so much.

The following evening, she rose and dressed for dinner.

"Perhaps tonight you will attempt to keep your clothes dry, Primrose."

"Yes, Lady Jane. It was not my intention to deliberately embarrass you. I just wished to help those people in that carriage, and then the little girl who was so upset over her dog."

"I know that, dear, it is just you are not aware of how delicate a young lady's reputation is. One misstep can bring about your ruin, and everyone here will know what you did."

Dear Lord, here we go again.

"Surely it is not that dire?" Primrose said, hoping it was the case. Her behavior had been well-intended, after all.

"But it is, dear. This is not like your father's cottage where you can do as you wish."

How she missed those days.

"You cannot go about digging up roots, and taking clippings just because it appeals. Here you are subject to fierce scrutiny, and as you are already at a disadvantage due to your age and circumstances, you must be more diligent in your behavior."

It was hard to believe that at the age of twenty-five she was old by society's standards. The thought was a depressing one.

Primrose busied herself with her reticule, hoping Lady Jane never found the small stash of clippings that were hidden under the bed.

"I understand and promise from this moment forth to behave exactly as I should."

"Then that is all I can ask of you."

They made their way downstairs, and the first person she saw upon entering the salon where the other guests had gathered was Benjamin Hetherington.

Botheration. Why, with so many other people present, was he always where she did not want him to be?

His eyes lifted briefly and caught hers. Primrose wasn't sure why she was suddenly short of breath, but she was. Perhaps she had contracted something from her impromptu swim after all.

"Have you completely recovered, Miss Ainsley?"

"I have, thank you, Lady Ryder."

The woman stood with her sisters, Mrs. Fletcher and Lady Levermarch. All were fair and beautiful, but it was Lady Levermarch who outshone them all. Primrose had never seen a woman who radiated confidence and beauty like this one. She'd actually seen men stop midsentence to stare at her.

"Your bravery put us all to shame," Mrs. Fletcher said. "It is normally something Phoebe would do, but you beat her to it."

"Yes, I was quite put out."

"Oh, I—"

"I'm not serious, Miss Ainsley," Lady Levermarch said. "What you did was a wonderful thing, and I admire you for it."

"Oh, well…." Her words fell away, unsure how to answer that.

"My dear friend raised her children to swim, as their property borders a river," Lady Jane said, much to Primrose's surprise.

"Do you have many siblings, Miss Ainsley?" Lady Ryder asked.

"Just a brother."

"And is he to join you in London?" Mrs. Fletcher asked.

"No, he and my parents are botanists. They are to travel to India soon."

"India." Lady Levermarch sighed. "How exciting."

Not to Primrose. She couldn't think of anything worse than being on a boat that long and going to a country where no one understood her. She was the Ainsley who did not want adventure. Actually, that was not exactly true. She'd like an adventure, but preferably within the United Kingdom.

"How sad for you to have them gone so long. I would miss my family terribly were they to leave me," Mrs. Fletcher added.

It should be sad, but actually it was a relief. Just like when your slippers pinched and you removed them at the end of a long evening. She'd tried to be like them, but every time it had been a disaster and Primrose usually just ended up being in the way, so she'd given up trying to please her family, and now tried to please other people who were usually more grateful.

"Phoebe was an absolute nightmare as a child," Lady Ryder said. "Always in trouble, and then as she grew there was her face, which was always a problem."

"Face?" Primrose looked at the beautiful Lady Levermarch, who was now rolling her eyes at her sister. She could see nothing but beauty in the woman.

"She is tolerably good-looking, and thus we had admirers calling constantly. Some sent her poetry that was really quite hideous. Poor besotted fools, all of them."

"They're jealous," Lady Levermarch said to Primrose. "I received all the looks in my family, as you can see. My sisters are really quite plain, wouldn't you say, Miss Ainsley?"

Primrose giggled, and then pressed a hand to her mouth, horrified that she'd been wrong to do so. Shooting Lady Jane a look, she was pleased to see her in conversation with the Dowager Duchess of Yardly, one of the elder guests here at Rossetter House.

"I do beg your pardon, that was rude of me."

"It's quite all right, Miss Ainsley. I assure you, we laugh at her all the time," Mrs. Fletcher said.

"I'm sure neither of you have reason to be jealous of your sister," Primrose said. "After all, you are both beautiful also."

"Thank you, Miss Ainsley, but let us assure you that neither Bella nor I have any wish to look as Phoebe does. It is more a trial than anything."

Lady Levermarch sighed. "'Tis the truth... but no longer,

as I now have a husband who sees to my every wish and scares off any man who looks at me."

"Is that what I do?"

The smile that passed between Lord and Lady Levermarch was filled with love. Primrose in all honesty had never wanted a man to look at her that way. That much emotion was surely a messy, complicated experience. Herbert certainly had never looked at her that way. Love was not in her future, as it had never been in her past.

"And now we are to go through to dinner, so let us proceed," Lord Levermarch said, holding out his arm for his wife to take.

They followed in an orderly manner, and when she reached her seat Primrose was horrified to find Mr. Benjamin Hetherington to her right.

"Good evening, Miss Ainsley." He motioned Primrose into her chair. "Lovely weather we had today. I hope you were able to see some of it from your room."

"Qu-quite lovely."

Looking left, she found Lord Levermarch. What was she doing seated so high up the table? Searching for Lady Jane, she found her closer to the duke.

"Is there a problem, Miss Ainsley?"

"Ah, well, I think perhaps I should be down there."

Mr. Hetherington followed her finger as it pointed to the bottom of the table.

"No, I think you are meant to be here."

"B-but—"

"Sit if you please, because when everyone has we will receive food, and I for one am famished."

Primrose sat. She then fussed with her glass, her skirts, and then when she had nothing else to fuss with, she looked straight ahead. The Dowager Duchess of Yardly was seated across from her. She forced a smile onto her face, and the elderly matron replied with something that resembled a snarl. The woman was one of the scarier members of society, and one Primrose kept her distance from.

"You have a book of mine, Benjamin Hetherington!" The Dowager Duchess banged her fist down on the tabletop to ensure she had everyone's attention. The cutlery and glassware jumped.

"Surely not," the man to her right drawled. "In fact, if memory serves it is you that have a book of mine... and one of Alex's, for that matter. So don't try your games with me, madam."

Primrose actually inhaled, making her gasp sound more like a wheeze. She shot Benjamin Hetherington a horrified look. He was smiling.

"Don't provoke her," Primrose whispered.

His smile grew.

The dowager harrumphed.

"What, no reply? Surely you can do better than a harrumph," he drawled.

The elderly woman's eyebrows drew into a fierce line. Her mouth puckered into a tight little circle, making all the wrinkles push up against each other.

"I expect to see you in the library tomorrow. I wish for you to explain about these steam engines. That book was hard to understand!"

"Very well, and I will break it down into simple language so it is not too taxing on your elderly brain."

"Dear Lord," Primrose whimpered, waiting for the explosion that would surely come after these words. Instead she heard a raspy sound. Looking at the dowager, she wasn't sure if her heart was giving out or she was laughing.

"She's laughing, Miss Ainsley, relax."

"It doesn't sound like a laugh. Are you sure?"

THE LADY'S DANGEROUS LOVE

"Yes. I know the Dowager Duchess of Yardly very well. That is a laugh."

"You, girl!"

Shock held Primrose rigid when she realized the woman was now speaking to her.

"Don't pick on her," Benjamin Hetherington said.

"I'm not, you young whelp. I was going to commend her on her bravery for plunging into the water to save that dog!"

"Oh well… thank you," Primrose said, unsure how to address the woman.

"Duchess," Benjamin whispered.

"But I am her inferior, so perhaps it should be your Grace?"

"Duchess will do."

As the woman concerned was now having a robust discussion with Alexander Hetherington across two guests, Primrose was sure she couldn't overhear their murmured conversation.

"You are no one's inferior, Miss Ainsley."

The words were spoken quietly, and they made her feel warm to her toes.

"I fear that is not true, but thank you for the sentiment, Mr. Hetherington."

"Rank and title do not maketh a man… or woman, as this case may be."

"The world we live in does not work that way."

"Well, it should," he said in that same soft, serious tone.

Primrose said nothing further, instead leaning to one side to allow the first course to be placed before her.

The soup came first, and thankful to have something to do, she took a mouthful, and tried not to make any slurping sounds. Everything on the table seemed to sparkle, from the crystal glasses to the silverware. It was a setting fit for royalty, and one she'd never believed herself capable of being part of.

"You swim very well, Miss Ainsley."

She swallowed and managed not to choke. Primrose didn't know what to say to that, so she ignored him and talked to his brother, who sat to her left.

"The soup is very nice, don't you think, Lord Levermarch?"

The surprise on his face was quickly masked. Beside her, Benjamin Hetherington chuckled softly.

"Ah... quite, but as yet I have only had one mouthful, Miss Ainsley."

"You will find it tastes wonderful," Primrose said, sounding like a complete simpleton.

"I'm sure I shall."

He gave her a gentle smile that made the corners of his eyes crinkle and his usually serious face appear softer. Of course, he only had to look at the beautiful woman seated across from him to do that.

Primrose took another mouthful and swallowed, allowing her eyes to circle the room. Servants stood dressed in livery, blending into the walls, seen but never heard. Everywhere there were signs of wealth and ducal opulence. Not that the duke and duchess flaunted that; in fact, quite the opposite. They were kind people with easy manners.

"Did you get the pond weeds out of your dress?"

She couldn't ignore him through the entire meal, or someone would notice... namely Lady Jane, who was always watching Primrose to ensure she behaved.

"There were no pond weeds in the river, Mr. Hetherington."

"I did not mean the river, I meant the pond... which you swam in earlier."

"Are you mocking me?"

THE LADY'S DANGEROUS LOVE

"Certainly not." His eyes twinkled.

"I took evasive measures to remove myself from a situation that was not a comfortable one. I wish to discuss it no further, thank you." Cool and calm, she'd said what needed to be said, and he would leave her alone now.

"You were not comfortable as I had compared you to a gout-swollen toe, which was unpardonably rude, but I hardly see that throwing yourself in the water fully clothed was the action of a sane mind. I am not such a terrifying man, surely?"

Primrose looked down at her soup and moved the spoon from side to side. She didn't really like turtle soup, contrary to what she'd said to Lord Levermarch.

"I am quite sound of mind, I assure you. The thing is, Mr. Hetherington, I can be a trifle impetuous. Once an idea takes root, I'm afraid I do not deliberate over it for long, and am likely to act, especially if I wish to leave the company of someone."

"Not a comfortable trait to have, I'm sure, and I have apologized for being rude."

She shot him a look. His eyes were on her, intent and searching. He was a handsome man, she could not say otherwise, and someone who she knew, just from brief observation, was popular... unlike her.

Looking to where Lady Jane sat, she saw a look in her eyes that was unsettling. The smile she bestowed on Primrose was a knowing one.

"Mr. Hetherington."

"Miss Ainsley." He bent his head slightly to listen to her

"Mr. Hetherington...."

"Miss Ainsley."

"The thing is, Mr. Hetherington."

"You have used my name three times in a short space of

time, Miss Ainsley. Is there any chance you could get to the point before you make it four?"

"I am attempting to explain something to you," Primrose said.

"I am quite intelligent. If you keep the words simple, I shall probably grasp them."

She glared at him. "My brother does that, and I dislike it."

"That being?"

"Insulting while smiling."

He lowered his spoon to the table and placed one hand on his chest. "I promise you I did not mean to insult you."

"Yes, you did, but that is neither here nor there as I have no wish to like you, or you to like me for that matter... which is the problem, actually."

"Is it?"

"Yes."

"If you stopped talking in circles and went in a straight line, perhaps I would understand what it is you are trying to get at."

Primrose took a sip of her soup while she put the words in order inside her head.

"I want you to ignore me for the remainder of the meal and afterward when we meet while here or in London. Be polite, but do not spend time in my company."

She'd shocked him, because his mouth opened slightly and his lovely eyes widened.

"I beg your pardon?"

"If I may speak plainly?"

"Please do."

"My mother and Lady Jane have hatched a plot to see me wed this season. My mother has no wish for me to return home, and Lady Jane is bored and sees me as something of a challenge."

"Good God."

"I have no wish to marry any of the men here," Primrose charged on, undeterred by his blasphemy. "I wish to return home and marry the man I care for."

His silence made Primrose wonder if in fact she'd made a fatal mistake in speaking her mind… again.

CHAPTER SIX

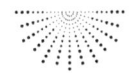

Shock held Ben silent for a while. Shock that the woman beside him was being brutally honest. He'd never met anyone like Primrose Ainsley before. Men were often brutally honest, but rarely the women of his acquaintance. Of course, he excluded his sisters-in-law from that thought, they were nothing but honest... brutally so. But a debutante... rarely.

"I see," he said, finding his voice, "and I gather the man you do wish to marry does not frequent society?"

"He does not."

"Where does he reside, if you don't mind me asking?"

"In the same village as my family."

"A farmer?"

"Herbert is a curate in our local parish."

"And does your father not wish you to marry this Herbert?"

She looked down at her soup as if it held the answer to his question.

"Miss Ainsley?"

"It's complicated."

"Because?"

"Because it is."

"Which is not an answer."

"Why do you care? Surely it matters nothing to you that I care for another, especially considering your high opinion of me."

Ben's sigh was loud enough for her to hear.

"I believe I have apologized for that and explained the reason behind comparing you to a gout-swollen toe."

"Surely you can see it is best we simply do not converse again, as we can barely speak a civil word to each other?"

Ben moved slightly so his soup could be removed.

"We have spoken a mere handful of words. You have no way of knowing if we could be friends or not, Miss Ainsley."

He looked at the woman seated beside him. Her dress was pale blue, simple except for the large bows under the puffed short sleeves. Her hair was in a bun with a matching bow pinned underneath it. She looked no different from any number of the women seated at this very table. Dressed as a young woman should be, and yet she was… very different.

"I have no wish for friends, and especially not someone like you."

"What is wrong with me, Miss Ainsley?" Ben was sure he'd been insulted again.

"Nothing, but I am trying to explain to you that I care for another and have no wish for Lady Jane to get silly ideas that perhaps you are interested in me," Primrose said quickly. "Please attempt to understand that."

"Perhaps if you speak more slowly, I may grasp your meaning."

"There is no need for sarcasm."

"There is every need."

"You're angry."

"A little, but more surprised, actually." He wasn't exactly

angry, more piqued. His ego wasn't monumental like some, but clearly he had one, as he was feeling quite put out at this woman's obvious lack of interest in him. *Curious.*

"Because most women want to solicit your attentions? Yes, I'm sure it is quite a shock to you that I wish the opposite."

"I'm quite sure my ego will cope," he drawled. "And does this paragon Herbert the Honorable share your feelings?"

"There is no need to be rude, and it's complicated."

She smiled up at the servant placing the second course before her. Ben had seen no one else do that. It was a sweet smile, and made her face come alive.

He snorted. "Of course it is. In fact, I'd think it accurate to say that anything involving you would be complicated."

"You don't know that about me!"

He gave her a pitying glance that had her muttering something beneath her breath.

"Did you just curse at me using flowers?"

"No."

"I'm sure you did, and I insist that you repeat it." The woman had him wanting to growl one minute and laugh the next. "Go on." He rotated a large finger in the air when she sighed.

Ignoring him, she placed some food in her mouth and chewed. Ben groaned as her jaw made a shocking click.

"Are you in pain?" She shot him a look. "You just moaned."

"No."

"Well then why did you moan?" She turned in her seat to look at him.

"Your jaw clicks when you eat."

"Yes, and always has. Pray tell me why that makes you moan?"

He took a mouthful of food and chewed, hoping she'd just

shut up. Unfortunately, she did the same, all the while watching him. Her jaw clicked again.

"You winced."

"I'll make you a deal, Miss Ainsley. If you tell me about your floral cursing, I'll tell you why I winced," Ben said.

She thought about that while she ate a little more.

"Very well. I will tell you, because after we leave Rossetter we will not encounter each other again."

"Are you not to see out the remainder of the season in London then?" Ben said, perversely put out by her dismissal of him again.

"Of course. But you are popular; I am not."

"Which means what?"

"How often have you seen or spoken to me at society functions, Mr. Hetherington?"

He would not feel ashamed because he had not made the effort to speak with her. He could not speak to every woman each evening.

"Explain about your floral curses, Miss Ainsley, before this discussion becomes an argument."

"Are you suggesting I'm argumentative?"

Ben simply looked at her, and she had the grace to look away first.

"Bluebell and Carnation is…, well, it's—"

"Hell and damnation."

"Yes. My parents do not like bad language of any kind. When my brother and I were younger and he was not quite so tedious, we decided to use a few flowers as curse words. Bluebell and Carnation. Hollyhocks, as it has a good sound to it, don't you think?"

"It certainly does," he said solemnly.

"Prunus Avium—"

"I beg your pardon?"

"Wild Cherry. This was used as the most insulting curse."

Ben laughed. He could not dispute the fact that Miss Ainsley was an entertaining, if slightly annoying dinner companion.

"How imaginative of you."

"We thought so, as it meant we could shriek them at each other and our parents couldn't be angry."

"You and your brother sound like you had a great deal of fun growing up."

"We did." She delivered those words in a cold, flat tone that told him something was off with her relationship with her sibling.

"Are you no longer close?"

"He is a busy man now."

Which told him precisely nothing.

"Of course. I understand he is a botanist like your parents?"

"Yes, he is."

"Hence the fact you wish to wed Herbert the Honorable, so you can stay close to them when they are in England?" Ben was shamelessly fishing for information now.

She nodded.

"Does this paragon, Herbert the Honorable, reciprocate your feelings?"

"Your brother is trying to attract your attention."

"Tut tut, Miss Ainsley. You cannot hope to marry a curate and continue to tell lies. My brothers are in discussion with their adoring wives."

"How do you know that?"

"I know my brothers."

"I don't understand."

She had rather a charming nose when it was wrinkled like that.

"My brothers love their wives, truly, madly, deeply, Miss

Ainsley. They are usually talking, touching, or simply looking at each other. It's nauseating."

"No, it's not, and if you want to know what I think—"

"I hang on your every word."

"You're an extremely vexing man, do you know that?" She was glaring at him again.

"It's my fondest wish."

She tried to swallow the smile he saw in her eyes.

"That's a pretty look on you."

"Thank you. Now what I was going to say, was that you are jealous."

"Of my brothers?" He'd never been jealous of Finn and Alex and wasn't about to concede to it now.

Primrose nodded.

"Hardly. My observation, Miss Ainsley, is that this love they share is an extremely uncomfortable condition."

"But a lovely one if a person finds that special someone to share their lives with."

"You have a silly look on your face, wipe it away at once."

"So you are a cynic, Mr. Hetherington."

"A realist. What my brothers and a few others of my acquaintance have found is not for everyone. This I have learned by observing some of the marriages of society."

"Thus, I want to marry a man I can respect."

"You have not once mentioned the word love, Miss Ainsley."

"Love is not for me, as it is for others. I merely wish to live a comfortable life with Herbert."

"Excuse me, but you just alluded to the fact that you believed in love in marriage?"

"I never said I didn't believe in it, I just don't think it's for me."

"What about Herbert the Honorable? Does he reciprocate your feelings?"

"It's complicated."

"So you said."

"H-he is not unaware of me... just not... well, he's not terribly aware of me either."

She shot him a look, and Ben could do nothing to stop the chuckle escaping.

"It is no laughing matter. If he were to just come about, I would not be here today. I could be home in Pickford."

"With your family."

"No, very likely on my own with the Putts."

"I'm almost afraid to ask who the Putts are."

The third course was placed before him, and Ben smiled at the servant.

"They are my parents' staff."

"Why are you alone with them?"

"You ask a lot of questions, Mr Hetherington."

She clearly did not want to continue with this line of questioning.

"Just being polite, Miss Ainsley. Now back to Herbert. Perhaps he believes in true love and is simply not wanting companionship?"

"I had thought this too when my advances were met with politeness."

This was too much for Ben; he started laughing again.

"Stop that!" she hissed.

"F-forgive me. What advances did you make?"

"Tell me why you winced when I ate?" she demanded. "I haven't forgotten that I shared my secret and you have not."

Ben picked up his glass and sipped. He wasn't sure he felt comfortable giving this woman ammunition over him. But fair was fair.

"Certain types of noise are very uncomfortable for me."

"Like a dog?"

"Extremely amusing, Miss Ainsley."

"I thought so."

"Chewing loudly, rustling—"

"Jaws that click?"

"Exactly. I have of course learned to deal with this ridiculous issue, but…."

"It's still there. You are just older now, so you have to cope with it?"

"Exactly," Ben said, surprised she understood.

"Miss Lydia is the local piano teacher in Pickford, and she is the same. She can't abide sitting close to me when we eat."

"Really? I've never met anyone else like me." Ben felt better knowing he wasn't the only one with his "condition," as Alex called it.

"Oh, I think there are more than just two of you, but it's my guess people simply don't talk about it, as it makes them seem odd."

"Are you saying I'm odd, Miss Ainsley?"

She raised a brow, and he barked out a loud laugh.

"Care to share the joke, Benjamin?"

As the words came from his eldest brother, Miss Ainsley turned to speak with him, and Ben had the ridiculous impulse to call her attention back to him. *Odd.*

"I have no idea what he has found humorous, my lord; he simply burst into spontaneous laughter. Is he quite all right?" She didn't add "in the head," but it was inferred that was exactly what she meant.

"I believe so, but he was dropped on his head often as a babe. Perhaps he is just now starting to exhibit symptoms."

"That is a possibility," she mused.

Ben decided that going forward it would pay to avoid this woman. She was a disturbing combination of wit and intelligence, both attractive qualities in a woman. Especially if you added a pretty face.

Not that she had shown him any partiality. In fact, the opposite was true.

"I am to go to the nursery and play hide-and-seek with the children and their parents in the morning. Would you care to join us, Miss Ainsley?"

God's blood, hadn't he just told himself not to engage with her?

"What… pardon?" she quickly added as she turned to face him again. "I have just told you why that cannot happen."

"It is my niece Amanda's sixth birthday, and her wish was to play hide-and-seek with adults, so we are obliging. I understand you want to avoid all contact with me, but that would mean you will miss all the fun. Besides, I am not proposing."

"I do not wish to have fun with you."

"Why do you wish to avoid all contact with my brother, Miss Ainsley? Has he done something reprehensible that I must thrash him for?"

The horrified look on her face at Finn's words made Ben smile.

"Of course not, my lord. I just have no wish…." She hesitated.

"She has no wish for Lady Jane to link her with any man but Herbert the Honorable," Ben added.

"Who is Herbert the Honorable?" Lord Levermarch enquired calmly.

"No one," she hastened to add.

Ben winced as her heel ground into his foot. Granted, it was not sharp, but she had put some force behind the action.

"Oh, come now, that is a heartless way to treat your future husband. Dismissing him like that speaks to your callous nature."

She could only be provoked so much, it seemed.

"Be quiet," she said through clenched teeth before facing Finn once more.

"Herbert is a curate in my village. He is a friend."

"For whom she holds no lasting passion, and yet wishes a comfortable marriage with," Ben added.

"I wonder if he has always been this way, my lord?"

"Irritating, do you mean, Miss Ainsley?" Finn said.

She nodded. "I have no wish to be rude, but perhaps he was not disciplined enough, my lord?"

"Oh, he was. Both of the twins were unruly and ill-mannered from a young age. It took all my strength to wrestle them into the halfway decent people you see before you, Miss Ainsley."

"You have my sympathies, my lord. The task must have been an onerous one."

"In the extreme." Finn's expression was solemn.

"I fear we are being maligned, brother." Ben looked across the table to where Alex sat.

"Has he started on our youth again?"

"He has."

"It is a tale he trots out at will, Miss Ainsley. I would not set a great deal of stock in it," Alex said.

He and his brothers bantered back and forth for a while, and he felt Primrose relax as she listened.

"Getting back to the game of hide-and-seek that started this crucifixion of my character, Miss Ainsley. Will you come?" Ben said a few minutes later.

"I will not."

"I wager you will, because you are of a curious nature, Miss Ainsley. In fact, I would bet my latest mill that I will see you in the morning, ready and waiting to partake in our game."

He couldn't be sure, but thought she said, "not bloody likely," under her breath.

CHAPTER SEVEN

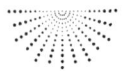

Ben saw Primrose's head as she peered around the edge of the doorway. Their eyes caught and held briefly, and then she disappeared.

"Come in, Miss Ainsley, we are just about to begin," he called.

"Oh no, I was just passing, but thank you" was her muffled reply.

"Passing to where?" Ben regained his feet. Patting his nephew on the head, he walked through the door. Primrose was attempting to scurry away.

"We are on the third floor, so unless you are wishing to scale the roof, I fail to see how you could be passing."

"I was strolling," she said over her shoulder, a forced smile on her pretty face.

"Again, this is hardly the place for a morning stroll. Strolling is usually done in the gallery, or the grounds. Perhaps the orangery, and even—"

"Yes, yes, I take your point!" she snapped, stopping to face him, now wearing a frustrated look.

He was smiling again, just like he had several times last

night through the meal he'd eaten seated beside her. Ben instantly removed it from his face. He could be pleasant and converse with this woman, but he would not be intrigued or interested by her.

"So what you actually wanted was not to miss out on all the fun, but you are unwilling to admit that fact. I believe I said as much last night, and that I would see you here."

"You are an annoying man!"

"Amen." Alex wandered past Primrose. "Try sharing your birthdate with the man, Miss Ainsley. It can be extremely taxing."

"I can imagine," she snapped.

"Come along, Miss Ainsley, there is fun to be had."

"I can spare a few minutes, thank you, Mr. Hetherington." She walked by Ben to follow Alex. "The nice one," she added for Ben's ears alone.

Ben was still smiling as he entered the nursery behind them.

The duke and duchess had painted the walls in bright, sunny colors and furnished it with comfortable chairs and plenty of toys. Three large rocking horses sat in a line on one wall. Shelves held books, and large soft pillows were scattered everywhere.

"Oh my." He followed Primrose's eyes and encountered the trunk filled with dress-up things, and beside it another smaller one holding dolls. The small house beside it was open, and they could see the little furnishings inside.

"Do you still have your childhood dolls, Miss Ainsley?"

She shook her head at Ben's question but didn't speak.

"Where is the birthday girl?" Alex asked.

"Here!" The squeal was loud enough to pierce eardrums.

Alex lunged at Amanda. The girl shrieked and hugged him close, her little arms wrapping around his neck as she kissed every inch of his face.

"Amanda," Ben touched the girl's shoulder after Alex had released her, "this is Miss Ainsley. Is it all right if she participates in the game of hide-and-seek? As it happens, she was just passing and heard all the noise."

Primrose smiled at the girl, and it was genuine and sweet.

"Happy birthday, Amanda. I hope I may call you that?"

"Of course." Amanda nodded regally, looking like her mother. Phoebe had perfected the art as a young girl also, Ben was sure. "And yes, you may play," she added as if she were royalty. "And now we are to begin."

Adults were already paired with children where possible, and the rules established. They were relayed for Primrose. She listened intently, and Ben just bet she'd remember each one clearly.

The Duchess of Rossetter , Lord and Lady Ryder, Finn, Phoebe, Alex, and Ben were the only adults who'd dragged themselves out of bed to participate in the fun, along with nine children.

"No cheating, Phoebe."

"I have no idea what you mean, William."

Will rolled his eyes.

The Duchess of Rossetter started counting, and everyone ran in different directions with absolutely no regard for the grand old furnishings lining the halls and filling each room. There were excited squeals as children ran ahead of adults.

Ben, who was paired with Samantha, the duchess's daughter, grabbed her little hand and ran down the hallway, heading left.

"There is a small alcove, Ben. We could hide in there, behind the curtains."

She had a lisp, as her two front teeth were missing.

"Lead the way then, Samantha."

They located it a few minutes later. Slipping inside, they settled in to wait.

"Are you enjoying having other children to share the nursery with during the house party?"

"Yes." She looked serious. "But I will also be glad when it is quiet again. But Mother and Father sneak us treats, as does every other parent, so I will miss that."

"And you little sneaks have told no one that you are already getting treats, so they keep coming."

"Of course. Sssh," she hissed loudly.

Ben fell silent. He heard the thud of the duchess's feet, and then she was there, smiling at them.

"Hello, sweetheart."

"Bother. We need to try harder next time, Ben."

"May I point out this was your hiding place, Samantha?"

The little girl gave him a serious look. "But you are the adult."

"I shall give it more consideration then."

They hid several more times, and Ben had fleeting glimpses of a smiling Primrose, who appeared to be enjoying herself hugely.

He and Samantha acquitted themselves quite well, even winning one round, and arrived back the last time to find two large trays of food and tea had been laid out on the nursery tables. His stomach was extremely grateful to see it.

"I cannot find Primrose," Alex said, looking at the plate of spiced apple cake.

"Well, she won't be in there," Ben said.

"You go and find her; I'm weak with hunger. She's alone, so it could be quite a small space she's hiding in."

"Alex, it is you who is in, therefore, you need to find her." Ben picked up a currant bun. It was glazed with sugar and smelled divine.

"Well then, she'll have to wait. This food needs eating."

Ben swallowed and thought perhaps it may be the best bun he'd eaten in quite some time.

"Someone must find her," Amanda said. "Or she will miss the birthday tea."

Ben stood his ground and glared at Alex, who in turn ignored him in favor of devouring a slice of apple cake.

"Very well, I'll find her, seeing as you are too lazy to do so," Ben said.

Alex simply smiled in that way that suggested he knew something Ben did not, which annoyed him enough to take another bun before walking out the door.

Ten minutes later, he'd checked every room and cupboard. Every nook and crevice. *Where the hell is she?* The rules were that you didn't leave this floor.

Standing in a smallish parlor, he turned a full circle. She wasn't behind the drapes or anything else in the room. Staring up at the tapestry, and the man in an intricately carved doublet, he wondered if she'd simply left and not told anyone.

"Did you see her?"

No comment was forthcoming, so Ben started to leave. His eyes fell on the windows. One was unlatched.

"Surely not?" Moving closer, he pushed it open slowly and leaned out to find Primrose Ainsley perched on a ledge. Looking down at the ground three floors below, he tried to think clearly and not give in to the anger and incredulity gripping him. She could have fallen, could even now be lying down there, broken and bleeding. Lifeless!

"Come inside." The words were calm, for all his need to roar them at her.

"The game has finished?" she said in a voice she would use to converse about the weather.

Ben couldn't bring himself to speak, so he nodded. One quick jerk of his head as he battled to subdue the anger inside him. He didn't usually get angry… not this kind of anger, anyway.

"Oh, and have I won?" Her eyes lit with excitement.

I'm killing her.

"Inside now."

"But did I win?"

She was inching along the building, her hands holding the wood above the window. Her white dress rose a few inches, showing him a pair of lovely ankles, and then the hem caught on a sliver of wood and rose further, allowing him a glimpse of pale, silken calves, before she pulled it free. The material made a tearing sound.

"Oh dear, Lady Jane is not going to be happy."

"She would certainly not have been had you plunged to your death!" His voice rose on the last word.

"I was perfectly safe."

"Give me your hand," Ben said when she was in touching distance.

"I have it. If you will just move back, I will climb in through the window."

Ben leaned out, wrapped an arm around her waist, and pulled her unceremoniously inside. She squealed, clung to his shoulders, and then she was on her feet.

"There was no need to do that!" Her hands were fussing with her clothes. Ben watched, fuming, as she inspected the small tear in the hem.

"Are you completely without sense!"

She dropped the hem, eyes wide as she straightened.

"What fool climbs out on a narrow ledge—"

"I am not a fool and was never in danger. The board I was standing on could comfortably hold both my feet." Her chin lifted, and the look on her face was anything but contrite.

"You were many feet above the ground perched on a narrow ledge! You could have slipped at any time. What if the piece of wood you were holding broke? These old houses are notorious for that kind of thing."

"I was safe, I assure you, and am quite nimble—"

"Nimble enough to fall several floors without hurting yourself?" Ben scoffed. "You are not a cat, Miss Ainsley."

"You're being irrational," she dismissed him, unwisely, with a wave of her hand. It just spiked his temper further.

"You," he pointed a finger at her, "are bloody infuriating and irresponsible. Twice you could have drowned, and now... to win a game, you take yet another foolish risk!"

"I am not speaking to you about this any further." She tried to go round him.

Ben grabbed her arm and pulled her close—so close that he simply had to lower his head for their eyes to be inches apart.

"I want you to acknowledge how foolish that was."

Her lips formed a line.

"Primrose." He pulled her closer still. She said nothing, so he kissed her.

Her squeak was muffled by his mouth. Driven by anger, the kiss was fierce. Ben knew he should ease back, knew it in the deep recesses of his mind where sanity lurked, and yet he couldn't make himself. She tasted like sin, her lips soft and sweet beneath his, and he could feel her breasts pressed to his chest. He wanted more of her, and that thought had him retreating.

"I'm sorry, I should not have done that." Releasing her, he stepped back.

She looked dazed, confused by his actions. Her lips were wet and pink, and his body hardened. He took another step back.

"Why did you?" Her eyes had cleared now. They weren't angry, just questioning.

"I was angry," he rasped.

"Do you kiss all the women you are angry with?" She

tilted her head to one side, as if she was inspecting some rare species of plant.

"Of course not. But I was exceedingly angry with you." Ben knew he sounded like a fool but had no other words to exonerate himself.

"I like to win," she said in a calm voice.

How was she calm, when his body was on fire?

"At the risk of your health!"

"Perhaps I was wrong, but it is my health to risk. I often climbed out onto the window when hiding from my brother. I'm sorry if that frightened you."

"You must have been absolute hell to grow up with."

Her smile was small, and Ben had a feeling she was taking this entire situation better than he. Which was surely not true, as he was the one experienced in these situations and she was the innocent.

"My brother often said that. Now if you will excuse me, I have a raging thirst, and I believe tea was to arrive in the nursery soon."

He stood to one side, as he had nothing to add to that, and she walked by, as regal as any princess, and left him alone—still fuming but also now aroused.

"Bluebell and carnation," Ben whispered. He followed minutes later.

When he arrived in the nursery, Primrose was engaged in conversation with the duchess. She shot him a look, then away again as he entered.

"You better have saved me a bun."

"Oh dear," Alex said, taking a large bite of the one in his hand. "So sorry."

Ben grunted something rude and took the tea Hannah handed him.

"I see you found her, then." Alex nodded to where Primrose stood. "She looked a trifle flushed when she entered. Where was she hiding?"

"On the window ledge… outside."

Alex choked. Ben stepped in as a brother should and whacked him hard on the back.

"Chew your food, Alex. Honestly, the children have better manners than you."

"Thank you, wife, for your support," Alex rasped, eyes watering. "Are you serious? You found her on the window ledge?"

Ben nodded. "Apparently she is a win at all costs kind of lady."

"Good Lord."

"Quite."

"I am taking Miss Ainsley to see a book. The rest of you behave… especially my children," the duchess said, heading toward the door with Primrose on her heels. "And the adults too."

"What book?" Ben said loudly.

"That old botany one my husband treats like his firstborn child," the duchess said. "Apparently, Miss Ainsley is an avid gardener also."

"I do not treat it like a firstborn child; it is far more important than him," the duke drawled, earning an outraged howl from his eldest child, Billy.

Ben studied Primrose. Her cheeks were flushed, and she looked excited. In fact, what she looked was adorable, and that did not sit well with him after what they'd just shared, so he looked away until she'd left the room.

Then he followed.

"Where are you going?" Will asked.

"I want to see this book," Ben lied. What he wanted was to see Primrose Ainsley again, and he had no intentions of examining that thought too closely.

CHAPTER EIGHT

Primrose battled to contain her excitement. She was going to see *the* book. It was just the thing she needed after that kiss. Her first kiss. Good lord, she'd not known such passion could be exchanged just from a meeting of two sets of lips. It had been swift and taken her completely by surprise. How could a mouth pressed to hers make her body tingle all over?

And not just any mouth, his mouth! Benjamin "Annoying" Hetherington.

Primrose had walked out the door of that room she'd been hiding in and exhaled slowly. She'd tried to steady herself. Her pulse had been racing and her body felt different. Being held by him had been wonderful. His passion and strength. She doubted Herbert would hold her in such a way, but then how did she know? Perhaps any man who held her would make her feel just that way?

She'd never thought herself capable of passion; indeed, she'd settled on a comfortable marriage in her future. Would she need to revise that now, in light of one single kiss? Unlikely. Primrose had realized early in her life that she was not easy to love. Perhaps that was why his kiss had made her feel so much. Someone had held her close, and she'd responded with fervor. Did she crave emotion so much that a stranger, any stranger, could make her feel what she had?

"You must see my night garden also, Miss Ainsley. Unlike my husband, I am not obsessed with books, but I do enjoy the gardens."

"You have a night garden?" Primrose breathed. She'd always wanted to see one of those. Pushing aside her troubled thoughts about the kiss she and Benjamin Hetherington had shared, she focused on the Duchess of Rossetter.

"Indeed, there is plenty in there and it is a wonderful sight. But you will have to go out after dark to view it."

"I would love to see it, thank you, and I shall make sure to take someone with me."

"That would be best."

Primrose walked through the old house admiring cabinets full of treasures that were many years old and paintings that were worth more money than she could hope to acquire in a lifetime.

"Good day."

"Mr. Sanders," the duchess said as he appeared before them. "What has you in this part of the house?"

"It's fair to say I was lost, Duchess. I had hoped to find the library, as the Duke told me it is one of the finest around."

"Of course he said that." The duchess rolled her eyes. "He actually believes it's the finest in the kingdom."

Mr. Sanders smiled, but did not reply.

He had only arrived yesterday. Tall, with an easy smile, he appeared a man of relaxed manners and a comfortable disposition—unlike Mr. Hetherington, who was anything but comfortable. In fact, he reminded her of how she'd felt when she fell in that blackberry bush a few years ago.

"Come along, I shall show you this library instead, as we

are heading that way and I am about to show Miss Ainsley a book."

"Excellent, I shall accompany you. How can a man resist such beautiful company?"

"This is actually the second library in the house, a small room that houses the most precious books in my husband's collection," the duchess said, entering the room. "I'll draw the curtains. They are kept closed so the books do not fade."

"I am not really a man who loves old books. Perhaps you could point me to the other library once we are finished here, Duchess," Mr. Sanders said.

"Oh, but surely you want to see *the* book?"

"*The* book, Miss Ainsley?"

"Lucian Clipper's *The History Of Plants*. It is the most extensively written and illustrated botany text ever created. He wrote it in 1532 and died the following year. This is the only copy in existence."

Primrose let her eyes move around the shelves after the duchess had opened the curtains and light flooded in. She inhaled the smell of old books.

"Someone should really bottle this scent."

"My husband often says that, Miss Ainsley," the duchess said.

The age of many of the books was evident by the spines.

"Are all these first editions?" Mr. Sanders asked.

"Most, yes. Mr. Stephens works for my husband, and it is he who hunts these down for him. Occasionally the duke will join him on a trip to procure a rare volume."

"May I see the book also?"

She didn't want to stiffen as Benjamin Hetherington wandered in, but after what they'd just shared, Primrose couldn't help it.

"I did not realize you knew the difference between a weed and a flower, Ben."

"Perhaps I don't." He gave the duchess a lovely smile that reached his eyes and made his face light up. Not that Primrose was impressed. It took more than a smile to do that. "But I do love old books."

"Oh, well then, that is an excellent reason to see this book."

"Miss Ainsley." He nodded to her as if they were mere acquaintances and his lips had not created turmoil inside her.

"Mr. Hetherington."

"Sanders, are you also interested in botany?"

"No indeed, Hetherington. I had hoped to borrow one of the duke's books to read, and apparently was searching for the wrong library."

"Here it is."

Primrose struggled to draw in a breath as she moved to where the duchess now stood. The case was glass, and it stood on a wooden pedestal.

"I am unable to open the case without my husband, as he has hidden the key. This book is his most prized possession. He guards it zealously."

"From you?" Benjamin Hetherington snorted.

"Yes, apparently I, and everyone else, cannot be trusted. It is only brought out when he is here."

"I-it's beautiful," Primrose breathed, leaning over the case as the duchess stepped back. "Look at the detail in the drawings."

She felt him move, and how she knew it was Benjamin Hetherington, Primrose was unsure, but seconds later his head was beside hers as he studied the book.

Inhale, exhale, Primrose reminded herself. It was something she'd done without thinking her entire life, so why was it suddenly so difficult now?

"His handwriting was very elegant."

She didn't speak, just focused on the book and tried to shut the man out.

"I have never seen a flower like that one, it is beautiful," he said.

"Nerium," Primrose said. "It is possibly the most poisonous plant in existence. It is rather bitter, however, which stops people from eating it."

"And that one?"

"One of the night flowers. They have a garden here at Rossetter ."

"Really?"

"Yes." Primrose nodded but didn't look to her right. "The duchess has told me I may visit it."

"At night?"

"I will take someone with me," Primrose said quickly. She crossed her fingers behind her back. She doubted anyone would want to view the garden with her, but she was now determined to see it and may have to do so alone.

"Did you know that it's said Christians believe that crossing one's fingers while lying invokes some kind of protective power of the cross to mitigate anything bad happening due to the lie?"

"How did you know I had my fingers crossed?"

"It seemed like something you would do. Plus, my brother does it constantly."

Primrose studied the book rather than saying something she may regret.

"What is that?"

He started questioning her again about the book and what it held on its magnificent pages.

"You really do know a great deal about plants, don't you?"

"Not as much as my family, and I prefer the species that are not rare and can be easily found."

"So you have no wish to accompany them on their travels?"

They were both still bent over the glass.

"No. Even if they asked me, I would not go."

"They haven't asked you?" He sounded shocked.

"It is of no mind." She dismissed his words, wishing she'd kept her mouth shut.

"If I apologize, will you look at me?"

"I have no wish to discuss that… that—"

"Kiss?"

She gave a sharp nod that nearly had her nose hitting the glass cabinet. "Nor do I wish to converse on anything but general topics with you from this moment on." Primrose kept her eyes on the book.

"The pages are quite faded."

Mr. Sanders was bent to her left now.

"It's extremely old. This is the only copy of this book in existence."

"One of my husband's ancestors had a fixation about botany, and it was he who paid an exorbitant sum for this book," the duchess said.

"It's magnificent," Primrose breathed.

"Excellent. Well, I shall try to get my husband to let you actually hold it, but I can promise nothing as he's foolishly protective of it. Always rabbiting on about it being highly sought and he will not have it stolen. We have all kinds of people visiting just to see it. Some have offered ridiculous sums of money, but it will never leave Rossetter while my husband is still breathing."

"I completely understand," Primrose said, reluctantly straightening. With a last look at the magnificent book, she turned away. "Thank you so much for this honor. I have long been enamored with *The History Of Plants.* Lucian Clipper was a revolutionary and before his time in some of his philosophies."

"I'm so pleased you enjoyed it. And I hope you will view my night flowers blooming before you leave Rossetter ."

"I certainly will, thank you."

"And now we are to have a light repast under the trees on the west side of the terrace. Then we will go into Twoaks to watch the boat race."

Primrose didn't want to watch boat racaoes, she wanted to wander through the gardens, but knew Lady Jane would not allow that.

"Are you to race in a boat, Hetherington?"

"I believe so, Sanders, and you?"

The man shuddered. "No indeed. I am a peaceful type of fellow." He then wandered off with the duchess, leaving Primrose with Benjamin Hetherington.

Hollyhocks!

"Hard to believe they used to clunk down these halls in armor."

"Is there an armory here?" Primrose leapt on the topic, as it was in no way personal or intimate like that kiss had been.

"There is, and it has quite the display. You shall have to view it, Miss Ainsley."

"Perhaps I will."

"Will you watch the boat racing, Primrose?"

"If I have to, and I think it better you call me Miss Ainsley."

"I shall try. What did you mean by 'have to'?"

"I am not really one for lolling about all day watching men do things I cannot… or more importantly, am not allowed to do."

He'd shortened his stride to match hers, and Primrose realized he was in fact a great deal taller than her. She'd never really taken the time to notice that in other men before. The hands he swung at his side as he walked would engulf both hers. Strong hands, hands that would keep whatever they held safe.

"Would you like to enter the boat race, then?"

"As a woman, I don't think that's an option, do you?"

"But if it were, would you?"

Primrose thought about that as they walked down the long hallway.

"I think I would. I like to do things that challenge me. Painting and sewing don't really do that."

"But gardening does?"

"Oh yes."

"Perhaps we could dress you as a man when no one is looking, and you can join the boat race."

She shot him a look and found his eyes on her. Primrose looked away.

"I'm not entirely sure why you are doing this?"

"Doing what?"

"The teasing, the… ah, the kiss, and all of it. If you are simply having fun at my expense because you can, then I beg you to cease, as it is not fun on my part. There are also plenty of young ladies here who would be more than happy with your attentions. Young, well-bred women who will simper and smile and tell you how wonderful you are."

"But not you." His words were deep and had lost their levity.

"Not me."

"And maybe that's why I seek you out, Miss Ainsley. You're different."

"No, I'm not. I'm bland—well, so my brother says—and a woman who is attempting to get through her first, and God willing, only season without attracting the attentions of a man."

"An extremely difficult thing to do when you are spirited,

beautiful, and interesting. I fear your brother has it wrong; you are in no way bland."

"I am none of those things, nor do I wish to be."

"You are, but that point will be discussed another day. Perhaps we could help each other?"

He stopped, wrapping his fingers around her arm. A shaft of sunlight came through the window behind him, burnishing his hair, making it appear as if he wore a halo. The man did not need divine intervention to make him any more appealing.

"We each have no wish to wed or draw interest from men or women. Perhaps instead if we showed interest in each other, the others, and I include my family and Lady Jane in that, would leave us alone."

"But if we are seen together, people will talk."

"True, but as you have no wish to live in society, you could easily decide against our furthering our acquaintance and walk away at the end of this. I will say there is no ill will between us, or something along those lines."

He did not look as if he was playing some kind of game. Could she do that? It would mean she could go home after the season and stay there.

"It is not quite that easy for a woman to walk away unscathed," Primrose said.

"We shall be seen chatting a few times, no more than that."

"I shall think about it" was all Primrose said as she started walking again.

"You do that, and remember your wish, Primrose. Marriage to Herbert the Honorable. That is what you still want, after all?"

Was it? Yes, Primrose told herself. Of course it was. Walking back to her room to get her bonnet, she wondered why she had a niggle of doubt now.

CHAPTER NINE

Benjamin wasn't sure why he'd proposed what he had to Primrose, but he did know one thing. The woman intrigued him like no other had before her. While he would never act on that, it would be enjoyable to spend some time with her. He had no wish for her to have feelings for him, and as she wanted to marry Herbert there was little risk of that happening.

Ben had come to the realization long ago that women were to be watched carefully, as they could turn on you as quick as a venomous snake. His mother had taught him that.

Yes, he had wonderful sisters-in-law, but he wasn't married to them, so they couldn't really hurt him… maybe his brothers, but he doubted that would happen.

It was actually a sound idea to spend time with Primrose and deter his sisters-in-law from the quest to see him married for a while. Yet when the season ended, wouldn't he be right back where he started, with Phoebe and Hannah still trying to find him a wife? But he could surely cry a broken heart for a while, which would give him more time without them hurling unmarried young woman into his path.

After visiting his room, Ben made his way down to the front entrance of Rossetter House. He found Alex there.

"What are you doing down here?"

"Waiting for you."

"How did you know I was coming down?"

Alex raised a brow.

"Right, that thing happened."

The "thing," as they referred to it, was simply something they'd always had. A knowledge that sometimes just popped into their heads that the other was close, or soon would be. Strange? Definitely, but as it was just a part of their lives, they lived with it.

"Where is your wife? You are not usually separated for long."

"Resting. She is tired, and there is the dance this evening."

"Hannah, tired?" Ben raised a brow. The woman had inexhaustible energy.

"She is to have a child, Ben."

"I know that, Alex. Her stomach gives her away."

"I told her to rest, actually. Hannah does tend to overdo things."

"Of course, and you are worried, which I'm sure is entirely natural. Each time Phoebe carried a child, Finn was frantic."

"Oh God," Alex groaned. "I remember and vowed never to be that way."

"But you will be." Ben patted his brother on the shoulder. "Come, a walk into Two Oaks for the annual boat race will make you feel better."

"Yes, I need a distraction."

"Do we have a boat?"

"I believe some of the locals have supplied them for us. Archery is planned for tomorrow."

"Yes, I heard that also."

"I will beat you as I always do."

"No, you don't!"

"More often than not."

"Rubbish. I always beat you and will continue to do so with very little effort on my part."

"What are you arguing about now?"

"Thea, how lovely to see you at last," Ben said, kissing her cheek. Married to Ace, she was the duke's and Will Ryder's sister. She'd wanted to marry Oliver Dillinger, and nothing, not even his lack of rank or birth and her exceptional one, had stopped that from happening. Unlike Ace, who was big and raw boned, Thea looked every inch the duke's daughter, with pale, flawless skin, and a haughty arch to her brow. She could have married any man but chose the one she loved.

"Yes, I am pleased to be out of my sickbed, I can tell you. Ace tends to hover if I'm unwell. As it was only morning sickness I was not in danger, but you cannot tell the man that."

"He loves you," Alex said, looking pale suddenly.

"Yes, that's all very well, but a large man like that hovering constantly tends to agitate me more than soothe."

"And yet I will continue to do so, my love."

"Hello, darling. I was just telling the twins about your annoying habit of hovering."

"I heard," Ace drawled, coming to his beloved's side. "And still I will not change."

Thea huffed out a breath, but slipped her arm through her husband's and moved closer to his side.

"Are you coming to watch the boat race?" Alex said.

"Of course, my foolish husband is competing."

"You taught me to swim," Ace added.

"But not that well yet."

"I'll save him if he falls in," Alex said.

Beneath the trees, large tables had been set with chairs and plenty of food and drink. A lovely setting on a sunny day, with Rossetter at their backs, it would take a hardened heart not to appreciate it. Ben looked for Primrose and found her talking with Mr. Sanders.

"You may have competition there, Ben," Ace said.

"Sanders?" Alex scoffed. "My brother is worth ten of him. Not that he's interested in Miss Ainsley, but if he was—"

"I'm unsure if I'm interested or not, but if I am that is my decision, thank you very much."

Alex's eyes settled on his face.

"But you could be?"

Ben shrugged. "I don't know yet." He left it at that. If Primrose agreed, then he had set things in motion. If not, he would say nothing further.

After yet more food, they began the walk into Two Oaks. Primrose was just ahead of him, still with Mr. Sanders, which shouldn't have annoyed Ben as much as it did. At least they had two other ladies accompanying them.

"Oh, Miss Ainsley, how are you finding your first season?" he heard Miss Hellier ask.

"Very well, thank you."

"But it must be something of a challenge, after all, considering your years…."

Ben heard the insult just as the others did. Primrose murmured something in reply that he didn't catch.

"And what of your family, are they to join you, Miss Ainsley?" Miss Robbins added. "Or will you be spending the entire season with the gracious Lady Jane?"

He'd been in society long enough to hear the innuendos in the words of those young women. People rarely spoke to him that way, and hearing it made the reality of Primrose's situation clearer. He thought about intervening, as obviously

Sanders was oblivious to what was happening, but then would she appreciate that? Likely not.

"Oh, Mr. Hetherington, is it not an exciting prospect?"

Miss Fullerton Smythe had moved to his side.

"What is exciting, Miss Fullerton Smythe?" Ben watched Primrose fall back slightly away from the group she'd been with, so she was now walking in front of him, alone.

"The boat race, of course!"

Pretty in pale lemon, Miss Fullerton Smythe wore a chip bonnet and white gloves and left him cold. Strange how that was the case, when with one look at the rigid back before him he felt anything but cold.

"Ah yes, of course. It should be fun."

She then chattered on about anything and a great deal of nothing, starting with the weather; he was soon bored enough to yawn. At least he could keep his eyes on that long blonde ringlet that trailed down Primrose's spine. Was she upset?

"Miss Fullerton Smythe, do you have a passion, such as books or plants?"

"A passion, Mr. Hetherington?" She pulled away from him slightly as if she was preparing to flee. He'd clearly shocked her.

"Something that excites you. I like steam engines." Ben wasn't sure why he had spoken those words, but it was too late to retract them now.

"Oh, well." She first looked left and then right. "Do you really wish to hear?"

"I do. Who are you checking for?"

"My mother. She has fiendishly sharp hearing, especially when listening to my conversations."

"And you don't want her to hear this one?"

"You asked a question of me, Mr. Hetherington, and not

about the weather, so I would like to give you an honest answer."

"Please do."

"Your interest is steam engines, which I'm sure are intriguing, but mine is wood carving."

Ben was sure she held her breath while waiting for his reaction.

"Really? How intriguing." He managed to keep the surprise out of his voice.

"It is." She exhaled. Her face lost that silly, girlish, simpering expression as she talked, and her voice even lowered to a normal pitch. "The trick is to find the right wood to use. I have many pieces in my rooms. Mother won't let me bring them downstairs… nor carve them anywhere but in my rooms or out in the stables."

"How does one go about getting just the right piece of wood?" Ben said, genuinely interested. He wondered if under those gloves there were several nicks and scratches on her hands. It was a very unusual hobby for a young lady.

"Well, I am not as skilled as I would like to be—"

"Yet," Ben qualified.

"Yet." She smiled. "I have found oak to be the best to work with." Miss Fullerton Smythe then launched into a full and detailed explanation that kept him interested until they were close to Two Oaks.

"Thank you for sharing your passion with me, Miss Fullerton Smythe."

"Thank you for listening, Mr. Hetherington."

"Your secret is safe with me. May I offer you some advice?"

"Of course." She looked up at him, and he saw she was genuinely interested in what he was about to say.

"Never give up your wood carving, as it obviously makes you very happy."

"My parents do not hold the same view as you, Mr. Hetherington. They believe no man will want a wife who, in their words, exhibits signs of an unbalanced nature."

"You are the least unbalanced person I know, and believe me, I've met a few."

"Thank you." She had lovely dimples. "Oh, I...." Her words fell away as Mr. Jeremy Caton walked by them. He lifted his hat and smiled at her, then carried on into the village.

Tall and lean, the man was an acquaintance but nothing more. Comfortable to converse with, third son of a viscount. He made his own way in the world.

"Miss Fullerton Smythe, are you all right?"

She gave her head a little shake, almost as if she had been in a daze.

"I am, thank you, Mr. Hetherington."

Interesting. Ben doubted Lady Fullerton Smythe would approve of her daughter within ten feet of a man third in line for a title.

"Please ensure that whoever you marry knows what you do beforehand. Not many men could resist a woman who does wood carving."

She laughed.

"My mother has lectured me for many hours on just that subject, so I fear you are teasing me."

"She's wrong. Now, my next suggestion to you is that you make friends with Miss Ainsley. She too has some interesting hobbies."

"Does she?" Miss Fullerton Smythe shot a look at Primrose's back. "My mother...."

Her words fell away as she blushed.

"Has no wish for you to associate with her."

"She has very particular ideas about most things."

"As do most mothers, from what I gather. Come along, I shall introduce you."

"Oh, we've met."

"But have you actually conversed on anything other than the weather?"

"It's the safest topic."

"I know. However, I want you to tell Miss Ainsley about your hobby; she will love it."

"Thank you, Mr. Hetherington." Her words were softly spoken.

"For what?"

"For being genuinely interested in my wood carving."

Ben felt ashamed of himself for not taking the time to speak with this woman before. Not taking the time to see that these young ladies had desires and interests just as he and his brothers did.

"It was my pleasure." He increased his pace, and Miss Fullerton Smythe kept up with him, and soon they drew alongside Primrose.

"Miss Ainsley, I believe you have met Miss Fullerton Smythe?"

Primrose's smile was wide and welcoming, even after what she'd just endured.

"Of course. Good day, Miss Fullerton Smythe."

"We are to sample the local bakery fare. I have heard there is none finer," Ben said.

"We just ate!" Primrose and Miss Fullerton Smythe said at the same time.

"I am a growing man."

"If you continue eating like that, some parts of you will grow faster than others," Primrose said.

Miss Fullerton Smythe looked shocked and made a choking sound. Ben swallowed his smile.

"As charming as this conversation is, I'm sure it's about to turn into frills and trim, so I shall leave you two ladies alone. I need to speak with my brother."

As he walked off, he looked over his shoulder to see Miss Fullerton Smythe lean toward Primrose and say something. He had a feeling these two women could become friends. Ben just hoped her mother didn't step in to stop that happening.

CHAPTER TEN

*P*rimrose frowned at the back of Benjamin Hetherington's head. What was he about, leaving her with this woman? They had barely spoken two words in the time they'd known each other, and those were about the weather.

She did not want to listen to more insults carefully veiled behind polite words. Primrose understood the order of things; she was beneath the other young ladies in society, and they wanted her to know that. She didn't have to like it, however, or stand idly by listening to those insults.

Yet more people who didn't like her. If she was not immune, this continual rejection would be unsettling.

Miss Fullerton Smythe's father was an Earl, and her mother very full of her own importance; she doubted either wanted their precious daughter to converse with someone like her.

"Miss Ainsley, will you walk with me into Two Oaks?"

"We are nearly there, Miss Fullerton Smythe."

"The short distance left then?"

"Of course. Thank you for asking, but I must be honest, shouldn't you be speaking with those other ladies?"

"I'm so terribly sorry, Miss Ainsley."

"Pardon?" Primrose looked at the young lady. She was beautiful in that flawless way some women had. Delicate bone structure, long curling lashes over soft brown eyes. Masses of lovely brown hair that was always styled perfectly. Her clothes were cut to perfection to sit on a lovely, delicate figure. Primrose could never be like that. She only had to walk three paces for a shoe ribbon to come undone or lock of hair to escape its confines.

"For not making more of an effort to speak with you when clearly I should have."

"Oh no, I completely understand," Primrose replied. And she did. She was not one of the favorable young ladies in society. She was here at the charity of another. Her family was not the type to inspire enthusiasm among ambitious parents and their offspring.

"You shouldn't. Did you know I like to do wood carvings, Miss Ainsley?"

"I—ah, no, I didn't know that." *That was a shock.*

"You think I'm quite mad no doubt for saying such a thing, but Mr. Hetherington told me to tell you. He said you had hobbies also that you may like to discuss with me? It is really quite a liberating feeling to speak about it, as before I have told no one."

Primrose looked at his back again. Broad, with wide shoulders encased in deep green. Did he introduce this woman to Primrose because he believed she had no friends? Which she didn't, but it was a humbling thought just the same, and one that made her feel warm inside.

"I'm sorry, I should just leave you alone."

"No!" Primrose took the arm of Miss Fullerton Smythe as she began to walk away. "Really, and I am interested in plants. I take cuttings wherever I go and hide them under my bed wrapped in something damp. The gardeners at Lady Jane's house help me."

Miss Fullerton Smythe's laugh was a great deal fuller than it usually was—and, Primrose thought, genuine.

"How wonderful. I make small woodland figures."

"Do you really? That's intriguing."

"Yes. My mother hates it, Miss Ainsley. My father tolerates it, and my siblings think I'm mad."

"My name is Primrose."

"I am Heather."

They shared a look, and then Heather squeezed Primrose's hand and they walked together over the stone bridge and down into the quaint town of Two Oaks.

"Heather, please come with me."

Lady Fullerton Smythe appeared at their side as they reached the first building. The militant look on her face did not bode well for her daughter.

"No, Mother, I am talking with Primrose, and quite happy doing so."

The woman's lips pursed, but she said nothing further, not wishing to make a scene, and walked away. But Primrose doubted the matter would be left there.

"I have no problem if you wish to follow her, Heather."

"No, I am asserting my independence, Primrose. It will do her good to see that I can do that occasionally."

People walked about Two Oaks at a slower pace than they did in London, where the streets were lined with horses and carriages and people bustling from one place to the next.

"It is lovely," Primrose said, noting the splashes of color coming from the window boxes. "I miss Pickford, even if it is not as beautiful as this."

"I'm always happiest at one of Father's estates," Heather said. "I wish I could stay there, but Mother would have conniptions if I even mentioned that fact. She pines for London when we retire to the country. It is my hope that one day I will marry a man who likes the quiet life as I do."

Primrose certainly understood that sentiment.

"I overhead the Duchess of Rossetter saying this morning that they have someone here in Two Oaks who does amazing carvings of birds. I believe they have a shop in the village."

"Let's see if we can find it then." Heather sounded excited.

They walked passed a milliners and a bootmaker. The Rossetter party drifted in and out of shops ahead of them, while Heather and Primrose kept searching for the carving store.

Thankfully she had lost sight of the disturbing Benjamin Hetherington.

"Miss Fullerton Smythe, do come and look at this bonnet. It will be quite lovely on you!"

"My mother put her up to that," Heather said out the side of her mouth to Primrose. "I will come soon, Miss Robbins," she called, waving to the young woman as they continued on down the street.

"Oh, but—"

Heather kept walking, dragging Primrose with her. They eventually located the shop. It was tucked away down a side lane darting off the main street. The only indication it was there was a small arrow with one word painted on it.

"Carving," Primrose read. "Not a great deal of thought went in to that sign. One wonders how just that simple word would lure people down that lane?"

"It's going to lure us, Primrose. But how can we duck down there without my mother seeing, I wonder?" Heather looked behind them to see if Lady Fullerton Smythe was close.

"Ladies, can I be of any assistance?"

Mr. Hetherington was smiling at them in a knowing way

that suggested to Primrose he was quite happy with the fact he had instigated their union.

"We wish to go down there to see the carving shop. To do that, we need a distraction," Primrose said, pointing to her left.

"Of the motherly intervention kind?" His eyes twinkled.

"The very one, Mr. Hetherington." Primrose tried not to smile, but it was difficult.

"Leave it to me. But give me a few minutes, and I will also expect some kind of carving as recompense. Perhaps you could pretend to look in that shop while I create a diversion?" He nodded to the confectionery shop window. "Not a terrible hardship, I imagine."

"No indeed." Heather tugged Primrose's arm. "I wonder if they have any of that toffee that everyone is talking about at the moment."

They were inspecting the window in detail a few minutes later when a loud shriek filled the air.

"Get it off!"

Turning toward the scream, Heather and Primrose found Lady Fullerton Smythe doing some kind of odd dance in the street while flapping her hands about. Beside her was Benjamin Hetherington.

"If you'll just come with me, I shall attempt to help you, Lady Fullerton Smythe."

They didn't wait to see just what he had done to Heather's mother; instead they hurried down the lane. The shop was tiny, a narrow place that was hard to walk into two abreast. The counter was manned by a wizened old man who looked them over as they entered.

"Good day to you."

"Good day. We hear you have some very fine bird carvings in your lovely shop," Primrose said. Heather, however, was already heading to the first shelf.

"Me and my Anne make them."

"Anne?"

"Women carve also, miss."

"Why yes, sir, they do," Primrose said loud enough for Heather to hear.

"'Tis rare to find such a place," Heather said, her voice filled with wonder.

"Well, be quick about it. Select what you wish, then purchase it so we can hurry back before we are missed."

Primrose's eyes fell on a small, scruffy owl. Its hair seemed ruffled, and it looked grumpy and disheveled. She didn't know why she thought of him while looking at it, but she did.

"I will take this," she said, giving herself no time to think.

Heather purchased three carvings, and soon they were leaving the shop.

"Oh, Mr. Caton, good day to you," Primrose said to the man entering.

"Good day. Did you find something to purchase? I have heard great things about this place."

"I-I, ah…."

Primrose shot her new friend a look. She was rigid, hands clenched into fists, and her face was now flooded with color.

"Oh indeed, we have found just the thing," Primrose added quickly. "We shall see you at the boat race, Mr. Caton."

His smile was gentle and directed at Heather. Was that longing she saw in his eyes?

"You shall."

Minutes later they were back out on the main street once again, and Primrose held the purchases in case Lady Fullerton Smythe questioned what her daughter was carrying.

"What happened in there, Heather?"

"With what?" Heather was looking down the street.

"Mr. Caton. You couldn't speak in his presence."

"I was worried Mother would arrive, Primrose."

She didn't think that was the entire truth but didn't press her further. After all, they hadn't known each other that long, and Primrose didn't want to destroy what could be a wonderful friendship.

"The birds in that shop were very detailed, Primrose. I so wanted to chat with that man about his techniques."

"Perhaps we can return before you leave Rossetter?"

"There you are!"

"Hello, Penelope," Heather said to the young woman who called to them.

"Your mother has had a terrible fright. It seems a spider dropped into her bodice. Mr. Hetherington saw it crawling down her chest. Luckily it was gone when she looked, but it was terrifying, as you'll understand. You need to come and see her, Heather. She was distraught."

Penelope, Miss Haversham, gave Primrose a look that suggested she'd just crawled out from under a rock.

"Come along, Primrose."

"No, Heather, you go, and I will see you later."

She didn't want to go, but she did… reluctantly. Primrose would be sure to drop off her purchases later.

"You owe me for creating that diversion."

"Miss Fullerton Smythe owes you," Primrose corrected the large, smug male now at her side.

"But you owe me for finding you a friend who has strange ways as you do."

"Collecting cuttings and having a love of botany is not strange."

"Your clicking jaw is strange."

"It's something I was born with, I can hardly help that. Besides, you have this issue with loud noises and people chewing, surely that makes you strange also, if not more so?"

"Me, strange?" He pressed a hand to his chest, his face a picture of innocence. "Many women would refute your claim."

"No doubt, but only because they see a handsome façade and not the complexities beneath."

They had started walking back toward the river that ran beneath the bridge. This would be the vantage point for the boat race, she'd been told. Rossetter guests were already gathering there.

"I am handsome? Why thank you, Primrose. I am also an open book."

"With many smudged pages." Primrose snorted, then looked about them to see if anyone had heard.

"You are safe, only I heard."

"You don't matter."

"Charming."

"I have given some more thought to your suggestion, and I believe it has merits."

"I thought you might."

"I will add smug to your list of faults."

"I am only smug when I am right."

"So clearly not often then," Primrose snapped.

"Ouch. I do believe you wound me, Miss Ainsley."

People had gathered on either side of the bridge, villagers and guests. Some had wandered down underneath to line the bank.

"If you will excuse me, Miss Ainsley, I must prepare to race. Save the rest of your cutting rejoinders for later, and we shall continue this discussion about you worshipping the ground I walk on for the remainder of the time we are here at Rossetter ."

He had walked away before she could say anything further. Primrose refused to watch him, so she walked to where Lady Jane stood, unfortunately, with Lady Fullerton Smythe.

"Are you enjoying yourself, Primrose?"

"Indeed, Lady Jane. Thank you."

"My daughter is the epitome of elegance, Lady Jane. Highly sought, and of course has all the right connections."

Bitch.

"Did you know that Primrose is the granddaughter of an earl, Lady Fullerton Smythe?"

Lady Jane may make Primrose grind her teeth regularly with her constant harping about society rules and the correct way to do things, but she could be extremely loyal.

"Oh… ah, I had of course heard something—"

"Yes. The current Earl of Pennworthy is her cousin."

Lady Fullerton Smythe looked like she'd swallowed that spider. Her mouth was opening and closing and her large chin wobbling. Primrose should not be enjoying the spectacle quite a much as she was.

"How unusual you did not know of the connection."

"Oh well… yes, of course I did, but had forgotten."

That was a big fat lie.

"Heather, dear," she called, looking around for a distraction. "Come here."

Heather arrived, eyes twinkling, and moved to Primrose's side.

"Yes, Mother?"

"Did you know that Miss Ainsley is the cousin of the current Earl of Pennworthy?"

"I didn't. How wonderful." She clapped her hands, making her mother's eyes narrow. "Come, Primrose, I have just the vantage point from which to watch the race."

Primrose let herself be pulled along the bridge.

"Here. We can see up and down the river. And how

wonderful that you found an earl to make you acceptable to Mother. Now we shall not need to hide our friendship."

"I don't think it's made me that acceptable, Heather. Those other ladies know about it, surely. In fact, peers know everything about other peers; it's a rite of passage."

"And watch out for my carving, Primrose. You just knocked them against the stone of the bridge."

"So, is that your true nature?" Primrose teased. "Bossy?"

"I can be."

"I can be like that too, so at least we will have some wonderful debates."

Primrose felt lighter than she had in days, and she had to thank Benjamin Hetherington for that. Today he'd kissed her and made her realize what could be between two people. If she never experienced that kind of emotion again, she could at least remember this day. Plus, there was now Heather in her life.

She'd woken up this morning the exact same Primrose who went to bed last night, but by midmorning she'd changed somehow. Now she had received her first kiss and made a new friend. Surely the day could not get better than that.

"We have known each other for an hour, perhaps two, and it is as if we have always been friends," Heather said. "I don't really have many friends, just acquaintances."

"No one really wants to associate with me because of my inferior birth and lack of dowry." Primrose went for honesty. "It does not bother me, but I must say it is wonderful to have met you… again."

"I am ashamed to say there are many aspects of society I find unworthy. So many rules and high standards. It's quite tiring."

"Very," Primrose agreed. "I'm always terrified of putting a

foot in the wrong direction. I shall return to Pickford and be quite happy to leave it all behind at the end of the season."

"That makes me sad, as we will not see each other."

"But we can write every week."

Heather sighed. "I don't want to marry someone I don't like."

They were huddled together looking back down the river, awaiting the arrival of the boats. No one could overhear their conversation.

"Then we must find a man you do like," Primrose whispered. "Is there anyone?" She looked at her new friend. "There is, I can see it in the way you're avoiding my eyes."

"You don't know me well enough to know that," Heather scoffed.

"Come, tell me who it is at once." What had happened in the wood carving shop slipped into her head. Could it be Mr. Caton that Heather had taken a liking to?

Heather looked left and right, then shook her head. "No, I don't want to voice his name."

"What a terrible chicken heart you are."

Heather just smiled and kept her mouth closed.

"I will find out, you know," Primrose said. "My brother says there is no secret in our entire village that I do not know. He thinks Wellington should have used me to interrogate people."

"They are coming!" Heather pointed to the river.

"I will not be deterred, but for now we shall watch the boat race."

And she was happy to do just that beside her new friend.

CHAPTER ELEVEN

*L*ooking upstream, she saw the first boat.

"Allow me to run a commentary for you." Lady Levermarch had arrived and positioned herself between Heather and Primrose. "You will not know some of the locals."

"Oh, yes please," Heather said.

The first boat appeared, and it was filled with people. In fact, too many people for the size. They were dressed in bright colors and wore scarfs on their heads.

"That is the Fletcher family, and they always dress like pirates. Mr. Luke Fletcher is married to my sister Isabella; he is seated in the rear. His family live in a lovely big house here in Twoaks."

"Twoaks is what the locals call Two Oaks, is that correct?"

Lady Levermarch nodded.

"There seem to be many people in that boat," Heather said. "I hope it will stay upright."

"It will. They've been doing this for years, and all know how to swim."

"How can they pass each other when the river is so

narrow?" Primrose looked up and down the winding ribbon of water.

"Race is a loose term for these events. It's really more a parade, and a great deal of the time is spent splashing each other. There"—Lady Levermarch pointed downstream—"is the only area wide enough for the boats to pass, so if they are to make their move it will be there."

Lady Levermarch continued with her commentary and infused it with wit that had Primrose, Heather, and those close enough to hear laughing.

"Lord Dobberly is something of an eccentric. That is his boat, and he always just sits in the back on a chair, dressed like Henry the Eighth. We fear if he is tipped in, he'd drown, weighed down as he is by so much clothing and gold."

He did look very grand seated in the rear of the little boat, waving regally.

"He runs the Two Oaks Derby."

"I've heard of that, it's run in winter," Heather said.

"Yes," Lady Levermarch sighed. "We, and many of the locals, have tried to get him to change it, but he will not yield. It has been run on December the twenty-first for many, many years."

"I've heard the race can be quite brutal," Heather added.

"My sister rode in it one year... the eldest one."

Looking for Lady Ryder, they found her with several children attached to her skirt.

"She has a far more robust constitution than appearances suggest."

"I've never done anything daring," Primrose said. "It is not in my nature."

"Rubbish. I saw you leap into that water to rescue that dog. If that is not daring, I don't know what is," Lady Levermarch said.

Was she daring? No, Primrose didn't believe it. She had

always wanted to do something out of the ordinary, but the opportunity had just never arisen. The most daring thing she'd done was help Mrs. Putt bake a cherry cake, and then deliver it to Herbert. He had not been pleased when she'd called on him alone and had hastily sent her away. He'd kept the cherry cake, however.

Herbert was definitely not daring.

"Never fear, ladies, there are still plenty of years ahead of you to be daring," Lady Levermarch added, leaning over the railing.

"In that boat are Jenny and Freddy. She was our housekeeper and married Lord Ryder's steward. They are wonderful."

The middle-aged couple beamed up at those on the bridge, smiles wide as they waved at Lady Levermarch and her sisters. Jenny, as Lady Levermarch called her, had flowers all over her hat, and Freddy wore a black waistcoat with brass buttons.

"Ah, now this is the boat I was waiting for. My husband and his brothers. One hopes they overturn."

"You don't want them to make it to the end?" Primrose asked, her eyes finding Benjamin Hetherington.

He'd taken off his jacket, like his brothers, and she could see the muscles in his arms working as he swung the paddle.

Primrose had told herself repeatedly that if she married it would be to a comfortable man, so why was she suddenly fixated on this one? Perhaps it was because he would never be anything to her and she felt safe doing so? Did that even make sense?

"Hello, darling!" Lady Levermarch waved to her husband. He waved back, the smile on his face filled with love.

I don't want that, Primrose reminded herself looking away from Benjamin Hetherington. *Besides, he said he had no wish to marry.* And he wouldn't marry her anyway. No, they

THE LADY'S DANGEROUS LOVE

were merely going to help each other get through the season, and then she'd go back to Pickford and marry Herbert.

Primrose tried to tell herself that this thought did not depress her, but it did.

"Come, we shall hurry down to the bank, then we can see the finish!"

In seconds Heather and Primrose were following Lady Levermarch—Phoebe, as she insisted they call her.

They made it as the two boats were neck and neck. She felt the excitement build. Primrose couldn't help the shriek that came out of her mouth. Looking to the bridge, she watched Lady Jane's mouth open, no doubt censuring her to behave like a lady, but she ignored it. There was too much fun to be had.

There were many boats now crammed on the river, all the occupants waving to those watching. People were shouting insults and encouragement, and soon Primrose was caught up in the excitement.

Looking at the water, she vowed that this time she would not end up in there. Today she would stay dry and not do anything to disgrace herself.

"Drop that stick at once, Amanda!" Lady Levermarch said to her daughter. "You will not throw that at your father."

The young girl had a cheeky look on her face.

"I wasn't throwing it at Papa, I was throwing it beside his boat so it splashed him."

"Oh, well then, go right ahead. I should like to see that also."

This woman really was like no other noblewoman she'd met before.

"You looked shocked, Miss Ainsley."

"Oh no, not at all."

"I find the direct approach works in life, or you shall

spend your days behaving in ways others want you to and not being yourself."

Wasn't that the truth.

Mr. Caton joined them then, saving Primrose from having to reply. "If I may suggest you do not go too close to the edge, ladies, as they will be attempting to splash each other and anyone they can reach."

Primrose looked at Heather. Her friend's cheeks were once again filled with color, and she was looking anywhere but at him.

"Jeremy, how lovely to see you!"

"I saw you this morning, Phoebe."

"Perhaps you did, but it is still lovely to see you again. Have you come to splash the people in their boats?"

"Lady Althea did ask if I would attempt to throw water at her husband, as she is unable to come down here herself."

He seemed a gentle man from what she had seen. Primrose thought he would be a lovely match for Heather, but doubted her family felt the same way.

"I'll splash him, too!" Phoebe yelled up to Lady Althea Dillinger, who stood at the railing. She waved.

"Excellent," Mr. Caton said.

"Have you been introduced to Miss Ainsley and Miss Fullerton Smythe, Jeremy?"

"Not officially." He had a lovely smile. "It is a pleasure to meet you, ladies."

They both curtsied.

"Would you like to see what I purchased in the carving shop, ladies?" He raised a small wrapped parcel that he held in one hand.

"I would!" The words rushed out of Heather's mouth with a bit more force than was warranted, but Mr. Caton did not seem to mind.

"We shall compare, then," he said gently.

Primrose handed Heather the bag holding their purchases.

"Excellent," Lady Levermarch said, slipping her arm through Primrose's.

"Pardon?"

"Nothing at all, Miss Ainsley. Come, we shall heckle people. It's something I'm particularly good at."

Primrose threw a look at Heather; her friend's head was lowered next to Mr. Caton's. Glancing up at Lady Fullerton Smythe, she couldn't read her expression, but doubted it was a happy one.

CHAPTER TWELVE

*E*very time Alex dipped his paddle, he managed to splash Ben.

"You will receive my paddle in the back of your head if you continue doing that," he growled.

"What?"

"That will do," Finn said as he always did and had done since they were children.

No one made Ben revert to childish ways quite like his twin brother.

"Your fair ladies are blowing you kisses," Ben said, looking up to the bridge, then beneath it to where Phoebe stood with Primrose.

"More like throwing stones," Alex drawled, waving to Hannah.

He wondered what had Primrose frowning. He watched Sanders move to her side, lean closer, and say something to her. Surely she could see the man was about as interesting as a bowl of gruel.

"Did you just growl?" Alex asked.

"What? Of course not. Gentlemen don't growl."

THE LADY'S DANGEROUS LOVE

"Actually, I heard it," Finn added.

"Move it, real men are coming through!"

Ben turned to see Will Ryder and his brother. They had Ace in their boat, which gave them considerable strength.

The river was just about at its widest part, and soon those with a competitive streak would be attempting to pass.

"Paddle!" Ben roared. And suddenly the race was on. They swept under the bridge.

"Gentlemen," Ace scoffed as they drew level. "You're all soft."

People on the bank waved and yelled encouragement, and Ben put his shoulder into the next paddle stroke. They surged forward.

"Oh, do hurry!"

He knew that voice. Turning his head, he found Primrose on the bank with Phoebe and Miss Fullerton Smythe.

"Paddle faster!"

"I'm trying!" Ben roared back at her.

He ducked as a paddle swung his way, and he turned to see Ace smiling.

"Sabotage!" Finn roared. The boats then slowed as the occupants resorted to splashing each other. Ace went into the water first, but they all heard the clunk as his head hit the side of the boat.

"He could have knocked himself out!" Ben roared.

"Can he swim?" Alex asked when he did not appear.

"Yes," Will said. "But not very well."

Everyone looked, but it was a cry from the bank that alerted him. Looking to where Primrose was running, he found her further downstream. Ace appeared, his body floating facedown in the water.

Someone screamed as Ben dived in, followed by the rest of the men. They swam as fast as they could, but to his horror, it was Primrose who reached Ace first. She held his head above the water.

"He's unconscious!" she yelled.

Ben could hear people yelling, but his focus was on reaching Primrose and Ace; he did so seconds later.

He held Ace from the left, and Alex moved closer and took the right side. Between them, they swam him to the shore.

Hands soon grabbed Ace and hauled him up onto the bank. Ben turned to find Primrose, but she was still struggling toward the bank. The current was a great deal stronger than it appeared.

"Grab her!" he roared at Will and Finn, who were closest.

They did, and towed her to the shore. Ben then grabbed her under the arms and pulled her upward.

"Is he all right?" Primrose asked, easing out of his grip.

"His eyes are opening," Mr. Caton said. "Come on, Ace."

"Oliver!"

Ben looked up to see Thea running down to them.

"Don't run!" Ace roared, struggling to sit. "For God's sake, slow down. I am fine!"

His face was ashen, but he seemed coherent. A trickle of blood ran down his forehead.

"I hit my head, but I am all right." He caught Thea close as she dropped down beside him, holding her as if she was made of spun glass. "I lost consciousness only briefly," he added.

"Yes, well, you are alive and rational," Thea said, patting his cheeks. "But obviously you shall need to be checked over by a doctor."

"Must I? I hate doctors."

"And yet I only need to sneeze and you call one."

"That's different," Ace grumbled.

"Come, we need to get you back and into dry clothes,"

Thea said. "But first I must hug Miss Ainsley close and tell her that she is wonderful."

"Oh no… really—" The words were cut off as Thea did exactly as she'd said she would. Uncaring of the wet now seeping into her clothes from Primrose's once again soaked dress, she squeezed her hard.

"Thank you, my dear."

"Yes, thank you, and you, Ben." Ace gripped his hand.

"Primrose." Miss Fullerton Smythe reached for her. "You are so incredibly brave. I was struck still with fear, but not you. You leapt in—"

"Recklessly," Ben added. "Without thought to consequence yet again."

"I was not reckless, I did what needed to be done!" She snapped at him. "You were too far away to reach him in time. He was about to go under again."

"And I cannot swim," Mr. Caton said, looking at Ace. "I will now be rectifying that."

"I am well, Jeremy," Ace said. Ben hadn't realized they were friends, but their hands gripped and held briefly, showing him he was wrong.

"Come, you need to get back to Rossetter and dry off—once again," he added as she shivered.

"I was not reckless," she said again.

She was actually daring to argue with him while standing there shivering like a drowned rodent. Her dress clung to her every curve, her bonnet was gone, and her hair hung in a long wet tail.

"Yes, you were, but now is not the time to argue. Now we need to get warm… again."

"I have no time to argue with you, Mr. Hetherington. Lady Jane is calling me."

Lifting her chin, and her sodden skirts, Primrose

squelched away as haughtily as you please. Leaving him with a feeling he couldn't quite define.

"She was incredibly brave, Ben," Finn said. "And likely right. She reached Ace just as he was about to go under again."

"She will drown one of these days. You cannot continuously plunge recklessly into water wearing a dress and always survive."

"Well, let us hope she does not make a habit of it," Alex added.

"One can only hope that three times is enough for one lifetime."

"Three?" Finn queried.

"I meant two," Ben lied.

"Did you?" Alex raised a brow, and Ben gave him a look that suggested retribution if he didn't back him up. "Two it is."

"You seem extremely interested in Miss Ainsley, Ben. Care to tell me what is going on between you?"

"There is nothing to tell you, Finn." His eldest brother clearly didn't believe him as he snorted, but said nothing further.

"As I said earlier, there is something between you and that woman. My question is, what?" Alex whispered in his ear.

Ben snapped his teeth together to stop from saying anything further and made his way up to the bridge behind the others.

A cart was plodding over the bridge as they arrived. It was hailed, and the wet members of the party were loaded onto it. Ben lifted Primrose, and she stiffened up like a board but offered him a curt thank-you. She then kept her distance from him and travelled back beside Miss Fullerton Smythe, who was clutching a parcel of something close to her chest.

Ben helped Primrose from the cart again when they reached Rossetter.

"Thank you, but I can manage," she said stiffly.

"I'm keeping up appearances," he whispered. "And yet another dress is assigned to rags."

"The other two were salvaged, and this will be also. I'm not sure why my wardrobe is such a concern for you, Mr. Hetherington."

Ben studied her, letting his eyes roam her face. She made him feel off-balance. They were the only words he could use to describe how he felt. He should cut all ties with her right now and stop this foolish charade before it truly began. So why didn't he?

Ben hadn't liked his reaction to seeing her in the water again. It had frightened him, and he tried to tell himself that was what he would have felt had any woman taken such a risk. But it wasn't convincing.

"Stop hurling yourself into the water," he growled, grabbing her elbow and walking her to the steps that led up to the front door.

"I have decided we will not be convincing should we undertake to deceive people about our intentions." She wasn't looking at him, but forward. "Good day, Mr. Hetherington. Come along, Heather."

Excellent. Surely that was for the best?

Miss Fullerton Smythe ran past Ben and up the steps to Primrose's side. He followed them into the house and stormed up to his room, where he stood at his window while a bath was drawn.

"Why her?" Ben couldn't work out why she intrigued him. She had a waspish tongue to match her attitude. He was no wiser once he'd dressed and made his way to where the other guests assembled for the dinner.

"I have wrapped this for you, Miss Ainsley. Water it daily, Jethrow said."

"Mr. Jones, how can I thank you, and Jethrow also."

God's blood, the woman was everywhere, Ben thought. Turning the corner, he looked over the edge of the railing to the level below. Primrose stood there dressed for dinner in cream silk, looking nothing like the drowned woman of a few hours ago. With her was a footman.

"'Tis nothing. Please let me know if I can be of any more help."

"I will, and again, thank you so much."

She touched the young footman's arm and then started back up the stairs. Ben took two steps back, which put him in the shadows, and seconds later she flew past him. He wasn't sure why he'd hidden, just as he wasn't sure why he followed her. But he did.

She ran down the hallway to the wing she slept in. Once there, she entered her rooms. Ben followed, standing in the doorway when he realized she was alone.

Primrose dropped to her knees, regardless of the fact she was creasing her skirts, and pulled something out from under the bed. It looked like a small wooden tray.

"There, you will be happy with your friends, and I shall give you another drink tomorrow. Good night, my beauties."

"Who, or should I say what are you talking to?"

She gasped as Ben came to where she still sat on the floor.

"What are they?"

"What are you doing in my room?"

"Following you."

"Why?"

"You looked full of nefarious intention. Now tell me what you were talking to?"

"Cuttings." She pushed them back under the bed.

"For?"

"Me."

His view of her was of a headful of curls pinned all over the back of her head. A cream satin ribbon was woven through them. The dress was simple, and yet also anything but from his position, which allowed him a view of the creamy swells of her breasts.

"Allow me to help you rise."

"I can—"

He picked her up by her waist.

"You don't have to argue with everything I say, Primrose."

"I know, I'm sorry."

Her words surprised him.

"We should not be in this room alone together."

"I know. You look beautiful tonight."

"Thank you, and you look handsome also."

Neither of them moved.

"We must go."

He wanted to kiss her. Instead he held out his arm, and they walked from the room.

"Oh, wait please!"

She ran back into the room and came back with something in her hands.

"This is for you, for creating the diversion." She looked nervous about how he'd react to the gift.

"You did not need to buy me anything, Primrose. I wasn't serious."

"I know, but I saw this and thought of you."

He opened it and found a small owl.

"It's scruffy and looks grumpy—"

"So you thought of me?" Ben was finding it hard to swallow. Of course, his family gave him gifts, but for her to do so, a woman he barely knew, felt different. Intimate in some way.

"You always look elegant, but sometimes your hair is

ruffled, or a collar is turned in. And that expression closely resembles the one you turn on me after I've thrown myself into the water." She was babbling now, clearly uncomfortable. "If I have offended you, I—"

"No, you haven't offended me, and thank you for my gift," Ben said, slipping the little owl into his pocket. "Now we must go down or they will come looking for us."

They walked for a few minutes before she spoke again.

"We cannot do as you suggested, Mr. Hetherington."

"Benjamin, and why not?"

Shut up, you fool, this is the best course for both of you.

"Because we continually argue."

"I call it debating."

She snorted, a sound he'd heard her make many times.

"You and Miss Fullerton Smythe seem to have hit it off remarkably well."

Her smile was genuine, and Ben felt it again, the pull this woman had on him. But he was a strong, intelligent man; he could resist her, and would. No woman would ever have control over him.

"She is very nice, and not quite what she seems."

"She does wood carving," Ben said, navigating the stairs with her at his side.

"She told you that?"

"She did, and I told her to tell you because I thought you and she may enjoy each other's company."

"I do like her. Her exterior would never suggest to me she had such a habit, and perhaps that is the lesson to be learned."

"That what we see is not actually the true personality of a person," Ben added.

"Yes. It is nice to have a friend, and I think she will be that."

"Excellent."

"Thank you for introducing us."

"You are welcome. I have been blessed with a close friend my entire life; I could not imagine life without Alex now."

"That must have been lovely for those occasions when you were nervous, or a bit unsure how to proceed."

"It was." Ben had never really known what it was to be alone with no one to confide in.

They walked the rest of the way in silence, and Primrose tried to withdraw her arm as they reached the room where the other guests were gathered. Ben didn't relinquish his grip on her.

"Good evening."

"Hello, Thea. How are you feeling now?" His family were tucked to the left as they walked in, chatting with their friends. But it was Ace and Thea who approached them.

"Like a ship that has run aground and is too large to be dislodged."

"And yet still so beautiful."

"Thank you, that is a kind thing to say."

"Explain to me why it's kind when he says it, and yet when I said those very words you snapped at me," Ace said.

"Because I can snap at you."

"That makes no sense to anyone but you, my love." Ace rolled his eyes.

"Good evening, Mr. Dillinger." Primrose slipped her arm from Ben's and sank into a curtsey. "Should you be out of bed?"

"Thank you, Miss Ainsley, and no he should not," Thea said.

"My head is a great deal harder than others, and the doctor has checked me over and declared me healthy. Stop fussing, Thea. Besides, I wished to thank Miss Ainsley personally now I can think straight."

"There really is no need," Primrose shook her head.

"There is every need. What you did today was incredibly brave, Miss Ainsley."

She hated this, being the center of attention. Ben could see how uncomfortable she was. Especially as around them people had stopped their conversations to listen in unashamedly.

"And I will add to that, should you ever need anything you can contact me and I will make sure you get it," Ace said solemnly.

"I-I, thank you, Mr. Dillinger," Primrose said, sounding nervous.

Ace was an honorable man, and he meant every word he'd spoken to Primrose. He would help her in any way should she need it, and for some reason Ben liked the idea of that. Ace was a powerful man, and having him in your debt was not to be taken lightly.

Ace leaned down and kissed her cheek. "Thank you for saving me, Miss Ainsley."

Ben wasn't jealous of that gesture, after all, Ace was married. However, it was strange how it made something tighten inside him just the same.

CHAPTER THIRTEEN

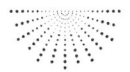

"She just leapt in. Honestly, the woman has no shame or grace."

Primrose overheard the words as they passed a group of ladies. She and Heather were in the ballroom, walking and talking after the formal meal had finished. Thankfully, tonight she had been seated some distance away from the disturbing presence of Benjamin Hetherington.

"Yes, she is something of a hoyden, but then considering her birth it is not surprising. Hard to believe she is related to the Earl of Pennworthy, and one wonders why he does not claim the association."

"Really? I don't wonder at all," trilled someone else. "If the association is even genuine, that is. I still have my doubts."

"It is all right, Heather, come along." Primrose tried to tug her friend with her when she realized it was she they were discussing. Heather, however, had stopped and would not be moved.

"Good evening, ladies."

"Miss Fullerton Smythe." They all shot Primrose a look,

but did not acknowledge her. Not one had the grace to look ashamed over what they had been discussing.

"We did not mean to eavesdrop on your conversation, and yet could not help overhearing that you were discussing one of us, loudly, in a very rude manner. In fact, my dear friend here, Miss Ainsley."

"Oh well, we were—"

"If I may suggest you study Debrett's—I believe the duke has a copy here—you will find that Miss Ainsley is indeed the granddaughter of an earl."

"Of course, we were—"

"What she did today was incredibly brave," Heather interrupted Lady Claire, "and had she not leapt into that river like a hoyden, as you so eloquently put it, the Duke of Rossetter's brother-in-law may not be with us tonight."

Not one of them spoke. Several lowered their eyes.

"Because a person is not born in the exalted circles of some does not make them unequal. I would even go so far as to say that anyone who would take the risk Miss Ainsley did today is the equal of anyone in this room, if not more so. Have a good evening."

They walked away then, leaving the stunned group of women grappling with what Heather had said.

"Oh, Heather." Primrose sniffed back tears as emotion choked her. "You should not have done that, b-but, oh you were magnificent."

"Do you know what, Primrose?"

"What?" She looked at her friend, dressed in rose silk, looking every inch a lady.

"I have come to realize since we became further acquainted today that you are worth twice these other women, and I will not hesitate to show that. I am just sorry that for so long I have behaved the same. I am exceedingly grateful to Mr. Benjamin Hetherington for opening my eyes."

"I don't think your mother will be happy with the change, Heather, and in such a short time." Primrose felt she needed to add, "There is the association with the earl, but it really does not affect my standing in society."

"Very likely, but I can no longer follow her every dictate. There is little doubt she will attempt to blame you, but I will not allow it."

"But, Heather, if I could caution you to…." Primrose's words fell away as her friend inhaled loudly. Heather's fingers dug into her arm.

"Ouch!"

"Forgive me," Heather said, her eyes on Mr. Caton.

"So, he is the one."

"Pardon?" Heather dragged her longing gaze from the man.

"The one whose name you would not give me earlier. Mr. Caton is the man who has caught your eye. I did wonder earlier, actually, when you couldn't find your words."

"Of course not." Heather turned her back on him.

"I think you are not being truthful, my dear new friend," Primrose said. "Oh, he is coming this way."

"What? No, we must leave… dear lord!"

"Take a deep breath, Heather. That's good, and another. Now turn around and smile that lovely smile that flashes your teeth and lights your eyes."

"I-I can't." Her friend's smile was frozen.

"Of course you can." Primrose forced her to turn by walking in a half circle with her. "Mr. Caton," Primrose gushed. "Is it not a wonderful occasion?"

"Indeed it is. The duke and duchess are to be commended. Good evening, Miss Fullerton Smythe." He bowed, and Primrose elbowed Heather, jolting her into a curtsey.

"G-good evening, Mr. Caton. I am pleased you are enjoying the evening."

"I do believe a quadrille is due to start." Primrose had never been one for subtleties, and she wasn't about to begin now. "I believe that is your favorite dance, Miss Fullerton Smythe?"

"Oh, well yes." Heather shot Primrose a frantic look.

"Well then, will you do me the honor of dancing with me, Miss Fullerton Smythe?" Mr. Caton held out one hand.

"Lovely, of course she will." Primrose nudged her friend forward.

With another frantic look, Heather allowed Mr. Caton to lead her to the dance floor.

"Miss Ainsley."

"Mr. Sanders, how are you this evening?" Primrose kept her eyes on Heather. Her friend had yet to speak a word.

"This night flower garden you have discussed has captured my interest."

"I have yet to see it, but hope to remedy that soon, Mr. Sanders. Also, to see some of the flowers in bloom."

"Because it is so rare to see?"

"That actually depends on the plants. As yet I am unsure what they have in the night garden here at Rossetter ."

"My dance, I believe."

Mr. Hetherington—Benjamin—appeared before her as the music ended, suddenly obscuring her view of Heather.

"I had not thought to dance," Primrose said, stepping to one side. Heather and Mr. Caton were leaving the floor.

"Why?" Benjamin followed her.

"Wh—pardon?"

"Are you ill or incapacitated?"

"Of course not!"

"Then you will dance." Ben held out his hand. "You'll excuse us, Sanders."

"Of course, we can continue our discussion on the night garden another time." The man bowed, then walked away.

"That was rude." She glared at him.

"No, it wasn't. I asked nicely. Now don't be a bore, Primrose, take my hand."

She did as he asked, slapping hers into his palm. He in turn placed it gently on his arm and led her out onto the floor.

"So, about my little proposition."

Drat, it was to be a waltz; and she would be in his arms again.

"I explained earlier why I believe that cannot happen."

"I'm sure as adults we can behave for a few weeks, at least for the remainder of the season."

Primrose thought about that, and about being close to this man for the remainder of the season. "No. I don't think it will work, and I have no wish for word to reach Pickford."

"Because you will wed Herbert the Honorable?"

He wore a deep blue jacket this evening, and his necktie and shirt were a startling white against his tanned throat.

"That is a very elaborate waistcoat." Primrose studied the pale blue and emerald creation.

"My brother," he sighed. "He dresses me, as, if left alone, I would be a fashion disaster, apparently."

"Surely it would not be that bad were you to take control."

"Not only do I have that other little issue I foolishly told you about—"

"The crunching, rustling issue?"

"Yes, that." He nodded. "But I am also colorblind, which means I sometimes struggle to tell the difference between red and green."

Primrose bit back her smile.

"I'm glad my inadequacies amuse you."

"I wonder if you should tell your future wife? It would only be fair to warn her, surely? But then it may also work against you."

"Very funny." He looked down at her and her stomach clenched. This close, he was devastatingly handsome. "And I have no wish to marry."

"What, never?"

"You dance well, Primrose." He changed the subject.

"Thank you, my mother taught me. Why will you not wed?"

"So, to cover the rules of our situation. We shall be seen in each other's company, showing others that we are exploring a relationship with the eventual ending being marriage."

"No, I do not think it will work, Mr. Hetherington."

"Benjamin," he said, relieved she'd stop questioning him about why he had no wish to marry.

"Mr. Hetherington."

"It will benefit us both, Primrose. You will be doing me a favor, at least for the remainder of this season, and I you."

"You shall be free of sighing, giggling women and their militant mothers?"

"Exactly."

"How taxing all that adoration must be." She tilted her head slightly, studying him.

"I am not one of your species, please don't inspect me."

She laughed.

"Oh dear." She swallowed her smile. "Lady Jane told me not to do that."

"Do what? Laugh?"

"It's meant to be more a soft, breathy giggle, and yet I've never quite mastered it."

"There's a way to a laugh?" He looked horrified. "Don't stop being you, Primrose."

"That makes no sense."

"Did Lady Jane lecture you about destroying another dress?"

"Yes, and made me vow to stay out of the water again."

She didn't want the dance to end, but it had to, of course. Just as he had to take her back to Lady Jane. Primrose knew no good could come from his proposition. Spending more time in this man's company would be dangerous to her, and she wasn't sure she'd walk away at the end entirely unscathed emotionally.

"Do you know Mr. Caton well?"

"No. I am acquainted with his elder brother, and he seems a good and fair man. Why do you ask? Surely you have not forgotten Herbert so soon?"

"Who?"

"Your beloved."

"Oh yes. And no, I was just asking out of curiosity."

He placed her hand on his arm as the dance ended and started walking.

"Or it could be that your new friend has an interest in him?"

Nothing escaped this man's eye.

"If you will just take me to Lady Jane, please."

"We can start implementing our plan right now by sharing a walk around the room."

He pulled her in closer, and Primrose could do little about it unless she wanted to create a scene.

"Lady Jane is smiling far too widely," Primrose whispered. "I have not agreed to your proposal."

"But you will," he said out of the side of his mouth. "Come, we shall visit the supper room and sample some of the treats."

"We just ate a large meal. Is there a time in your day when your stomach is actually full?"

"Very rarely."

The room had plenty of guests.

"Eclairs," Benjamin said, towing her with him to the table. "They are my favorite."

"I thought all food was your favorite." Primrose reached for a small piece of peppermint candy and popped it into her mouth. It made a satisfying crunch.

"Must you?" He stopped with the eclair halfway to his mouth.

"Oh, I must." She picked up another piece and crunched again.

"Your jaw clicked."

"Did it?"

"Loudly."

"Primrose!"

She turned to find Heather behind her.

"Hello, would you like some of this wonderful peppermint candy? I highly recommend it. Stand right here and eat it with me." Primrose passed the plate to her friend.

"I really don't—"

"No, you really do." Primrose handed a piece to her. "It's the best I've tasted."

"Shrew," she heard Benjamin hiss.

"Mr. Caton, Primrose. I just danced with him," Heather whispered.

"Yes, how was it?"

"Wonderful."

"If that is the case, why are you frowning?" Primrose held the plate closer to her chest as a large hand came around to remove it.

"Primrose, Mr. Hetherington wishes to eat some of the peppermint candy."

"I'm not sharing it," she said, taking another piece and biting into it loudly. His groan was her reward. "Eat another piece, Heather."

"I don't want another piece. Now put that plate down and listen to me."

"Yes, put the plate down, Miss Ainsley," he mimicked Heather.

She turned and slapped the plate down. Benjamin picked it up and walked down the table to place it at the end.

"What is the problem, Heather?"

She grabbed Primrose's hand and they shuffled sideways until they had reached a wall offering some privacy. Benjamin, she noted, was still circling the table, and no doubt eavesdropping.

"You should not have lured me into dancing with Mr. Caton, Primrose."

"Why? You like him, and he likes you."

"That is not the point," Heather said, obviously agitated. "Does he? Like me, I mean?"

"Very much, is my guess. His eyes are constantly following you wherever you go."

"Are they?" Heather sighed.

Primrose nodded.

"It doesn't matter, he will never be good enough for my mother. His brother may be titled, but he is not."

"But if you care for each other—"

"That matters for nothing in our world, as you very well know, Primrose."

"Well it should, and it is not as if he was not born into a titled family with a great deal of money."

"My mother wants me to be a lady," Heather said.

"You are a lady."

"You know very well what I mean, Primrose."

"Sorry, I should not have teased you." No one knew better than she about how society saw a person who was beneath them. The thought was a depressing one.

"Don't give up, Heather, please" was all Primrose found to say. "I'm sure we can make this work somehow."

She looked at Benjamin and caught his eye. She saw the sympathy in them and hated that her heart beat just a little faster because of it. The man was far too appealing in almost every way. The thought of leaving society at the end of this season and not seeing him again was suddenly a depressing one.

CHAPTER FOURTEEN

*W*hen she was sure Lady Jane was snoring peacefully, Primrose pulled on her sturdy boots and shawl over her day dress. It was close to 2:00 a.m., and the perfect time for her to inspect the night garden.

She'd told the duchess she was eager to see it and the woman had winked at her and said it was not located too far from the house if she chose to go alone. Primrose took this as an invitation to do exactly that.

Perhaps she had meant for her to visit it just before retiring for the evening, and not at 2:00 a.m., but she was awake, and surely could not get into trouble going for a quick walk.

She hadn't been able to sleep anyway. Visions of Benjamin Hetherington and their kiss had kept her awake. Then there was Heather and her feelings—which were clear for anyone to see—about Mr. Caton. Something must be done… but what?

Primrose hoped a brisk walk in the gardens would clear her head and help her sleep.

Opening her bedroom door, she closed it softly behind

her. Tiptoeing to the stairs, she hurried down. Reaching the front door undetected, she opened it and stepped outside.

The left hand path that led behind the house was the one she had been told to take. Hurrying along the front, Primrose turned at the end.

"Oomph!"

"Hollyhocks!" Primrose shrieked as the person she collided with stumbled backward, then fell, taking her with him. She landed hard on a broad chest. "Oh dear." She tried to scramble off the body, but her foot got caught in her skirts and she tripped, somehow resulting in her front being pressed to theirs.

"Be still, Primrose!"

The words were more a breathless rasp, but for all that she still knew who uttered them.

"Benjamin, I'm so sorry!"

Dear Lord, not him again.

"You're certainly heavier than you look," he wheezed, easing her off his chest. Seconds later they were both standing.

"I have heavy bones, so the doctor once told my mother. Please forgive me, I did not know you were there when I—"

"Hurried recklessly around the corner?"

"Umm, yes." She bobbed a curtsey. "Begging your pardon once more." Primrose started to walk away, but a large hand secured itself around her upper arm.

"You don't honestly think I would let you walk away, do you? It's an ungodly hour, and you're clearly alone. Surely I deserve an explanation?"

"I don't have to give you one," Primrose said. She wanted to get out of this man's company and view the garden.

"No, you don't, but you're not simply walking about alone in the dark. So you either tell me, or I take you back to your room."

"You're out here." She squinted up at him and saw that his jaw was clenched and his eyes narrowed. "Why should I not be?"

"Yes, I am."

She waited for him to elaborate, but he didn't.

"I'm not telling if you won't."

"This is not the schoolroom, Primrose. But if you must know, I was simply walking as I could not sleep."

"Oh. Well, I'm sorry for that."

"As am I, because now I have a crushed windpipe and bruises."

"Oh dear, I am sorry. Does it hurt terribly?"

"No, I was teasing you. Now tell me why you are out here when you should be sleeping and dreaming blissful dreams of Herbert the Honorable."

I was actually thinking about you.

"There is no need to mock me."

"Probably not, but it is a great deal of fun, and in a small way a repayment on all that deliberate peppermint candy crunching."

"People cannot go about eating quietly just because you cannot stand the sound, Mr. Hetherington."

"I know, but it's my fondest wish that they try."

Primrose harrumphed.

"You called me Benjamin before."

"I should not have."

"Are you meeting someone?" He sounded angry about the possibility and she wasn't sure what to make of that.

"No! Good Lord, do I look the type to do that?"

"There's a certain type?"

She gave in. "The duchess has a night garden, and it is my fondest wish to see it. This is the first night I've had the chance to."

He laughed softly. "Of all the things I thought you would

say, that was not one of them, but of course it had to be about a plant."

"Yes, well, it is my life's work not to be predictable."

"You are certainly that. Are you to steal more cuttings?"

"It is not stealing, it is… well, it's harvesting them."

"Harvesting them," he mused. "Sounds a lot better than theft."

"Well, good night then, and if you would keep this to yourself I would be most grateful."

"As I have never seen a night garden, I think I shall accompany you."

"No! I mean, thank you, but no. It would not do for anyone to see us together."

He grabbed her arm again, then turned her toward the path that ran around the house. Primrose felt the imprint of his fingers right through to her skin. She did not like being so aware of this man.

"As everyone is slumbering, I hardly think that is likely to happen, and anyone who is awake at such an hour is doing something they should not, like you, so lead on."

"Do you mean discreet liaisons?"

"Miss Ainsley, I'm shocked. I'm not sure an innocent like you should know about such things."

"My mother may not show a great deal of interest in anything but botany, but she talked to me at length before I left about many things that happen in society."

"How very forward thinking of her. Why does she only show interest in botany?"

"It's her life's work."

"And you are her daughter, so surely she shows interest in you?"

Primrose was not about to discuss her family relationships with him, of all people.

"Thank you for offering to accompany me, Mr. Hetherington—"

"Benjamin."

"—but I really don't need you to, so please return to your bed."

"And yet I am accompanying you. We cannot have some rogue gardener seeing you and deciding he wishes to lure you into his shed."

"Very amusing."

They walked in silence, the only sound their feet crunching on the shell paths.

"I like the night," Primrose said, feeling the need to speak. The silence between them did not feel comfortable to her. "It's nice to be alone… well, nearly alone, with your thoughts."

"Quite" was all he said.

They entered the gardens, and the scents were different from the day. Clearer somehow. Primrose identified each as she passed them.

"What's that?" He pointed to a tall sprig of flowers.

"Hocks."

"And that?"

This carried on as they passed plants, until they'd moved through a gate. The path they then followed was winding, and at the end was another gate. The hinges creaked as Benjamin opened it. A large stone wall encased the entire garden, and Primrose felt her heart thud harder.

"What's that?" He pointed at another plant.

"Are you testing me, or are you really this ignorant?"

"I beg your pardon?" He stopped, and the moonlight told her he was not amused by her insult. His mouth formed a line, and his brows met in the middle in a fierce frown as he stood before her looking large and forbidding. Primrose, however, did not scare easily. Her brother had been trying to achieve that for years. Perhaps if she continued to needle him, he may return to the house.

"I believe you understood the question. Now if you will excuse me, I have need to keep moving, as I do not want Lady Jane aware I am missing."

"For the record, I am not ignorant, I just have not made a study of plants. Do you know how a steam engine works?"

"Not in detail, but I have a little knowledge."

He made a scoffing sound that her brother often used when she attempted to discuss something botanic with him.

"In the boiler, there would be a firebox where coal would be shoveled. It would be kept burning at high temperatures to heat the boiler to boil water, producing high-pressure steam. The steam expands and leaves the boiler via pipes into the steam reservoir. The steam is then controlled by a slide valve to move into a cylinder to push the piston. The pressure of the steam energy pushing the piston turns the drive wheel in a circle, creating motion for the locomotive," Primrose said.

"How do you know that?"

"My father and mother have two servants in our house. Mr. and Mrs. Putt. Mr. Putt is interested in steam engines, and you cannot walk five paces without tripping over some kind of journal in the kitchens."

"Why are you in the kitchens?"

"I like it there. Don't be a snob, Benjamin."

That silenced him, and they walked on. His fingers were still on her arm, and loath as she was to admit it, Primrose was starting to enjoy the feeling.

"I love steam engines," he said softly. "I love the mechanics of them. I love the noises they make and the smells. I love that they will change so much for so many."

He spoke with passion, just as she'd heard Mr. Putt do many times.

THE LADY'S DANGEROUS LOVE

"Did you know that steam power will enable mills to operate away from a water source?"

"I didn't know that, actually, and believe me when I tell you I know a great many things."

"Quite the know-it-all, then?"

"My brother often says that, but it is not as if I set out to know everything. I just… well, I do."

His chuckle carried on the still night air.

Primrose sighed. "My family rarely talk of anything but botany when they are home, so that left reading. I have learned a great deal from books."

"Like I said, a know-it-all."

"It is hardly my fault, and I fail to see why I should appear dimwitted to make anyone else feel better."

"But I thought it was important for a woman to do just that. How could a man see you as a future wife if you are more intelligent than he? Surely the Honorable Herbert will not want a wife who bests him in everything?"

"But for the next few weeks, that is not a problem, is it?" But it was a problem, actually. Herbert could be a little pompous at times, often telling her things with a great deal of ceremony that she already knew. Once she'd tried to correct him, and he'd been wounded.

Could Herbert kiss me like Benjamin did? Could he make my heart beat just a little harder inside my chest?

"I have no wish to marry a man who does not respect my intelligence." Primrose shot him a look and noted the smile, and her anger fled as quickly as it had come. "You're teasing me."

"A bit."

"It's all very well for you to do so, but you must understand that it is a concern. Men do not want a woman who sits about the place reading newspapers and doing anything other than needlework and other 'ladylike' pursuits. I have no wish to do that." Primrose spoke honestly out here in the dark. It was only them; no one would overhear their conversation. It was liberating to speak her mind finally.

"Then don't, and I'm sure your Herbert won't mind if you can outthink him."

"Much easier for you to say than for me to carry out," Primrose snapped, taking her arm from his. "I fear Lady Jane has an ulterior motive, as does my family, and will do whatever it takes to wed me to someone this season. I cannot be a burden to my parents indefinitely, so I must accept."

"I'm sure they all have your best interests at heart—"

"Indeed? How is it in my best interests to end up wed to a man I cannot tolerate?"

"I'm sorry."

"I don't want or need your sympathy. Plus, you are not really sorry." Primrose felt the full weight of her life then. How what happened was completely out of her hands. She had no say in the direction her life would take. The injustice of that nearly choked her.

"Primrose—"

"It is the reality of many a young lady," she interrupted him again. "Perhaps you and your kind should think about that when comparing us to gout-swollen toes!"

Primrose was not terribly good at holding on to her temper or tongue when something annoyed her.

"If you'll—"

"Good evening, Mr. Hetherington. I think it best you return to the house now." Primrose stormed away, deciding it was time to put some distance between herself and *that man*. She was not usually someone who allowed herself self-pity, but right then she wanted to give in to a good bout of it.

CHAPTER FIFTEEN

*B*en watched Primrose walk away from him, chin raised, skirts swishing. With a few misplaced words he'd angered and likely hurt her. His intention had never been that; he'd simply wanted to tease her, but it had happened and now he needed to make amends.

After the ball, he'd gone to bed feeling on edge. The night had been spent dancing, talking, and watching Primrose. She'd danced with Mr. Sanders twice, which while not scandalous was a clear indication that the man showed an interest in her. Did she feel the same way? What of Herbert? Thoughts had swirled around and around inside his head, angering him.

Ben never lost sleep, and the fact that it was because of a woman unsettled him more. He did not allow women to interfere with his life in any way. He'd made this vow many years ago.

He'd decided on a walk in the cool night air to clear his head, and it had been working until Primrose landed on him.

He found himself walking in the direction she'd taken instead of doing what he should have and turning around.

She was standing beside a bed of flowers, staring down at them.

"I'm sorry."

"Go to bed, Mr. Hetherington. You can never walk in my shoes, as I cannot walk in yours. There is little point in us continuing to converse, as neither of us can speak without annoying the other. In fact, I'm calling a halt to this silly idea of yours."

"Again?"

"It's for the best."

"I understand the plight of some women is vastly different from mine, Primrose. I am not completely oblivious to such things."

She sighed, which he couldn't interpret, but didn't speak.

"And I am sorry you believe your family see you as a burden."

The plants at their feet were just shadowy figures, their fragrance subtle in the cool night air.

"I did not say that."

But she'd implied it, and it hurt her deeply that they didn't want her. Ben wondered how a family could treat one of its members that way.

His mother had seen him and Alex as a burden.

"I truly am sorry."

"Please just go away and let me view the night garden alone."

"I don't want to leave you out here alone. Primrose, can we not be friends?" He didn't want to add that he'd had several people comment on his closeness to her already, and that his plan seemed to be working even if she didn't want it to.

"No."

She walked on down the row, and through the opening at the end which he hadn't seen until that moment; an arch in the wall. Ben followed and found himself in a very different garden.

Dark, and to his eyes, overgrown. There were large plants everywhere. Their shadows were quite sinister at night.

"Primrose?" He couldn't see her, but heard her sigh.

"Why are you following me?"

"I'm not entirely sure but think it could be that I'm scared of the dark."

Her laugh was quickly muffled. "I think it best if you don't call me Primrose." It was the clipped tone she used sometimes when she wasn't impressed. Strange how he already knew she had different tones.

"What would you prefer? Medusa, perhaps?"

"Extremely amusing, and if I had a head full of snakes, I'd certainly set them upon you and have you gaze upon me so I could turn you to stone."

"Ah, but then all those women you say admire me would be distraught."

"Your mother clearly did not discipline you enough as a child, Mr. Hetherington. In fact, I would go so far as to say you were spoiled atrociously."

"My mother abandoned us, actually. My eldest brother was correct in that it was he who disciplined and actually raised Alex and me."

Primrose fell silent.

"Where are you?"

"Did she really abandon you?"

"Yes. Tell me where you are?"

"Look right."

Squinting into the darkness, he found her crouched under a large plant.

"I believe there is a special place in hell for parents such as yours, Mr. Hetherington."

"Very likely." Ben wasn't sure why her words made his

chest feel warm, but they did. "But as she's not dead yet, we shall have to wait to send her there."

"I'm sorry."

"For what?

"Saying what I did. I did not mean to hurt you." Her words were mumbled.

Ben dropped down beside her.

"I'm not hurt, Primrose," he lied. In fact, his mother leaving him had left a dark stain on his soul, but not even Alex knew that.

He'd never told his brother how he'd gone to his mother's room, the only woman he'd ever loved, the day she'd told them she was leaving. She'd opened the door to his knock, and he'd thrown himself at her, wrapping both arms around her waist. Her French scent had wrapped around him, and he'd held her tight, sobbing. He'd told her he loved her and didn't want her to go. She'd wrenched him off her and laughed in his face.

"There is no such thing as love, you silly little boy, and the sooner you learn that the better it will be." She'd pushed him out of her room, then slammed the door in his face.

He'd learned, all right. Learned to not ever let a woman get close enough to hurt him again.

"We got the better end of the deal with Finn raising us," Ben said calmly.

Thoughts of his mother no longer hurt him, but the memory of that day... now that, he held close. He made himself remember the pain so he would never make the mistake of giving his heart to a woman again.

"He was hard but fair, and he loved us."

She sniffed.

"Why are you weeping?"

"I'm not."

"That was a sniff."

"I have allergies."

"They came on quickly."

"I do not like to think of two small boys being upset and watching their mother leave them! Must you continually challenge me?"

He touched her cheek, just one finger that he ran down the soft, silky skin, and all the fight drained out of her.

"We didn't watch her. At the time we had my father's dueling pistols and were attempting to use them on the household furniture, for target practice." Which was the truth. Ben had wept in a dark cupboard after his mother had cast him aside. When he was done, he'd washed his face and vowed never to shed another tear over a woman.

Her laugh was more a gruff little bark.

"We were heathens, and it took my brother's arrival and the subsequent harsh words and discipline to straighten us out. Lord knows where we would be now if Finn hadn't arrived."

She looked up at him, and as his eyes had adjusted to the darkness around them, he could see her. Lord, she was sweet. She looked away first, and back down at the plant.

"Can I ask you a question, Primrose?"

She nodded.

"Why do you take risks? All that plunging into the water, and then climbing out onto the window ledge. Why do you do it?"

He knew she was thinking about how to answer him.

"I am alone a great deal, and rarely have anyone care what I do or say. It may seem as if I am reckless, but in fact it is just that I do as I wish most of the time without anyone there to tell me otherwise. As to why I've jumped into the water twice beside the incident at the pond," she shrugged. "I like to help people."

Her words had been even, no emotion clouding them.

Ben thought them incredibly sad. Why did no one care about what this lovely woman did or said? Why did she feel the need to constantly help others?

"I am actually quite cautious, and I would never do something that would cause me harm."

He snorted but said nothing further.

"Is that some special night garden plant?"

She made a hmm sound. "This is an Evening Primrose."

He let her talk, explain what it was and its origins, and when his thighs started to cramp, he rose to his feet, taking her with him.

"I find it hard to believe you are not close with your family, considering your passion for flora and fauna."

"I have no wish to travel to wild climates to find rare species as they do, so we no longer have a common ground." Her words sounded indifferent, but Ben knew she was anything but.

"Family shouldn't need a common ground."

"There is much they still wish to explore; it is not their fault that occupies their time."

He let the subject drop, as it was clearly uncomfortable for her.

"So you like the more common species of plant, then?"

"I like a flower or plant for its beauty or uses," she clarified in that prim little voice she used that had his fingers itching to grab her and... *do what? Kiss her? Shake her?*

"And now we must leave."

"But I am not finished," she protested... loudly.

"And yet you have been out here long enough, and as you have no wish for Lady Jane to find you missing, I think it is time for bed."

She harrumphed, but allowed him to lead her from the garden.

"Mr. Hetherington?"

He'd had, by his calculations, five minutes of peace before she started talking again.

"Miss Ainsley."

"I will ask one last time that tomorrow we put distance between us, as I have decided this is for the best."

"I shall see how I feel when I rise."

"What does that mean?"

"It means I shall see what mood I rise in; whether I wish to speak with you or not."

"But why?"

"I do not want to ignore you, Primrose. I want us to be friends."

She turned to face him, her eyes bright under the moonlit sky. He felt it again, as he had every time he had contact with this woman. That little uncomfortable jolt of awareness. Ben knew it would pass, he'd experienced it before… perhaps not such a severe case, but he put that down to the complexities of the woman before him and the kiss they'd shared.

"Why?"

"I think you need more friends."

Her hands went to her trim hips.

"We cannot be friends, they would see it as more." She nodded toward the huge house looming before them.

"You are also one of the more interesting women at this house party."

"That is hardly fair. Do you personally know each lady at this party whom you so blithely label as uninteresting? Know their circumstances or what is behind their behavior?"

"Ah—"

"I didn't think so," she scoffed, further annoying him. Ben didn't like people scoffing at him, mainly because his brothers did so constantly.

"If I may—"

"Perhaps if you took the time to speak with them, and not

assume a preconceived notion they are after your vast fortune and connections through marriage, you may see their true characters, Mr. Hetherington."

He could lean closer and put his hand over her mouth, and would have it firmly in place before she was aware he'd moved.

"Your arrogance is quite something, as is your overinflated opinion of your worth, sir."

Ben took one large step, which brought him close enough that the toes of his boots brushed hers. He then leaned in and kissed her again.

Shock had her mouth dropping open, which was perfect as far as he was concerned, because he could take the kiss deeper. Lifting a hand, he held her head at just the right angle.

Slipping the other around her back, he eased her closer to his body. Those lush curves felt wonderful pressed to his chest. Even through their layers of clothing, he could feel this woman, and his body reacted as it had earlier.

"Oh dear," she whispered as he eased back slightly to take a breath. "That should not have happened again."

"And yet it did." Ben kissed her again because he had to.

"I-I—we must s-stop."

She lifted her head, and her expression did not dispel the lust rampaging through him. Her eyes looked up at him with longing. A simple kiss, and he was hotter than Hades.

"Primrose," he said softly.

She pulled out of his arms and stumbled back a few paces, shaking her head.

"No." The hand she lifted was small and pale. "That was... it was f-folly, just as it was the last time."

Her stutter told him she was affected too.

"It didn't feel like folly." Ben believed in honesty. "It felt very nice... again."

THE LADY'S DANGEROUS LOVE

"Yes, it was."

Her reply made him smile. Only Primrose would tell the truth in such a moment.

"But we should not have done it."

"Primrose, look at me." He lifted her chin so their eyes met. He could lose himself in her, he realized, and the thought was like someone dousing him in cold water.

What the hell was he doing? He'd just reminded himself why he didn't have feelings for women, and here he was... *hell!*

"I need to leave because there will never be anything between us, because we are not suited. We are not suited, and you know that as well as I. I am unsure what that was about... the kisses." She waved her hand at him. "I can guess it was merely curiosity, or perhaps that is something men do..., however, it is not—"

"I beg your pardon?" Ben felt his calmness flee. "Are you suggesting I kiss innocent woman in a willy-nilly fashion?"

"Yes, I am. And now I am leaving, before this discussion gets out of hand."

"It's already out of hand!" he roared as she turned, picked up her skirts, and ran away from him.

Ben followed, but she was surprisingly fleet-footed and had a lead on him in seconds.

"Damn it, woman, will you wait!"

She didn't, of course, as he'd known she wouldn't. He gave up and let her go. Surely no harm could come to her in the short distance between here and the front door. He arrived just as she slipped inside.

"God's blood." He followed slowly. "What is wrong with me?"

He was behaving differently, and it was all because of her. Somehow, she'd broken through the protective shield he'd put around himself to keep from being hurt. It was a terrifying thought.

CHAPTER SIXTEEN

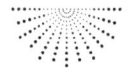

"Why are you still sleeping?"

Ben swam up through the depths of sleep.

"I have never known you to sleep this late. Are you ill?"

Forcing his eyes open, he found Alex at the foot of his bed, looking immaculate in a waistcoat of burnt orange and cream.

"Sod off." He lobbed a pillow at him.

"There is a carnival in the next village over from Twoaks. Apparently, they have excellent jugglers and acrobats. We are going, but we must eat first. Now get up."

"Twoaks? Have you become a local?"

"Our brother is now a local, and thus by association so are we."

"Thus," Ben mimicked. "Haven't you a wife now to annoy?"

"Heggley, draw his bath and fetch his clothes, if you please. The puce waistcoat with the silver lining will do."

Ben, who had closed his eyes hoping it was all a bad dream, opened them again in time to see the besotted look on his valet's face. He loved Alex. Worshipped him, even. He also never questioned a word Alex said.

"You are both making me ill, leave at once."

"Make that water extremely hot, Heggley, so we can rid him of his foul humor. Although, now that I think about it, cold may be better."

"Will you just leave!" Ben hurled a pillow down the bed. Alex caught it, annoyingly.

"You have twenty minutes."

He was ready in nineteen; however, only because he wished it so.

Wandering out onto the terraced area where a table laden with food was set up for the guests this morning, he did a quick survey of those assembled. His relief was acute when he noted Primrose was not there.

In the sobering morning light he had come to the realization that she could be a serious detriment to his long-held rule. He would never give a woman power over him. She intrigued him by no other means than being different, and now he knew what he had to do. Ignore her.

She'd been right, what he'd proposed was foolish, and the end result would likely not have been pleasant for either of them. Ben had stopped thinking clearly, and he blamed her for that also.

"Ahhh, Ben. How wonderful of you to join us."

Ignoring Alex, he greeted the other guests seated at his table. One was Miss Penelope Haversham, who had made her interest in him no secret.

"Miss Haversham, how lovely you look this morning."

"Oh thank you, Mr. Hetherington!" She smiled, and it did absolutely nothing for him. No flicker of interest. Perfect.

He took the seat next to her.

"Can you believe some of the guests have gone to the carnival already? Early risers." She shuddered. "It seems both

Miss Ainsley and Miss Fullerton Smythe are among them." The look she shot Ben told him that people had started to notice his interest in Primrose.

"As my brothers will attest, I cannot abide rising early," Ben lied. Usually he had been the first up in the household.

"Oh, neither can I." She gave him another smile.

He knew Alex was staring at him, but he ignored him and rose to fill his plate with food. This was the right course. Primrose had been right; nothing but trouble could come of them pretending an interest in each other. Just as it would if he gave in to the feelings she created inside him. It was a fleeting fancy, as they all were. Distance would put an end to his intrigue, he was sure of it.

He ate, talked about nothing of interest, and then they all assembled for the journey to the next village.

"So what was that at the table?" Alex moved up beside him.

"What was what?"

"The flirting with Miss Haversham?"

"It was flirting, Alex."

"I understand that, Ben, but I had thought you and—"

"If the next words out of your mouth are Miss Ainsley, then don't speak them. I have no feelings for that woman."

He felt his brother's eyes on him, but he thankfully said nothing further. In case he changed his mind, Ben nudged his horse into a gallop, leaving the other guests behind. Alex kept pace with him.

The day was clear and the sky blue. Cows grazed in pastures, lazily swishing their tails to remove flies, and for the most part it was idyllic.

The village of Chipping Nippley, which they were at present riding into, was larger than Two Oaks (contrary to what Alex said, they were not locals and could not call it Twoaks), but Ben didn't think it was as picturesque.

There was no river greeting them, or quaint shops butted together like books on a shelf.

"Apparently Edward I, also known as Edward Longshanks—"

"Thank you, Alex, I know who Edward I is."

"Yes, well, apparently when he rode through Chipping Nippley he was ill and could not go on, so he stayed here for two weeks while he recovered."

"Who told you that?" Alex wasn't above telling a story to Ben that had no truth to it whatsoever with the hopes that he'd recount it and look like a fool. Ben often did the same thing to Alex.

"The duke, just this morning. Look there, see, that tavern is called The Longshanks."

It was, but still not enough evidence to convince Ben.

"And there is Edward I Cobblers."

The shoe shop had a crown perched over the doorway. In fact, every shop had some reference to the man Ben now believed had stayed here.

Alex said nothing, he just wore a satisfied smile that Ben ignored.

"You'll be here for the Longshanks Fair?"

"We are indeed." Ben smiled at the elderly woman standing on the roadside. "I have heard that the great man himself stayed here many years ago?"

She leaned to the right, putting her weight on one hip, and sucked in her bottom lip.

"You'll be right about that, young sir. Graced us many times, he did. Said it was his favored place to stay. Left us many of his possessions."

"Did he really? How wonderful," Ben encouraged the woman.

"A feather from his favorite cap, and his most prized possession, his drinking vessel."

"Well, I will be sure to inspect these items."

"They're dotted around the village. You'll see there, in the front window of The Longshanks, that's his drinking vessel."

Alex and Ben dutifully looked. The vessel was something of a disappointment for Ben; he'd expected something gold and jewel-encrusted.

"It's quite plain." Alex voiced Ben's thoughts.

"He was not a man of grand gestures, was our Edward Longshanks. He was humble."

"Well then, that must be why," Ben soothed the woman, who had now sucked her lips inside her mouth. "Now if you can point us in the direction of the fair, I would be grateful."

"Through the village, take a right at the driveway, then you'll see an open gate. You'll want to enter the pint and pie run."

"Pint and pie run?"

She gave Ben a look that suggested he wasn't the most intelligent person she'd met that day.

"It's through the woods. You have to stop and eat a pie and drink the pint before you can recite the riddle the fair maiden hands you."

"Right," Ben said, not sure what else to add.

"Mind you," she cackled, "not many of them are actually maids, if you get my meaning."

Alex barked out a laugh.

"Yes, well, thank you kindly for your information."

"If you have a penny to spare, I'll see it makes it into the village for the Longshanks fund."

"I almost hate to ask," Ben muttered to Alex.

"For preserving his memory." The old woman glared at him. Her hearing had obviously not deteriorated with age.

Ben dug about in his pockets, as did Alex. The woman took the coins with a brisk nod, then walked away.

"I think you insulted her with your disparaging comment about the vessel," Ben said, leading the way.

"Very likely. I wonder if there is actually a fund."

They studied the shop fronts and saw the entire village had devoted itself to Edward I.

"Was this village even here back then?"

"Very likely," Ben said, "but it was possibly just one or two structures of some kind."

They crested the hill and saw color everywhere. Flags fluttered on tent roofs, and stalls had people lined up viewing their wares. Ben saw a small platform had been set up, and on it was a juggler throwing drinking vessels in the air.

"Exact replicas of the one we just saw in that window."

Alex was laughing too hard to reply.

Soon they were wandering with the rest of the party from Rossetter. Of Primrose he saw no sign, which had Ben relaxing.

They walked between stalls. Ben dug into his pockets for money often, and was soon munching on treats. Hannah purchased shawls for the baby, as did Thea. Ace and Alex hovered. Ben knew he would never be like that, as he wasn't going to be a father.

He tested how that felt inside him. Strangely, it left him feeling hollow. Logically, he knew there wasn't a viable reason not to marry, and it was likely he could be happy like his brothers. But the memory of that searing pain when his mother deserted him had not eased in any way for Ben, and he never wanted to experience it again.

"Right. I have entered us into the pie and pint race," Finn said. "I will beat you both."

"You?" Ben scoffed. "You're too old to beat us."

"Did you hear that, Will? Apparently we are too old."

"I know I am," the Duke of Rossetter said. "But I shall cheer you on with a pint in my hands."

"I'll show you who is too old, Benjamin." Will scowled at him.

"I was wondering about the riddle and the fair maiden?" Alex said.

"I think we have to carry the mugs to the finish line and hand them to her," Finn added. "And she hands us a riddle to read."

"You will not be kissing any maidens," Phoebe stated loudly.

"Good day to you all."

And with those five simple words, all the good resolutions and calm Ben had achieved fled. Turning, he found Primrose standing behind him with Mr. Sanders and Miss Fullerton Smythe.

Hollyhocks.

CHAPTER SEVENTEEN

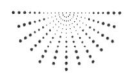

"We have purchased a great many things already."

Primrose kept her eyes on Heather as she spoke to the Rossetter party. Benjamin was there, and the smile he'd given her had just the right amount of civility. It was a smile he would give anyone. That was exactly what she wanted, she reminded herself.

He had obviously come to his senses and realized that putting distance between them was for the best. There could be no more wonderful kisses or teasing. No more debates or letting her guard down, Primrose thought, shooting him a look.

His hat was in a large gloved hand, his hair ruffled. The jacket was a sedate brown, but the waistcoat was far from it. His brother, she thought. He would have selected it, as she doubted Benjamin would ever pick something like that.

"Come, Mr. Hetherington, we are to watch the acrobats."

The jab of pain she felt just under the ribs was surely from the fudge she had just consumed, and not because Miss Haversham had slipped her arm through Benjamin's.

"Excellent. I love acrobats," he added.

She trailed along behind with Mr. Sanders.

"Are you to enter the pint and pie run, Mr. Sanders?"

"I am not the kind to do so, Miss Ainsley. I shall leave that to more enthusiastic members of our party."

"Of course."

He was as different from Benjamin as night was to day, and that was a good thing, Primrose reminded herself.

"Uncle Ben, there is a giant here!"

His niece ran toward him. He moved away from Lady Haversham and caught the little girl as she launched herself at him.

"Is there really? Do you know, I have never seen a giant."

He hugged her close before lowering her to the ground.

He'd told Primrose marriage was not for him, but she had to wonder why. He was obviously good with children and had a kind heart. Plus, he was a good brother; she had seen that too.

"Primrose."

"Yes, Heather?"

"Will you walk with me to the fortune teller's tent?"

"Of course, if that is your wish."

Taking her friend's arm, she turned them away from the Rossetter party and headed in the direction of the tent that had purple and gold stripes and thick fringing.

Entering, they inhaled the musky scent.

"You have come to have your fortune told by the great Zvonka?"

The young girl could have been no more than ten. She wore a dress of blue silk and a belt that had many scarves tucked into it. On her head was another scarf; this one had beads sewn all over it. On her fingers were rings, and she had at least ten bracelets on her arms.

"Yes, please," Primrose said when Heather stayed silent.

"Come this way."

"You're coming." Heather's fingers latched on to Primrose's arm.

"I don't want my fortune told."

"I don't care, you're coming."

She had little choice but to follow. Entering another room in the tent, they found a woman seated at a table. The scent in here was stronger. She was dressed like the child, but her eyes were ringed in black.

"Sit."

Heather fell into the seat on the other side of the table.

"You also." The woman, presumably Zvonka, waved Primrose into another chair the girl retrieved.

"No, I'm just watching."

"Sit!"

She sat.

A cup of tea was thrust into Heather's hands by the girl. Primrose also took one.

"Hold it with both hands and look into the liquid. Pour into it your heart's desires and dreams," Zvonka said in an eerie voice that had the hairs on the back of Primrose's neck rising.

She wasn't exactly a sceptic, but neither could she bring herself to believe that some tea leaves arranged in a cup could hold her future. But for Heather's sake, she was willing to do this.

"Pour the liquid into the bowl Kezia holds." Zvonka nodded to the girl.

They did as they were told, and then Kezia left, and suddenly the air thickened with tension. Looking around her, Primrose wondered how that was possible. Surely it was the same air they'd just been breathing.

"Focus!" Zvonka yelled.

"Right. Sorry," Primrose muttered.

Heather shot her a nervous look.

Zvonka took Heather's cup and looked inside. She stared into it intently for what felt like minutes.

"You are unhappy?"

"Oh, well—"

"You want what you cannot have."

Heather slumped back into her chair.

"You are healthy, but others are determining your future for you, as is the way of your people."

"Isn't it your way, then?" Primrose asked. Zvonka scowled her into silence once more.

"I see a sword; there is a battle coming in your future."

"Oh dear." Heather's hands twisted together.

"But also love. It will be up to you if you stand up for it. Up to you to grasp it with both hands."

The cup was then lowered to the desk.

"Th-thank you… I think," Heather whispered, now clearly unsettled.

"You." She picked up Primrose's cup and stared into it. "You are a difficult girl."

"I'm not really, I just like to—"

"Do not speak!"

Primrose snapped her teeth together.

"You have much to face soon too. Many things to overcome. I see love for you also, but many, many obstacles are in your path before you can achieve it."

"Well, they do say the path to true love is not an easy one." Primrose tried to lighten the suddenly tense atmosphere.

"Oh dear, that's not good, Primrose."

"She will overcome these trials and live a happy life with the one she loves," Zvonka said quickly, obviously realizing her client was upset. "Now I am tired. Please give Kezia your money. I must rest and regain my strength before my next client."

"Of course." Heather hurried out of her seat, grabbing Primrose's hand, and they left the room. They paid the young girl and were soon outside.

"Heather, you realize that she cannot possibly know your future."

"She said I was unhappy, Primrose, and I am. She said I want what I cannot have."

"Yes, but that could be a lot of young women of noble birth, surely."

"No. She knew how I felt. Knew my feelings of unrequited love."

"Love? Surely it has not come to that yet? I mean, you and Mr.—"

"Don't speak his name, please!"

Primrose fell silent.

"And I do love him. We talked last night for quite some time where my parents could not see us. I had the first real conversation with the man who has intrigued me since I arrived in London."

"But how is that possible, Heather, on such short acquaintance? You don't even know his character," Primrose said. "Surely you have only seen him a handful of times."

"I know what I feel, and I have never felt this way before."

She studied her friend, saw the glimmer of tears in her eyes.

"I'm sorry, Heather. Are you sure your parents will not find him favorable?"

Heather shook her head. Primrose took her hand and squeezed it hard.

"I'm worried for you also, Primrose. There is true love in your future, but so much to overcome to reach it."

"Heather, you really should not believe every word that woman said. She cannot know what is in our futures."

"But she did. Don't you see, Primrose, she knew what was

inside me, and she knows there is trouble ahead for you. Do you think it involves Mr. Hetherington?"

"What? No! Why would you say such a thing?"

"You have been talking to him a great deal, and you get a look on your face when he is near."

"No, I don't!" Primrose tried to calm down. "He annoys me. The man is arrogant, and I feel someone needs to put him in his place, so I have been... putting him in his place, I mean."

"Really? I thought there was more to it than that."

"Absolutely not."

"If you say so," Heather said, much to Primrose's relief. But she would not be persuaded that Zvonka did not know their futures, so Primrose gave up trying and hoped that in time her friend forgot about the wild prophecies.

"Come, ladies, the pie and pint race is due to start," Mrs. Fletcher said when they returned to the Rossetter party. "We are to wait at the finish line to greet the men. Apparently, we count the mugs in their hands, and they must recite the words on a card we hand them. The one who can do so clearly and has the most mugs, wins."

"Good lord, that doesn't sound like much fun," Primrose said.

"Men." Mrs. Fletcher shook her head. "They are indeed an unusual breed."

All the women gathered nodded in agreement.

CHAPTER EIGHTEEN

*B*en rolled up his sleeves as he looked left and then right.

"Why do I let you talk me into these things, Alex?"

"Because you love them," his twin said.

Alex, Ben, Finn, Will, Ace, Luke, and Jeremy Caton were participating in the pint and pie race with some of the locals.

"This is the second time in two days I'm having to exert myself," he heard Ace say. "You noblemen are a curious lot."

"Says the man who smashes his fist into a man's stomach for fun," Finn said.

"Yes, but often it's your brother's stomach, so there is a great deal of enjoyment involved. As yet, I am unsure if this will produce the same emotion."

"True, but I have got a few jabs in of my own," Ben added. He and Ace sparred a lot in London.

Ben looked around him. He had no idea where Primrose had wandered off to; he just hoped she stayed out of the water... if there was any nearby.

"Damn," he muttered. *Stop thinking about her.*

"Pardon?"

He waved Alex's question aside. Ben vowed silently that she would no longer intrigue him.

"If I can have your attention, please."

A woman who could only be described as buxom waddled out in front of the men. She wore a grubby white dress with plenty of lace and frills, and a bonnet the same.

"My name is Mrs. Higgs, and this is my husband, Mr. Edward Higgs."

He was staggering out behind her carrying a large bell. The handle was worn and spoke of its age.

"This here bell was used by Edward I on his visit to Chipping Nippley, this village being a particular favorite of his."

Ben looked at Alex. The corner of his brother's lip lifted.

"The tankards of ale you'll be drinking from are exact replicas of his. You will carry them with you to the end. At each stop, someone will watch you drink the entire contents and eat the pie. Cheats will be disqualified."

"They take this quite seriously," Will said out the side of his mouth. "Joseph cheated once and was disqualified, and he's a duke."

"This whole Edward I business is very intense."

"Completely. They have several events each year to celebrate him. There are more Edwards born in this village than in any other in the United Kingdom."

"The winner will receive one bushel of Squire Edward's corn," Mrs. Higgs added. "Follow the path down the hill and into the forest. Ribbons on the trees will show you the way." She went on to explain all the rules. "If you wish to purchase a tankard to remember your day here in Chipping Nippley, they are available at the Blacksmiths for 3 shillings."

"It's tempting," Ben said out the side of his mouth.

"And now we start!"

Her husband counted down from five and rang the bell, and they were off.

Ben jabbed Alex in the ribs as he took off; passing Finn, he did the same.

All Mrs. Higgs's rules were forgotten as they crested the hill and started down to the forest below. The locals, Ben noted, were already in a steady trot, unlike the others, who were sprinting.

"Clearly they know something we don't," Ace said, keeping pace with Ben.

"I'd say that's likely, as they enter each year."

The first stop was set up on a low-hanging branch. Pies were in a basket, and the pints lined up on the branch. Ben ate his pie in four bites and gulped down his pint.

"You may go," the woman who was manning the station said when Ben had finished.

He ran on, this time more slowly, as the beer and pie were now swirling around inside him.

"Pie was good," Will grunted, passing him.

"Beer was better." Finn did the same.

Ben stuck out his foot, and his brother stumbled but managed to stay upright.

"I'll make you pay for that later."

"Only if you can catch me!" Ben ran by him, tripped on a fallen branch, and hit the ground cursing. His friends and family jogged by laughing.

Swearing, he regained his feet and caught them. The next station had sweet pies, which Ben washed down with his ale.

"Jeremy, are you an ale drinker?" Ace asked the man.

Caton's face was a bit pale.

"Not really."

By the fourth station, Ben had to admit that things were getting a little hazy. The clang of the tankards was a constant accompaniment as they tried to hold them and keep themselves upright.

Ace had taken off his necktie, explaining that he was not a

nobleman and appearances were not important to him. He then threaded all the tankard handles through it and hung it from his shoulder. Luke, who declared he wasn't a nobleman either, did the same thing.

"Our birthright certainly becomes a hindrance at such times," Alex said, jabbing Ben in the ribs and winding him, which nearly brought up the pies and ale. Taking several deep gulping breaths, he managed to keep them down.

Clearing the station before the others, Ben found a tree trunk large enough to hide behind and waited. His brothers squealed in the same tone as Amanda when he leapt out in front of them. It was most satisfactory.

"Is the path winding more and more?" Luke Fletcher squinted. "I feel like it tish?"

"It's your eyes," Will said in that slow, concise way people did who had drunk too much.

Five pints down, and it was fair to say they were all pickled. The slightest thing had them laughing like loons, except Ace, who appeared to show no effects at all.

"'Scus he's too bloody big," Jeremy Caton said. "Holds as much liquid as an ox."

For a man who rarely spoke a word, his tongue had certainly loosened with the ale, Ben thought, as he attempted to focus on the track before him. Will was up ahead and weaving all over the place.

"She's sooo sweet."

"Who?" Ben asked Caton as the man sighed loudly.

"Miss Fufferton Smythe."

He had a silly look on his face. Ben would never smile like that over a woman... well, he hoped he wouldn't, but then there was Primrose. He sighed loudly.

"Wasssh your step!" Ben said as Caton stumbled.

"My ffeet no longer appear to belong to my body."

THE LADY'S DANGEROUS LOVE

Ben knew how he felt. The trick of holding the tankards and keeping himself upright was almost herculean now.

"One more to go!" Finn bellowed, loud enough so the next county could hear. His brother's hair stood off his head, and his jacket bore a tear in the sleeve from where a branch had snagged it. Had Ben been able to, he would have enjoyed the sight hugely. However, he was simply focusing on survival at this stage—and keeping the contents of his stomach down.

They had long since been overtaken by the canny locals, who obviously knew the trick to the race. All had given the Rossetter party a look that suggested they were idiots. Clearly they knew a thing or two.

The last station was manned by the elderly lady who had spoken to them when they rode into town.

"Hello." Alex leaned over to peer at her. "How lovely it is to see you again."

"Nobles" was all she muttered, handing them pies. Her mouth formed a straight line.

"Thish is not going down well," Finn muttered.

"Weak is what you all are." Ace ate his in a few bites, then downed the pint. He then stood chatting with the old lady, whose name was Meg, while the others attempted to do the same.

The problem was, the pie didn't want to go down.

"Eat a few mouthfuls, then take a drink," Ace said, watching Ben. "I'm hoping it's not going to take much longer, as the light is fading."

"Bastard," Will hissed.

Jeremy Caton burped, and Alex made a retching sound.

"Weak is what they are, Meg. Saddens me to think I call them friends," Ace added.

Ben managed to swallow the last mouthful of his beer. He

rocked back on his heels, and a large hand came out to steady him.

"Not long now, Ben."

He focused on Ace. The man was ridiculously large.

"I need to lie down."

"Soon."

Ace managed to herd them all out on to the track once more, staggering left and right; he was like a shepherd with an unruly flock. Somewhere in the recesses of his mind, Ben realized that he was seriously inebriated. Everything seemed larger and louder to him now.

"Excellent, we're there. Just up ahead, gentlemen, your women await you," Ace said as they came out of the woods. Ben saw a crowd of people. His eyes searched the women, but they were swaying... or was that his eyes. Then he saw her: Primrose "she never stops talking" Ainsley.

CHAPTER NINETEEN

Primrose had been eating the fudge Heather kept feeding her and listening as she continued to regurgitate every word Zvonka the fortune teller had spoken.

"I was there too, Heather."

"I know, but you must listen to what she said, Primrose. You are obviously about to face some trying times—"

"I will return to Pickford and live in my house until I can convince Herbert to marry me. That hardly seems trying."

"But you may not convince him."

"I will," Primrose said with false confidence.

"I'm glad my mother decided not to accompany us today. The duchess told her that she would watch over us, which was very nice of her, don't you think, Primrose?"

"Very nice."

While Lady Fullerton Smythe had allowed Heather to associate with Primrose a few times, it was not to be a regular occurrence, or so she'd told her daughter last night.

"She may be an earl's granddaughter, but she is still not worthy of too much of your attention, Daughter, and in this your father and I will not be questioned."

Heather had spat the words out in an angry tirade when she joined Primrose this morning.

"Heather, we are friends now, so please do not go against your parents' wishes for me. Our friendship will not change if we do not spend a great deal of time together." She felt she needed to explain this to her.

"I know that, but I choose to spend time with you. It is liberating to speak as I wish."

"Oh, well then." Primrose felt humbled. "I like having a friend, too."

"Good Lord, what is that noise?"

The words were spoken by Lady Althea Dillinger. She and Mrs. Hetherington had decided to make the journey to Chipping Nippley even considering they were with child.

"Exercise is good for expectant mothers," Lady Althea had said when Primrose enquired if she needed a seat. "Contrary to what others will tell you, Miss Ainsley, it is better to keep moving than take to your bed. I have a new physician, Dr. Siblinguyer, who explained this to me."

Not that Primrose saw children in her future, but she would remember that piece of advice, as it was unlikely her mother would ever offer up any.

"I do hear it," Heather said, looking to the forest.

Loud singing could be heard, and it was getting closer, and then suddenly there they all were. The men from Rossetter who had decided to partake in the pie and pint race, staggering out of the trees.

"Primrose," Heather said, her eyes on the men. "I think those men have overindulged."

"Mightily," Lady Ryder said, holding back laughter.

They had their arms linked, all except Mr. Dillinger, who was walking at the rear. He looked like a farmer herding his stock. Arms wide, he kept nudging the staggering men to keep them moving.

"Mother of God, look at them." Lady Levermarch looked amused. "It is so rare to see my husband unraveled that I will enjoy this moment immensely."

"They will have sore heads tomorrow," Mrs. Fletcher said. In her hand was a card, like they all carried, with the verse each man must recite.

The clang of tankards was almost deafening.

"I'm not sure what's worse, the singing or the clanging," Lady Althea said. "At least my husband appears in control, although one can never tell with Ace. He's a canny devil and can hide most emotions."

"Well. You ladies need to get them to recite the words." Primrose tried to hand her card to Miss Haversham, who in turn looked horrified at the approaching group.

"No, you must do it. I..., aha, there is something that needs my direct attention." She fled.

"I fear she may have just realized that men have more to them than what she sees in the ballrooms of society," Lady Levermarch said. "Good riddance. The woman is far too mouthy for my liking."

"Primrose."

"Yes, Heather?" Primrose couldn't drag her eyes from the approaching men... more importantly, one of them. Benjamin Hetherington. He was singing at the top of his voice, and he wore a silly grin. He looked so sweet that she felt it again, that squishy feeling inside her.

"Mr. Caton does not look like Mr. Caton."

"Who does he look like then?"

"A drunk and rather silly Mr. Caton."

"Still the same man, but you are just seeing another side to him. Perhaps this will be the moment you realize he is not the man to whom you've given your heart."

"Primrose!" Heather gasped. Primrose dragged her eyes off the approaching Benjamin in time to see her friend looking around her. "You should not speak to me like that."

"Why? Surely between friends it is best to speak the truth?"

"Well, yes, but I told you that in confidence." Heather anxiously examined the faces around once more.

"I did not shriek the words; only you heard them."

"I can't love him." The words were torn from her friend.

"Therefore we must avoid discussing him altogether?"

Heather looked in pain, but as the men were nearly upon them, Primrose let the subject drop.

They staggered up to their wives, the ones who had them, wearing sloppy grins.

Lord Ryder couldn't seem to get his tongue around the words he was meant to recite, so he was not declared the winner, which had him roaring his disapproval. His wife grabbed him by the hand and led him away.

Primrose had watched the locals come in a short time earlier. Only one had recited the words, but he'd only drunk four pints.

"'Lo, Miss Hainsley... Primpyrose." Benjamin reached her, and the waft of his ale-laden breath nearly dropped her to her knees. "I have c-completed the pie and pint run."

"There are several other ladies who have cards, go and find one of them," she whispered.

"Wh-what?" His eyes nearly crossed as he attempted to focus on her.

"Go and get someone else to give you a card."

His smile was sweet and made her stomach clench tight. *Oh, this will never do.* His shirt was untucked, and he'd lost two buttons on his waistcoat. Grass and twigs clung to his hair. He looked like a man she could touch and care for, a man of humble origins.

"I—ah… wants you," he said slowly, slurring his words. He then listed sideways but managed to stay on his feet.

"Oh very well." She held out her hands to take the tankards he thrust at her. "Five tankards," she said, and one of the locals took them from her. "Now read this." She held out the card.

He squinted, rocked back on his heels. Primrose grabbed his arms to stop him falling.

"'Slots of words," he mumbled, still squinting.

Primrose had thought it quite a simple verse by Keats, but she guessed it wasn't when you were five tankards of ale down.

"Keats." He looked up at her, still smiling. "Romantish."

Primrose refused to blush at his words.

"Though one moment's pleasure
In one moment flies—
Though the passion's treasure
In one moment dies—"

His words had gone from slurred to sober in seconds as he recited the verse.

"Excellent!" The woman who had taken the tankards congratulated Benjamin, but like Primrose, he didn't move. His eyes had caught and locked on hers.

"Primrosh." His whisper was ragged. "We c-cannot… this is—"

"Yes." She shook her head and backed away. "Well done, Mr. Hetherington. You are to be commended for consuming all that ale and reciting Keats. I'm quite sure the p-pies were very tasty also." She was babbling as she kept walking backward. He didn't move, his eyes simply followed her, and then they rolled back in his head and he slumped to the ground.

"I have him, Miss Ainsley," the Duke of Rossetter said, passing her.

"The winner is Mr. Dillinger!"

She tore her gaze from Ben, who was being hauled back to his feet, and looked for Heather. Dear Lord, Mr. Caton had her in his arms. Oh, this was not good with so many onlookers.

"Come, Heather, we must leave at once. Your mother will wonder where we are!" Primrose gripped her friend's shoulder hard.

"I—I—"

"Now, Heather."

"Of course." She pulled away from Mr. Caton and walked away.

Primrose looked over her shoulder and saw devastation written in every line of Mr. Caton's flushed face.

It was not until they were in the Rossetter carriage, returning to the house party, seated beside Miss Haversham and her mother, that Primrose was able to inhale deeply.

She felt Heather's hand squeeze hers on the seat, but that was the only gesture portraying the devastation her friend was feeling.

Heather had fallen for a man her parents would never countenance her marrying, and the path to true love and happiness had just become a great deal more treacherous to navigate for her.

Primrose would recover. Yes, she would be lying to herself if she didn't acknowledge now that she felt something for Mr. Hetherington, but it was merely a simple infatuation and nothing more.

Dear Lord, let it be simple.

CHAPTER TWENTY

Two nights later, Primrose tossed and turned in bed. The man was playing havoc with all her preconceived notions of men and women and the relationships they undertook.

She'd put distance between them since the pint and pie run, and he had been happy with that, seeming to avoid her where possible also. Not that she'd seen anything of him or the other men—other than Mr. Dillinger—the day following. Most had remained in bed.

The problem was, now that they were having no contact, she missed it. He was funny and intelligent, and yes, mocked her. No one had done that before, and she found she quite liked it.

"Contrary is what you are," Primrose muttered, throwing back the covers.

When he did converse with ladies, it was that silly Miss Haversham and her group of twits, as Heather liked to call them.

She couldn't define exactly what she felt for Benjamin

Hetherington, only that she'd never felt that way before. But it was decidedly odd.

Taking her candle, she pulled on her dress and slippers, then let herself out of her room. It was late, in fact very likely the early hours of the next day, but she didn't want to lie in bed thinking about that man any longer.

Exercise, her father always said, helped with sleep.

Taking the stairs up, she was soon walking the hallway to the second library. The duke had told her she could go in there at any time, and he would ensure a new page was turned each day for her to read. As yet, his wife had not convinced him to let Primrose hold the book.

To be honest, this was just as exciting: seeing a new page every day, with more words and pictures. Perhaps she would take a book from the shelves and read that tonight. The duke had said she may.

The sound of voices had her blowing out the candle and merging into the shadows. Primrose had no wish to come across someone conducting a tryst and have to answer questions as to why she was wandering the halls.

"It's this way, but be quiet."

"We need to be quick."

"Very, then we must leave before anyone rouses."

"I've packed my things, and the note has been left on my nightstand."

Primrose didn't recognize the voices. What were they discussing? She had a feeling something was not right.

Placing her candle on a small table, she followed on tiptoe as the men moved away. They climbed the stairs, and Primrose followed. She was sure they were up to no good as they headed toward the library.

She heard the slow thud of feet as they entered the small room. Peering inside seconds later, she could see very little, as the curtains were drawn.

"Cut the glass."

Dear Lord, they were taking the book! Primrose turned to leave and alert someone as to what was happening.

"Not so fast." A large hand banded around her waist, and another over her mouth. "Inside."

She was forced through the door and it was shut behind her.

"We have a problem. Get the book fast, we need to leave now!"

Primrose opened her mouth to scream as the hand lifted off her mouth, but before she could something was stuffed in there. Her hands were tugged behind her back and bound, and then her feet. She was lifted and thrown over a shoulder.

"No one speak again."

They walked through a silent house, and Primrose tried to wriggle, but the man who held her had a hand clamped over her legs. She didn't know where they were going as she couldn't see, and the jostling upside-down position was making her nauseous. Inhaling through her nose, Primrose tried to stay calm. She would need a clear head to deal with what came next.

The cool night air hit her minutes later.

"Take her to the carriage, quickly."

How was she to stop them and raise the alarm?

She was jostled as they started running, and her stomach rolled. Primrose had never been able to cope with a rolling carriage like her brother had. On the rare trips she had accompanied them, they had stopped to accommodate her travel sickness. Yet another difference between her and her family.

"Open the door."

She was thrown onto a seat, then two men joined her.

"Move, Miss Ainsley, and I will simply shoot you."

In the dimness, her gaze sought the owner of that voice.

Mr. Sanders was staring calmly down at her from the opposite seat.

"You have made my situation extremely uncomfortable, Miss Ainsley. I need a moment to work out what it is I will do with you."

"I say kill her."

Primrose's eyes shot to the other man, but she did not recognize him. She tried to dislodge the rag in her mouth, but it was wedged tight. She made a gagging sound, but no one removed it.

"No. It is bad enough that we have riled the Duke of Rossetter by stealing his prized book. I have no wish to rile more people and have them chase me down."

"Then what?"

"Perhaps she will have to come with us for a while. We will leave her somewhere to be released in a few days. By the time she can get word back to Rossetter , we will have left these shores."

"You're the boss."

"Yes." Mr. Sanders leaned closer, so close his face was only a few inches from hers. He smiled down at her, and looked nothing like the man she knew. This one had a sinister cast to his face that made her shiver. Primrose closed her eyes and tried to think. She would have to get herself out of this, as no one knew she was being taken. But that was nothing new for Primrose; she was always alone.

BEN WANDERED through the gardens and down the drive toward the stables. He couldn't sleep... again. It was becoming quite a habit, and he blamed it all on her. Miss Primrose Ainsley was destroying his peace, and he wasn't entirely sure what to do about that.

Once the ten-piece orchestra tuning their instruments

inside his head after the pie and pint run had moved on and he could think rationally again, he'd remembered what he'd felt like when he'd seen her on the finish line. The drunken euphoria he'd experienced just because she was near had been very real. His usual self-preservation filter had been lowered, and the instinct to go to her, hold and kiss her, had been strong. Instead he'd made a fool of himself, and she'd run for the hills.

He'd realized when his head had cleared that he could no longer deny she had somehow slipped under his usually impenetrable defenses. However, Ben had no doubt that he could dislodge her; it would just take time and dedication to the cause.

He'd tried to itemize all her flaws, but that didn't make her any less appealing. She was irritating and opinionated, but only with him. In fact, with others she was all that was sweet. The staff loved her, as she was constantly smiling or offering them a kind word. She talked too much and didn't seem to care overly what he thought of her, but he found those traits charming. What did that say about him?

He'd reasoned that she was attractive, but no more so than others; in fact in some cases a great deal less. That hadn't worked, as all he could think about was her lovely body and soft lips.

Avoiding her had made him wonder where she was, but he'd stuck to that as best he could over the past two days, and even spent time with other young ladies at the house party. He'd been bored as stiff as his shirt points in no time, but he'd kept up the façade of disinterest in Primrose. Not that she appeared to mind. She'd been spending a great deal of time with that idiot Sanders.

The sound of a horse snorting dragged him from his disturbing thoughts, alerting him to the fact that either one had broken free from the stables, or someone was up ahead.

Moving to the left, he blended in with the trees and walked slowly forward. This part of the drive was hidden from the house and could be accessed from the side of the garden through a series of paths.

"Did you get it?"

"It's inside. You'll have to ride up there with Bob, John, as we have another package to carry now."

They spoke in hushed tones, but their voices carried in the still night air.

"What is it?"

One of the voices was cultured, the other not. Ben moved closer; his curiosity was piqued. The meeting appeared to be of a secretive nature.

"A lady saw us when we stole the book. I had to bring her before she alerted someone."

Ben's heart dropped to the soles of his feet. Why did he believe the lady they referred to was Primrose? Surely she was tucked up in her bed dreaming of him, and if not him then at least her cuttings.

"What lady? Don't tell me it's one of them toffs. That'll bring trouble down on us, it will."

"It's no one important, only Miss Ainsley. No one will be overly worried about her disappearance for a while. They'll be curious as to what's happened to her, of course, but not as worried as if it was one of the others."

What? Of course people would be worried if Primrose went missing! How dare someone suggest otherwise!

"Get up with Bob and hurry about it, or someone will see us!"

Ben had no time to return to the stables for a horse. There were crossroads not far from Two Oaks; if he delayed to saddle a mount, then took the wrong road, he may never see Primrose again. A sharp pain in his chest told him that would haunt him forever.

Moving out of the shadows, he saw a large, lumbering carriage start rolling down the driveway. It had yet to pick up speed and was obviously trying to make a quiet getaway.

Ben started running. It had a rear seat, and he saw no shape in it to suggest it was occupied. When he was close enough, he jumped, catching the edge of the seat. Pulling himself up and onto it, he tucked himself down low as the carriage began to pick up speed.

He knew Primrose would be terrified inside, distressed, and wondering if she'd ever see her friends and family again, but he couldn't confront anyone yet. If he did and the driver panicked, the horse may veer out of control and the carriage could crash with Primrose inside. Ben could not allow her to be hurt. No, he was best to wait and see where they stopped. He would rescue her then.

He wondered who the man with the cultured voice was. He couldn't put a face to it, but he would, and then he would be made to pay. No one was abducting Primrose and getting away with it.

When would someone realize he was missing? Would he rescue Primrose and be back before the sun rose? Ben thought about the knife he usually carried that was still in his rooms at Rossetter . Unarmed, with only his wits, he lay between Primrose and whatever these men intended to do with her.

At least he always carried money. Finn had instilled this in the twins. 'You must always be prepared to bribe someone.'

He worked through plans inside his head as the miles passed. Ben was good at that, better than Alex. He was the rational twin. Looking for landmarks, he soon realized they were headed to the coast; he just wasn't sure where or why.

Thinking back over the conversation he'd heard, Ben guessed the Clipper book was inside the carriage. It was extremely likely that if Primrose had seen them attempting to steal it, she would have taken action and not given a thought to her well-being.

Bloody fool.

He was now the only person who could ensure her safety.

Ben soon fell into a doze with his cheek pressed to the carriage, so he wasn't sure how long they'd been travelling when it began to slow. From the cramping in his thighs and the glow of approaching dawn, he guessed it was some time.

As the carriage slowed to roll into a courtyard, Ben took the opportunity to climb off the back. His legs didn't want to work, and he landed on his backside. Hitting the ground hard snapped his teeth together and jarred right through his body, but he was soon up and running until he was concealed by the stables.

Moving as close as he could, he stopped within hearing distance of the carriage that had now halted before the two-story inn. The door opened, and out stepped two men. Primrose was still inside.

Sanders! The man had fooled them all. He'd come across as easy in his manners, and almost awkward. But what he'd been doing was infiltrating the house with the purpose of stealing the book.

"I've given her a healthy dose of a sleeping draft, so she's slumbering."

"What's that wrapped around your hand?" the other man, who Ben didn't recognize, said.

"The bitch bit me."

Ben heard a muffled chuckle.

"Yes, well, I taught her respect."

Anger had his fists clenching, but he made himself stay hidden. He could not help Primrose if he charged in and got captured himself.

"Right. Bring the book and her. I have already paid the

proprietor a great sum of money, so no questions will be asked."

"You go on and rest easy in your soft bed, your majesty," Ben heard the other man mutter as Sanders walked away.

Creeping closer, Ben watched as he reentered the carriage, then appeared with Primrose in his arms.

Seeing her defenseless, arms hanging and head lolling, had his anger climbing. He wanted to charge over there and grab her, but knew again he had to show patience, no matter how desperate he felt to reach her.

Slinking back into the shadows as someone led the horses away, he moved behind the stables and waited.

CHAPTER TWENTY-ONE

Her head felt thick and her body lethargic as she struggled to open her eyes.

"Wake up, Primrose."

"C-can't."

Something cool was laid over her face.

"You must; try harder."

"C-can't." She closed her eyes and fell back into sleep.

"God's blood, you are a trying woman."

Cracking her eyes open, she tried to find the owner of that voice, but his face swam.

"Up you get."

He was whispering in her ear, and his breath tickled, making her laugh.

"Sssh! You have to be quiet now, Primrose, while I untie you."

"'Kay," she managed to get out. Her tongue felt ridiculously large inside her mouth.

She was lifted then, and they were moving.

"F-feel bad." Her head started to swim.

"Hold on."

Scrunching her eyes tight, she breathed through her nose in an attempt to battle the nausea. She felt them going down, and then relief as cool air brushed her face. They walked for a few more minutes, and then she was lowered to the ground. Managing to get to her knees, Primrose tried to shake the fog from her head.

"I'm sorry to have to do this, but it is a necessity."

Before she could draw another breath, her head was plunged into cold water. Spluttering, she tried to scream, but she was submerged again.

"Don't scream; they'll hear us."

Now awake, Primrose glared up at Benjamin Hetherington.

"You'll still be woozy, but at least you're awake now."

"Was that absolutely n-necessary?"

"Absolutely."

Primrose bit her lip to keep from shrieking at him. Her face was wet, as was the front of her dress. Looking skyward, she saw the sun just beginning to rise.

"The book!" Primrose tried to regain her feet, but a large hand stopped her.

"We are not going back in there for a book."

"It's not just any book, but *the* book."

They were crouched beside a horse trough, the one she'd just been dunked into. He was close, so close she could smell his scent. Until that moment, Primrose hadn't even realized she knew it so well.

"Why are you here?" Scrunching her eyes shut several times, she fought to clear her vision. When that didn't work she cupped the water and drank deep.

"Horses have been drinking out of that."

"They have excellent taste." She drank another handful.

"I saw the carriage and heard that you had been captured and were inside, so I jumped on the back."

"That was terribly brave of you."

"Wasn't it, though. You'll be forever in my debt now." His eyes were on the inn they had just left. He was on one knee, one hand braced on the trough. Primrose thought he looked wonderful.

"It's hardly chivalrous to expect payment for your good deeds."

He laughed, just a soft snuffle, but it made her lips twitch.

"Perhaps we can leave this discussion for another time. Are you feeling all right, Primrose?"

"My jaw is a little sore, and my head is still fuzzy, but otherwise I am well."

Gentle fingers lifted her face and studied it.

"Who struck you?"

"Mr. Sanders."

The fingers tightened briefly and then fell away. She watched him pull off his necktie and lower it into the water. He then pressed it to her jaw.

"I'll kill him for you."

"I-I don't think that will be necessary." She wasn't entirely sure if he was serious or not.

"No one should strike a lady."

"Benjamin, I'm all right… really. Thank you."

His jaw was clenched, the muscles bunching and releasing.

"There are too many of them for us to do anything anyway," Primrose said. "However, I think it best we hide and then follow them when they leave."

His eyes were suddenly focused on her.

"We are leaving now. Returning to Rossetter ."

"No, we cannot do that."

"I'm not arguing about this, Primrose." He regained his feet and started to walk, towing her with him. As she was stumbling, he held her pressed to his side. They were soon out of sight, nestled in some bushes. Primrose sat once more, as her legs were still unsteady. "I will steal a horse, and then we're leaving."

Primrose grabbed his lapels to stop him moving.

"We have to get the book back."

"Don't be foolish, we cannot do that. Our best course is to leave and set the authorities on to doing so."

"No, Benjamin, don't you see, it has to be us. If *The History Of Plants* leaves here, it will never be seen again."

"For heaven's sake, woman, it's a book!"

She could see he was frustrated, but Primrose had to make him understand.

"But not just any book. If it is lost, then we shall never benefit from it again, because if it goes offshore it will sit in some private collection in some dark, dingy room."

"You don't know that!" His whisper was hissed in fury. "It could be going to a school for all you know. Besides, the duke keeps it in a dark, dingy library."

"But he lets people who wish to see it do so, and that is the point here. We will never again learn from its many wonderful pages if it leaves these shores. Don't you see, Benjamin, we must do this. It is our duty to Lucian Clipper and those who came after him."

"You cannot actually be serious?"

"Historians and botanists regularly visit Rossetter House to read that book. Some of the workings in there are taught at universities and schools. You must try and understand its significance."

"I am not a fool," he snapped in a tone that suggested she'd hurt his feelings. Surely not. The man was so confident in everything he did or said, respected by his peers and adored by women.

"I understand that, and that is why I am appealing to you. We must get that book back."

"Primrose." He sighed her name. "It is too dangerous. If you insist, I will follow them and send you back on horseback or in a hired carriage, but I cannot allow you to get hurt again."

"You would do that?" Something warm and heavy settled inside her chest.

"If I did not, I fear I will never get you to return to Rossetter ."

"I will not be going, but it is a very generous gesture." Primrose could do nothing to stop the yawn that overcame her.

"You will be going back to Rossetter , make no mistake on that."

Primrose struggled to her feet, determined to make a stand. Unfortunately, her legs did not obey her. She fell in a heap on her backside.

"My legs don't appear to be working."

"Whatever sleeping draft they gave you will take some time to dissipate."

"I'm not leaving, Mr. Hetherington."

He was looking out from their hiding place beyond the stables, his eyes going from left to right and back again.

"You called me Benjamin before. I would like you to continue to do so, especially considering the circumstances we find ourselves in."

She didn't say anything, just hid another yawn.

"Come, we will find somewhere more comfortable for you to sleep, then be ready when they are to leave."

"No. I have no wish to leave this place for fear of missing them, or fear of you letting them go."

His hesitation told Primrose her guess had been correct.

"We need to move further down the road. Once there we can get a horse, and hopefully food. Besides, that carriage will not be leaving anytime soon."

"Why?"

"I managed to disable it, but that will only be a brief respite."

"That was very clever of you."

"You sound shocked."

"No, I'm not. I know you are an intelligent man when you wish to be."

"I don't have time to lock horns with you over that comment right now."

She was lifted with ease into his arms.

"I can walk."

"Yes, I've seen how well that worked for you."

"Y-you cannot carry me!" Primrose had never been held like this before. Perhaps by her father when she was young, but not in a great many years.

"Yes, I remember now from the last time I carried you how heavy you are. My back will be uncomfortable for days."

Was he laughing at her? She couldn't tell, as his face was calm. Primrose had her arms around his neck and a perfect view of his side profile. His jaw was strong, cheekbones pronounced. The man should be carved in ivory from this particular angle.

"What are you looking at?"

They were walking down the side of the road, close enough to a group of trees should they hear a carriage.

"You have a large mole with several long hairs sticking out from it."

"No, I don't."

"It must be a trick of light, then."

He turned then, and his face was suddenly there. *Good Lord, the man is disturbing.*

"I see somewhere we can hide, and very likely a place we can get horses. You do ride, I hope?"

"Not really… and definitely not in this dress."

His eyes ran over her body, and even in the weak dawn light she felt where they landed.

"What does 'not really' mean?"

"It means not really, but I will do my best considering our situation is dire."

"How extremely brave of you."

"Was that mockery?"

"Yes. You've jumped recklessly into water, and climbed out a window to win a game of hide and seek. But horse riding in a dress is beyond you?"

"I don't like horses."

"Which means what exactly?"

"I can't ride, and have never learned!" Primrose did not like admitting such a weakness, but now was a time for honesty only.

"Good Lord, there is actually something you can't do. I must remember this moment."

"Sarcasm is beneath you."

"Come, I see a barn. We can hide in there," he said, ignoring her. Leaving the road, he walked through the grass.

"Please put me down, I'm sure my legs are working now."

He did; she staggered a few steps, then landed on her bottom again.

"Happy now?"

"Of course I'm not happy!"

He bent to pick her up.

"I just don't want you to tire yourself."

"Have some faith in my stamina."

"You don't seem to be breathing hard. Are you hiding that in some way?"

"I do plenty of things that ensure I can cope with carrying damsels in distress should it be required."

"Like what?"

"Boxing."

"Really? I have always wanted to see that."

Benjamin moaned. "Not another one."

"Another what?"

"I know a lady of noble birth who is rather enamored with boxing and even has her own punching bag hanging in her rooms."

"Really? Do you think I—"

"No."

"But—"

"No."

"I'm sure Herbert will be more lenient," she said.

"He's a clergyman; how have you come to that conclusion?"

Primrose sighed, because nothing else really fit the moment.

CHAPTER TWENTY-TWO

*B*en walked into the small barn. It smelled of the usual scents: hay, horse, and manure, but the new scent now mingling in the air was Primrose.

It wasn't exactly sweet or spicy, but a mixture of both and exactly right for a woman like her.

Contrary to what he'd said to Primrose, his arms were tired, but he wasn't showing her that. His pride could not take the knock she'd give him.

He found a pile of hay and lowered her onto it.

"How is it you are here, Benjamin? I-I had thought I would need to extricate myself from this mess alone."

And she'd been frightened, even though he knew she would never admit that to anyone.

"I couldn't sleep and was out walking. I came across the carriage and heard them saying you and the book were inside. I jumped on the back."

"Did you really? That was extraordinarily brave of you."

Why did those words make him feel ten feet tall?

"But how did you manage to get me out of the room in that inn?"

"When everyone was asleep, I crept into the inn. The man who'd been stationed outside your door to watch over you was snoring and had fallen sideways."

"That was a very good deduction, knowing that I would be inside that room."

Her eyes were clearer now, lacking the slightly unfocused gaze she'd had before.

"I think it was a fairly simple leap to make, don't you?"

"Yes, of course. Go on with your story." She waved a hand at him.

"The man was snoring. I walked over him, unlocked the door, and strolled in. You were also snoring—"

"I was not!"

She looked like someone who had taken a tumble in the hay, sitting there with her hair down, clothes wrinkled, deliciously rumpled.

"Thankfully, when I roused you, you didn't shriek, and even managed to keep quiet as we left."

"I am quite capable of being quiet should I need to be."

"Really? I have not seen much evidence of this, but if you say so," Ben teased her.

"I need to say thank you again, Benjamin."

"If you must."

She rolled her eyes.

"But seriously, thank you. Not many people would have done as you did, and I am extremely grateful that I am out of Mr. Sanders clutches. You do know it was he who was behind this entire thing, don't you?"

"I do. I saw him when the carriage stopped. As to not many doing as I did, I'm sure your family would have wanted to rescue you."

"No, probably not."

"You're not serious?" Ben didn't believe her. "You are of their blood."

"And a burden to them." The words were spoken softly.

"You are not a burden."

Her smile was sad.

"I am, actually, but thank you for saying otherwise. My family… well, they don't need me, you see. I am not easy to…" Her words fell away. "Never mind."

"What were you going to say?" He stood over her, looking down at her now lowered head. "Tell me what you were going to say, Primrose."

"Nothing. I am tired, and therefore my tongue has loosened."

He thought about pressing her, but then remembered that he didn't need to know more details about this woman.

"All right. Now you stay here while I go and find us some transport."

"Promise you'll come back!" She lunged for his hand as he turned to leave, gripping it hard.

"You think I'd leave you here?" He dropped to his knees at the fear in her voice. "I would never leave you alone, and I had hoped you would understand that about me by now."

"I'm sorry." Her voice wobbled. "Perhaps what has happened has upset me more than I realized."

The last few hours were taking their toll on her. Her spirit had dimmed, but Ben knew it would not be for long.

"Which is completely understandable. It's not every day young ladies are snatched from house parties and whisked away in the middle of the night."

"At least you saw. My hero," she said around another yawn.

"You are safe now, Primrose." He gathered her into his arms and held her tight. She didn't resist, but burrowed into him, her hands gripping his shirt, holding him close. He felt her tremors then.

"You are such a brave girl, Primrose. Not many women of my acquaintance would have endured what you have and not dissolved into a puddle of tears."

She sniffed, then eased back.

"Thank you for following me, Benjamin."

He cupped her cheek, using his thumb to wipe her tears. So beautiful and full of life. She would never be anything to him, but if he were to choose a mate, it would be someone like her.

"You're welcome." He leaned in and placed a soft kiss on her forehead. "Now rest, and I shall return soon. I promise."

She didn't answer, just lay down on the hay and let him cover her with his jacket.

Ben made himself walk away. He'd promised her he'd follow that carriage when it left with the book. He'd lied. He was getting her out of here as fast as he could. An investigation of the barn left him empty-handed, so he headed to the house and knocked on the front door. It was soon answered by an elderly man.

"Good morning, sir. I have need of a horse. I am willing to pay handsomely for it."

The man had faded blue eyes and wore a shirt that had seen many washes.

"I have no horses save one, and it's a pony I attach to my cart."

"Well, thank you all the same. If my wife and I may rest in your barn, we shall be gone in shortly."

The man nodded, and Ben handed him several coins. The old man was curious, and who wouldn't be considering there was a perfectly respectable inn that would offer them a bed and food only a few minutes away. But he didn't question Ben, and for that he was grateful.

He would have to go back to the inn, but to do that he had

to ensure the carriage holding Sanders had gone, or they'd recognize him. Ben had no issue going a few rounds with the man one-on-one, or even taking on a second should it be required, but he knew Sanders had three men keeping him company, and doubted he'd come out on the right side of the ledger with four men in a fight.

Keeping to the fields and out of sight hidden in the trees, he retraced the path to the inn. Daylight was slowly creeping in, and the courtyard now had people wandering about seeing to the chores.

Ben ran to the stables and around the side. Staying pressed to wood, he moved as close as he could to the inn.

The front door burst open, and out strode Sanders.

"She's gone!" He was roaring at the man accompanying him. "How the hell can that be when you were guarding her door!"

Sanders looked different. No more the amiable gentleman, his stride was aggressive, as was his voice.

"I want her found!"

Not while I'm still breathing.

"Search everywhere. She cannot have gone far considering the sleeping draft I forced down her throat!"

The man at his side ran into the stables, presumably to speak with the other henchmen. Ben waited and watched; a few minutes later, he had his break. If he could get that damn book, Primrose would not be quite so incensed when they left.

"The carriage! One of the wheels is loose!" The men ran back out of the stables.

"What?" Sanders roared, following them back in.

When they had disappeared, Ben slipped unnoticed into the inn, and headed upstairs. After searching the room Primrose had been in, he checked the ones on either side. None had the book.

Making his way back downstairs undetected, he slipped into the kitchens. He found two staff there, a young boy and a woman.

"Good morning."

The woman looked up from the pastry she was rolling. Her eyes ran over Ben, noting his necktie was mussed and he wore no jacket.

"Can I help you, sir?"

"I am in need of food for my journey, please."

"Of course. If you'll step outside and wait in one of the rooms, I'll parcel you up something and have it brought right out."

"I have something of a sore head, do you mind if I step outside the kitchen doors briefly to take some air while I wait?"

She chuckled.

"Mr. Henry's ale can affect a man in that way."

"That it can."

The food was handed to him minutes later, along with a flask filled with ale.

Slipping around the stables, he ran back to Primrose, eating a large wedge of pie on the way. The pastry melted in his mouth, and was a close second to the pies he'd eaten in the pint and pie run.

Entering the barn, he found her still nestled in the hay. She looked almost angelic with her mouth closed. Dropping down, he settled beside her and closed his eyes. Just a few minutes and he'd wake her, and they'd leave for Rossetter .

He woke slowly, as he always did. Alex said it was like watching a bear come out of hibernation. Slowly orientating himself, Ben opened his eyes.

Primrose.

Turning his head, he found her still sleeping, curled toward him, hands under her cheek. Sweet, he thought. At least, she was when she wasn't awake and taking him to task.

He ran a finger down her cheek, and her nose wrinkled. Touching her plump lower lip, he traced the contour, then down to her chin. Unlike him, she didn't wake slowly.

Her eyes shot open and locked onto his.

"Dear Lord, what is the time?"

He envied that. Alex woke alert.

"I'm not sure, as I slept myself."

"The carriage!" She bolted upright. "We must stop it."

"It may already have been repaired and left the inn, Primrose."

She fell back into the hay.

"Drat."

"Drat?"

"It seemed to fit the moment."

"No flowery curses?"

"I don't have one to fit the occasion."

"How about Lupin?"

She laughed, a soft, husky chuckle.

"Why are you and your family not close, Primrose?"

The thought bothered him. He was sure earlier that she'd been about to say she was not easy to love.

"Because they have no time for anything but what they see as their vocation."

"So therefore there is no room in their lives for anything or anyone else? That sounds unfair."

"Life is not fair, Benjamin. You are extremely lucky if you have not worked that out yet." Her eyes were on the roof above her head.

"I have been treated unfairly in my lifetime, Primrose."

"By your mother when you were just a boy?"

He managed a nod. Even the reference to his mother made him tense. "But surely you and your brother—"

"My brother and I were once close," she interrupted him.

"What happened?"

"My parents infected him with their obsession for botany. They tried with me, but every time we went away, I would get sick. Homesick, travel sick, or seasick. It was a weakness in me, and therefore I was no longer welcome. Weakness is not welcome in the Ainsley family."

"It's not a weakness, Primrose. It's something that is inside you and has been since birth. Just like your annoying clicky jaw."

"It only annoys you."

"Oh, I'm sure there are more people, they're just too polite to mention it."

She snuffled. Not exactly a laugh, but not a sad sigh either.

"Benjamin."

"Yes, Primrose."

"What are you afraid of?"

"I don't understand the question," Ben said to give himself time. But he did, only too clearly. He just didn't want to answer it because he couldn't lie to her.

"What is deep inside you that frightens you?" Her words were nearly a whisper, but as he was only inches away he heard them.

"Pineapple makes me shudder. And moths, I've always had an abhorrence for them. They fly about your head, and I'm sure once I swallowed one."

"That's not what I mean as you very well know."

"Tell me your fears first, Primrose."

"It's not really a fear, it's the truth."

"Let's hear it then."

"I have a character flaw—"

"Just the one," he scoffed.

"I'm unlovable." She said the words so calmly, it took Ben a second to take in their full meaning. He'd been right about what she was going to say earlier.

"No, you're not!"

"The statistics prove it, and I'm all right with that. I've accepted it. Hence, I wish to wed Herbert, as he and I will never love each other."

"Wait." Ben rolled onto his side to face her. "You don't actually believe that nonsense, do you? You are totally loveable."

"It's all right, Benjamin, it doesn't hurt me, and like I said, the statistics prove me right."

"Of course it bloody hurts!"

"There is no need to roar at me. You asked, and I told you."

"What statistics do you have to back up this ridiculous statement?"

"My family don't love me, and neither does Herbert." She spoke in that prim little voice that he loved.

"Four people is not an accurate set of statistics."

"Yes, it is, and as I've had exposure to those people for many years, the data is more than accurate."

"Lord save me from a woman who actually thinks she knows how to use her brain," Ben scoffed.

"That's insulting. My intelligence is equal, if not greater, to any man's."

"Yes, it is, so how about using it."

She harrumphed. "Now you need to share your fear, Benjamin."

Not bloody likely. Ben knew that his fear would sound as ridiculous as hers had. His, however, would never change, and he would never allow a woman to have the ability to hurt him again.

She turned her head to look at him. Their eyes held for long seconds.

"Primrose, some man will love you one day, I promise."

"No, that's not for me."

He moved closer. "Yes, it is. You are kind and giving and have a lovely personality. Please promise me you will not give up on love?"

"Benjamin, there is no need for this. My understanding is based on fact. I like facts, they make life simple."

"Rubbish." He leaned over her until their eyes met and held. "Admit to me you are loveable."

"I'm not." She lifted a hand and touched his cheek. Just a brief brush of one finger, and Ben gave in to the inevitable and kissed her.

"We shouldn't do that."

"No, we shouldn't." He kissed her again, this time taking it deeper. "But we will, as no one is here to see us."

"Benjamin." She sighed his name into his mouth.

"Primrose." He nibbled her jaw and down her neck. "Just a few harmless kisses." *Harmless,* he scoffed silently. Kissing her was like setting tinder to paper.

"Oh, that feels nice."

He knew she'd be the kind of woman to tell a man exactly how she felt. The kind of woman who would want to experience all the wonders a kiss could give her.

"How about this?" Ben placed his lips on the skin above the bodice of her dress.

"N-nice also."

This was wrong on so many levels, but surely a few kisses would not hurt. No one would ever know they had shared them. He wanted to stop her hurting. Stop her thinking she was unlovable. Surely he could do that with a few kisses.

He returned to her lips and took her mouth again for another hot, searing kiss.

"Open for me, Primrose."

She did, and he eased his body over, half on top of hers, and seconds later was lost. His head swam, his mind emptied of all but her, and he'd never felt quite so desperate in his life before.

CHAPTER TWENTY-THREE

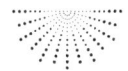

*P*rimrose wrapped her arms around Benjamin's neck and held on. His kisses were heating her body, making her feel weak. Her limbs felt like they were infused with warm liquid. Before, when they'd kissed, it had been lovely, wonderful even, but this... this was all-consuming.

"More," she whispered as he moved to her neck again.

"If you insist." His words were gruff and told her he too was affected. "But I want you to tell me you are loveable first."

"No."

She felt his hand on her thigh, hot and heavy, stroking up her leg, and she wanted it on her skin. Wanted to feel the wonder of their flesh touching.

"Tell me," he ordered her.

"I would be lying to you if I did, and I-I try not to do that."

She shivered as he kissed the edge of her jaw. His other hand wandered upward to slip under the edge of her bodice and stroke, so close to her breast. Her nipple grew tight and ached. Then he tugged the material aside and cupped the full flesh of one breast.

"Oh, Benjamin."

"You have lovely breasts, Primrose."

They'd really just always been there, on her chest, but now she was quite glad of that fact, as they felt wonderful under his large hand.

He took her lips in a hot, bone-melting kiss. Exquisite did not begin to explain what this felt like. She now understood the poems and odes that people wrote about passion. Understood how people did foolish things in the name of love. Right then, she would do anything he asked of her.

Not that this is love, she reminded herself quickly.

"I must stop," he whispered against her lips.

"No, I don't want you to." She was desperate for him to continue. Desperate to have the tension building inside her eased. Desperate to feel wanted by someone for once in her life.

The hand at her breast squeezed, and one long finger stroked over a nipple, making her shudder. His other hand was on her leg, moving higher under her skirts, stoking the flames of need into a furnace inside her.

When his mouth left hers again, she grabbed his shoulders to urge him back, but he ignored her, moving lower, and then she felt his lips on her breast.

"Dear Lord, Benjamin." Primrose thought what they'd been doing had been wonderful, but when his mouth closed over her nipple, she was fairly sure she could have swooned —had she been the type to do so, and standing upright.

The hand under her skirts moved in between her thighs, and Primrose made a squeaking sound and clamped them together.

"Let me do this for you, Primrose." His voice was hoarse. "I want this for you."

She let her thighs fall open. He stroked her there, tracing a single finger down the soft folds, sending her into a riot of delight.

Hollyhocks, she was surely going to explode with the pleasure of it all.

And then he stopped, just when she was sure something was about to happen.

"Why have you stopped?"

"Sssh." He placed a hand over her mouth. "I think I hear someone."

Primrose wasn't sure how, as all she'd heard was a roaring in her ears.

"B-but, Ben—" The rest of her words were muffled by his hand.

"Be quiet," he whispered in her ear, pulling her skirts down and hoisting her bodice up. "Hide."

She scrambled to her feet, pleased that her legs were now working, and hurried to duck behind a half wall. Benjamin followed. Crouching beside her, he handed her a small bundle.

"Someone is coming in here; you must be quiet."

"I can hear they are coming, and I know to be quiet."

"Is this you being quiet?" His face was inches from hers.

She shut her mouth.

They listened to the sound of feet entering the barn.

"The carriage will be ready soon, but he wants us to check here, before we leave, for the woman."

The hand on Primrose's arm gripped her harder. She was then forced backward onto her bottom. Seconds later she was in the dark with a cover thrown over her head. It was smelly, and she choked back the gagging sounds. Benjamin wasn't in here with her, so where was he hiding?

"Good day, gentlemen, what can I help you with?"

"You!"

"He's one of them toffs from that house. I saw him one day when he came into the stables."

"Grab him!"

Primrose didn't know what to do. If she showed herself, they'd take her too, and then there would be no way of escape. She heard the sound of a fist meeting flesh and hoped it was not Benjamin on the receiving end.

"Throw that over him, he's a strong bugger!"

"Christ, there's three of us, and he's putting up a good show!"

She heard more scuffles, and then suddenly they stopped.

"Right, let's get him back and see what Sanders wants done with him."

She waited a further five minutes, counting them off in her head. They were the longest minutes she'd ever waited. Primrose then threw off the cover and took a large breath.

"This is not good," she whispered. "Not good at all."

Benjamin had shown himself because he feared they'd take them both otherwise. The gesture spoke of the man she already knew he was. The honorable, protective man who loved his family and friends.

Grabbing the bundle of food, she left her hiding place and let herself out of the barn. Checking the way was clear, she crept to the trees. They would hide her from the road and anyone travelling along it. Reaching the end, she crouched and watched the inn. There was no sign of Benjamin, but there was no sign of the carriage either. Both were likely still inside the stables.

Opening the bundle, she ate a piece of cheese and half a slice of pie. Primrose needed her strength. Drinking some of the ale, she shuddered. She'd never developed a taste for it. She then tried to come up with a plan.

Somehow, she had to follow that carriage and rescue Benjamin; she just wasn't sure how yet. Clutching the bundle, she dashed along the road into the courtyard. Veering right, she made it undetected to the stables and found a door at the rear. Dare she go through it?

It was vital she remained undetected, but she had to see what was going on. Leaving the food outside, she dropped to a crouch and slipped through the door.

"It's lucky there's no other travelers about. Someone would be highly suspicious if they saw us carrying him back here."

"He's in the carriage now, away from prying eyes."

They were discussing Benjamin. She hoped they had not hurt him.

"The sooner we leave, the better. That busybody Miss Ainsley will be trying to raise the alarm by now. She will have a way to walk, as the next village is some distance, but she's a determined sort."

She recognized Mr. Sanders's voice now. *Am I a busybody?*

"Do you think she knows we have him?"

"I doubt it. My guess is Hetherington somehow came upon us and realized we had Miss Ainsley in the carriage. He then followed, and was about to attempt to grab her when you grabbed him. You did search that barn, didn't you? There was no sign of that infernal woman?"

"Yes."

"We did."

"Aye."

They were lying; if they had searched, they would have found her.

"Why didn't he grab her last night?"

"Maybe he tried and couldn't find her. Plus, I was guarding outside her door, so she must have left by the window."

"From the second story?" Sanders scoffed. "She'd break her bloody neck!"

"She must have tied the sheets together."

"Did you check that?" Sanders asked.

"No. But how did she get out when you'd given her that sleeping draft? Maybe you didn't give her enough."

"I did wonder that at the time," Sanders said. "She's a devilishly tricky woman. I endured many days with her, and that was not easy, I assure you. That woman is a challenging one."

"There you have it, then," another voice said. "She's obviously woken and worked her way out the window and down to the ground."

"Let's hope she had a fall and hurt herself, and it festers," Sanders snarled.

Charming. His words merely reinforced what she already knew. Primrose was not a loveable person. Benjamin had tried to tell her differently, but she knew better.

"That'd be the best outcome."

"No one's asking you. Now get this coach fixed. We need to get moving!" Sanders roared.

"It's fixed."

"Then why are we talking and not moving! I'm going to get my things, then we're leaving, and this time we're not stopping until we reach Dover."

"We'll need to change horses."

"It will be done with haste," Sanders snapped. "Now get the horses harnessed, and let's go!"

Primrose heard the sound of feet.

"He's a mean bastard, that one," she heard someone mutter.

"Aye."

Peeking around the edge of the partition, Primrose saw the coach. The men were focused on the front and harnessing the horses. Studying the vehicle, she saw the seat that Benjamin must have ridden in at the rear. Dare she climb aboard and hope no one decided to use it? It looked precarious, and her stomach rolled at the thought of being balanced up there for hours. But what choice did she have?

The waiting as they prepared to leave stretched her nerves to breaking point. Especially as Benjamin was inside that coach just a few feet away, no doubt trussed up like a goose.

She didn't want to think about him hurting; it made her stomach ache. Primrose decided she had to move now and get into that coach or she would be left behind. There was no way she could catch it when it started moving. No doubt she'd ended up face-first on the road. Plus, she didn't have the darkness to conceal her like Benjamin had.

Inhaling a deep breath, she scurried to the rear of the carriage while the men were still busy with the horses and climbed up and into the seat. Crouching in the small space, she closed her eyes and prayed no one found her.

She didn't have long to wait before the coach was lumbering out of the inn with one more occupant than they realized. She settled in and hoped her stomach did not get too unsettled.

Visions of what she and Benjamin had done in that barn filled her head now that she had time to think. Time to remember how wonderful he had made her feel. She should be shocked at her wantonness, and yet she wasn't—perhaps because she'd never felt that close to a person before. Whatever the reason, she would never regret that small moment in time. A moment where she experienced what it felt like to be wanted. A moment she doubted she would ever recapture.

CHAPTER TWENTY-FOUR

*B*en had been in bad situations in his life. There was the time he and Alex got into trouble in the gambling den and hadn't been able to pay their debts. Finn had stepped in to save them from being beaten and likely thrown in the Thames. Another time, they'd invited two young ladies on a picnic, only for their fathers to come instead. Ben hadn't known he and Alex could run that fast.

This situation, however, was something he would have to extricate himself from alone. He had no problems with that; since his brothers had married, he'd been running solo a lot. He'd enjoyed aspects of that but did miss Alex, as once they'd been inseparable.

"We won't have to drug him, because we should reach the port before nightfall."

Sanders sat to his right, and another man to his left. Ben was trussed up like a goose on the floor between them. A pillow would be nice, as his head was banging on the floor.

"The Duke of Rossetter is a powerful enemy to have, Sanders. As are the other men at that house party, especially my siblings."

THE LADY'S DANGEROUS LOVE

"They will not find me, Hetherington, as I will be long gone from here with the expectation of a great deal of money in my immediate future."

"I hope you put a great distance between us, as my eldest brother is somewhat dogged in his need to protect my brother and me. He has been known to travel far and wide to seek retribution," Ben said in a conversational tone. "Then there is the fact that I will likely want to seek some of my own."

"I am not frightened of you and your brothers, Hetherington. You will never find me."

"May I ask what you've done with Miss Ainsley, as she appears not to be in this carriage."

He'd thought long and hard about what to say with regard to Primrose and decided that his not knowing her location was the outcome best for her.

"Somehow she escaped. The woman's trouble, and I knew that from the start."

"Watch what you say about her, Sanders. Miss Ainsley is my friend."

Sanders scoffed, making Ben's fingers itch to strike him.

"She has a great deal to say for herself. It's hardly surprising she is not a society favorite," Sanders said.

Yes, she did, and Ben realized that was what he liked most about Primrose. She was no retiring, meek miss, his Miss Ainsley.

His Miss Ainsley.

He tested the words and found he liked them. Memories of her full breast in his hand and the taste of her on his lips were things he would carry with him for some time.

I'm unlovable.

Her family needed to be shot for letting her believe that. The woman was totally loveable. Hell, if Ben wasn't who he was, he was sure he could love her... but he didn't and wouldn't.

"She will have raised the alarm, Sanders. You will be caught in no time." Ben looked to the other man seated across from Sanders; he appeared uncomfortable.

"We will be gone before then."

"And dare I ask what you'll do with me?"

"Shoot you if you don't shut up!" Sanders snapped.

"Shooting a viscount's brother... let me see. I think someone can be hanged for that."

"Here, we can't shoot him!" The other man looked a bit green now.

"Shut up, you fool. I need to think!"

"Clearly not one of your strong points," Ben needled him, "or you would have started by now."

"I've infiltrated your ranks for the last year, Hetherington, to execute this plan, and none of you knew who was in your midst," Sanders scoffed. "So I think we can say that thinking is indeed an asset of mine."

Ben made a scoffing sound as he wriggled to get comfortable. His bonds were tight; he knew this as he'd been trying to free himself since they'd dumped him in the carriage.

"Sanders, we tolerated you, but that was all."

The man's face tightened in anger.

"Any chance I can occupy a seat? The coach springs are not making my current situation comfortable. Plus, I have no wish to hurl the entire contents of my stomach over your boots... then again...."

He hoped Primrose had indeed gone for help and that she was now safe. The woman was reckless, but he reminded himself that there was no way she could have followed him. She didn't know how to ride, so a horse was out of the question, and she wouldn't have been able to get on this coach undetected.

"Pull him up."

Ben bit back the moan as his ribs gave a sharp jolt of pain and the abused muscles in his shoulders ached.

"Many thanks." He nodded to the man he was now seated beside.

"You're welcome, sir."

"Don't be polite to him!" Sanders roared. "He's a nuisance and nothing more."

"It makes me nervous that his family will be after him now."

"You let me worry about that."

They traveled in silence, and from snatched glimpses of landmarks, Ben noted they were heading to Dover.

"My guess is the book you stole is leaving these shores?"

"Very good, Hetherington. I am to receive a large sum of money for it."

"We certainly won't miss you, but the book belongs here." Ben kept his voice calm, as if he was conversing over the breakfast table. He didn't want this man to know he was in fact seething with rage. He'd touched Primrose. Struck her, and Sanders would be made to pay for that.

"Well, now it will have a new home," Sanders mocked. "With someone who will take excellent care of it."

They stopped to change horses, and Ben was gagged and forced back down onto the floor, and then they were off again. As the day dwindled into early evening and the sun lowered in the sky, they reached the port of Dover. Ben had once again been forced onto the floor and gagged for the last few miles, and his body was protesting loudly.

The carriage rolled into a barn and stopped.

"Leave him in the carriage for now," Sanders ordered. "Raise your head and I'll have the guard shoot you, Hetherington. Yell for help, and the same thing will happen."

He wasn't sure how he was to do that, as he was gagged.

The men left and he lay there listening to the sounds of activity outside the carriage. The horses were unharnessed and led away, and then there was silence. Just him and whoever was outside guarding him.

He lay there until dark, and then some more. He heard the rumble of voices, and then that stopped too. A loud snore told him the man on guard was now sleeping. Sanders would not be pleased if he knew that once again they were sleeping on the job. Not that he could do anything about his situation. The ropes were tight, and his hands and feet were now numb, which was not a good sign. In fact, the only thing keeping him from moaning in agony was Primrose Ainsley.

He focused on her, remembering her lush breast in his hand and the feel of her sweet lips under his. She was an innocent, Ben knew that, but she'd been responsive and eager.

Was she safe?

Surely by now she'd reached help and sent word to his brothers.

Please be safe.

He heard the handle on the coach door. It wasn't a decisive movement. Squinting in the darkness, he saw the door open a crack. The small hand that reached inside landed on his face, one finger nearly dislodging his eye.

Christ!

The hand moved to his mouth and pulled out the rag that Sanders had stuffed in there, and Ben took a deep breath.

He knew he couldn't speak, just as she did. Instead he watched her slip through the door and into the carriage. Ben bit back a grunt as she kicked his head climbing over him onto the seat.

"Ben!"

Leaning over, she placed a hand on his chest. His eyes must be shooting flames as she looked into them.

"Hurry up!" he mouthed.

Something in his gaze had her scurrying down the seat.

"Slowly," Ben hissed.

She did as he asked, and the coach didn't sway, thank God. He felt her hands tugging at the rope that bound his ankles. Her little hiss of frustration had him tensing, but no one heard.

He was going to kill her. Wrap his hands around her neck and squeeze. What the hell did she think she was doing, taking such a risk? Bloody little fool; if anyone looked in or came to check on him, they'd both end up in trouble. She could be captured and harmed. The thought made his blood run cold.

She finally undid his feet. Ben rolled, and she started on his hands. The pain of blood moving into his feet had his teeth gritting. Pins and needles followed.

He was too scared to acknowledge her bravery. Terrified, angry; so many emotions chased through him that they nearly choked him as he silently urged her to hurry.

His hands were harder for her, as he'd been constantly working on them and had likely tightened the knots. She hissed, and he could hear the rasp of her breath as she struggled.

"Get me out," he whispered after a few more tense minutes.

"Your hands?"

"Later. We need to move now."

She kicked him in the ribs as she tried to scramble out of the carriage. Ben bit back another grunt of pain.

He sat upright as she opened the door, then with a series of maneuvers, managed to swing his legs so they were out the door. Sliding out, he motioned to her to close it behind him.

"Move," he whispered into her ear.

She ran into the darkness with him following. Ben struggled to coordinate his movements with his hands tied behind his back, especially as his feet were struggling to work. His balance was off, and he was listing from side to side, but he managed to keep up.

There were plenty of buildings frequented by people they could go into, but he wanted somewhere private. He needed to get his hands free so he could strangle Primrose.

Ben took the lead and circled a tavern. Slowing to a walk, he crept along the rear wall.

"We need something to free my hands."

"Right." Primrose started looking about her as if something would magically appear.

"A knife," he said in a sharp tone.

"Right," she said again, still looking.

"A sharp one."

Her eyes fell on the back door of the tavern, and before he could stop her, she'd ducked inside.

"God's blood!" Ben followed but did not enter. If she screamed, he be in there in seconds. Seconds later she came out.

"I didn't mean for you to simply walk in there!"

"I have a knife. I took it off the bench. It was just sitting there, and no one was looking."

He grunted something, not willing to concede how well she'd done. Anger was still riding him.

"I don't want to hurt you."

"Just cut the rope, Primrose."

She did, sawing gently through it. She only nicked him once.

"I'm sorry!"

"It's fine. Let's go." Clenching and unclenching his fingers, he then shook them hard to get the circulation moving. Grabbing the knife in one hand, he took her fingers in the other, securing them inside his in case she disappeared again.

"Where?"

"Be quiet."

"Oh, well I just—"

He placed his hand over her mouth, then leaned down until their eyes met.

"Not one more word, do you understand?" Smart girl that she was, she nodded.

They moved around the front to the tavern and walked beside the buildings and shop fronts down the street until he thought they'd put enough distance between themselves and Sanders. Ben doubted he would stray far from the carriage while he was supposedly still inside.

"Look!" She nudged him in his sore ribs again. He sucked in a deep breath.

"What?" he snapped.

"A sign, they have rooms for let."

Ben pushed the knife into his boot and tugged her hand, perhaps a little harder than necessary, and soon they were walking up the steps and into the white weatherboard house.

"Good evening."

A woman was knitting behind the reception desk.

"We would like a room, please."

She looked him over, taking in the fact he had no necktie or jacket, and then Primrose, who looked rumpled. Her hair was down, and her dress torn.

"We had an accident. Our horses bolted, scared by a-a bunch of grouse which we unsettled. The carriage wheel broke, and it rolled onto its side. We've had to walk a great distance, and I fear we are very hungry."

Ben glared Primrose into silence as she finished speaking. God's blood, the woman would surely not be fooled by such a ridiculous tale.

"Oh, my dear, how awful for you. But at least you are not injured."

"No indeed, we all escaped unscathed," Primrose continued.

"Well, you and your husband have no need to worry, we have a room that will suit you for the night. Are you to sail in the morning?"

Primrose nodded. "We are. Hopefully our driver will have the carriage fixed by then and arrive with our luggage."

"You'll be comfortable here until morning, I can assure you of that."

"Oh, how very kind of you."

Ben was sure there was smoke coming from his ears. His rage was an unreasonable inferno and rising by the second.

"We'll need half the money up front, you understand. We've had a few scoundrels leave without paying their bill," the woman said.

"No. Really? That's shocking," Primrose replied, appearing ready to settle in for a nice long chat.

"Here." Taking the small purse he carried around his neck out, he handed over some notes, and a few more to keep her from asking any questions.

"I want food and a bath. Is there anywhere we can get some clothing?"

The woman nodded, happy to do anything he wanted. "I'll see to it. Your lovely wife is about the size of my daughter."

"This is indeed kind of you, and of course we will be happy to pay. You have a lovely establishment here," Primrose said.

Ben was fairly sure the top of his head would explode if he didn't get Primrose up those stairs and into the room. He would have plenty to say to her then. First, he had to get her to shut her mouth!

"Right, if you'll follow me, please." The woman took one look at Ben's face and hustled around the desk.

They followed her up the stairs and into a room. It looked clean enough, and the bed somewhere he could sleep for a week and half, which was what his body was craving.

"I'll send someone up with your bath, food, and those clothes,"

Ben shut the door behind the woman with a decisive snap. Turning, he noted that Primrose had placed herself on the other side of the bed. Her eyes were suddenly wary. Perhaps she had noted his mood after all.

"What the hell did you think you were doing!"

CHAPTER TWENTY-FIVE

She tried not to wince at the roar. Primrose had felt his anger from the minute she opened the carriage door to find him lying on the floor.

"When?" She played for time.

"Primrose—"

"I couldn't let them hurt you," she rushed to add.

"How the hell did you follow us?"

The words were fired at her like bullets from a gun. Primrose dug her toes into her shoes to keep from retreating as he stalked closer.

"I... ah, I climbed on the back like you did."

"You did what?"

This time his voice didn't rise but stayed dangerously low. She winced.

"You bloody fool. Do you have any idea what could have happened? Why didn't you go for help?"

"I couldn't let them take you away, because then we wouldn't know where you were."

The words sounded rational to Primrose. Rational and completely the right thing to do, she reassured herself.

"Christ!" The word was an angry hiss. "You should not have taken that risk. The entire journey, all I could think about was that you were now safe, and yet you weren't. You spent it on the back of the coach!"

"I did what I thought was right!" Primrose felt the heat of her own anger take hold. "I did what you did... felt you needed to do."

"You took a foolish risk and could have been hurt. They could have captured you again! You could have tumbled from your perch and no one would have known!"

He prowled toward her, looking like a large beast seeking vengeance. His eye was darkening, and she found other bruises on his jaw. Dark hair stood off his head, and he was many miles away from the nobleman she had come to know... had thought she knew.

This man was bordering on a feral beast. Primrose should be scared.

"I did what I thought was right." She raised her chin. "You rescued me, and I rescued you."

"So we're even?" he scoffed. "This is not a game, Primrose. These people would kill you in a heartbeat to get what they want."

"I'm not a fool, so don't treat me like one. I did what I thought was right," she said again. "You may be stronger and a man. Therefore, in your opinion it was your responsibility to keep me safe. But I didn't see it that way. I wanted to ensure you w-were safe too."

"Don't cry." His words were flat and cold.

"I'm not, I'm angry."

"So am I, but you don't see me crying. Tears don't affect me like they do other men... especially when a woman uses them for emotional manipulation."

The injustice of his words robbed Primrose of speech. Luckily, it was only a momentary condition.

"How dare you suggest my tears are not real! I don't know what women you've been associating with, but I assure you these are real." Primrose swiped a finger under one eye and waved the damp appendage at him.

He looked at her then. A long, hard stare, and then his lips twitched.

"Your nostrils are flaring."

"That's because I'm bloody furious," Primrose snapped. "My brother used to run for the hills when he saw me in this state!"

"I'm not scared of you."

"And I'm not scared of you." Primrose braced her hands on her hips, defiant.

"You should be," he muttered, closing the distance between them completely. He wrapped an arm around her waist and hauled her to his body.

"Thank you for rescuing me." He whispered the words into her hair. "I'm sorry if my words upset you."

"Your words told me that you have a deep-seated mistrust of women. Is that the fear you would not share with me?"

"No."

Primrose was sure he was lying, and the sudden tension in his arms suggested she was right.

"Is it because of your mother?"

"No." Cold and hard, that one word told Primrose she'd touched a nerve. But now was not the time to pursue the matter further, and to be honest, she was too tired. Standing here in his arms was the first moment's peace she'd had since he'd been captured.

"I still wish you'd run away to safety, Primrose."

She rested against him, placing her head on his shoulder and simply enjoying the feel of his strength around her. Slipping her hands around his waist, she felt all the tension and fear finally ease.

"I'm tired."

"Me too," Primrose agreed.

"We will eat, then bathe. But first I'm going to find out what I can about when Sanders is leaving. He's getting a boat to France, I'm sure of it. And it's there he'll hand over the book."

"I'll come with you."

"No." He cupped her cheeks. "And not because I'm trying to protect you. Okay, maybe there's some of that. But it will be easier for me to get information if I am alone. I also want to send word to my brothers. So please stay here, Primrose."

"But what if they see you?"

"They won't. But if I am not back in an hour, then you can come looking for me. This time I give you permission, because let's face it, there's no one here to stop you."

She nodded.

He kissed her softly, then released her.

"I will be back soon, I promise."

Primrose felt ill as she watched him walk to the door.

"Are you sure I shouldn't come with you?"

"No."

"But—"

"No. Now be a good girl and stay out of trouble." His smile was gentle.

"Mr. Sanders said I was a busybody," Primrose blurted. For some reason, those words had hurt her.

"You are, but in a very nice way." He opened the door, but stopped before stepping through. "By the way, I like a woman with opinions."

He shut the door gently behind him, leaving Primrose to wonder what that actually meant. She was never one to just accept a comment, she had to chew on it, tear it apart, and then usually reform it into something completely different.

She wasn't a confident person no matter the persona she portrayed.

A knock on the door a few minutes later had her hurrying to open it. A maid stood there.

"I have a tray of food, and the bath is following, Madam."

"Thank you." Primrose pressed a hand to her stomach as it rumbled. The food she'd eaten seemed a long time ago now.

He will return.

"I have some clothes for you and the gentleman, ma'am," the maid said. "I'll leave them on the bed."

"Thank you."

When she'd left and the tub was filled with steaming water, courtesy of a footman, Primrose decided on a wash first. Stripping, she climbed in and sighed. The water felt so good. She scrubbed herself and washed her hair with the coarse soap provided. Once she was done, she dressed in the chemise left by the maid. It was too big, but clean. Wrapping a blanket from the bed around her, she ate.

Leaving a healthy portion for Benjamin, Primrose pulled a chair up to the window and sat to wait.

SHE WOKE as someone lifted her.

"Benjamin?"

"Yes, sleep now."

"Are you all right?"

"Yes. Sanders is not leaving until the morning."

"Oh, that's good news. We can still get the book back."

He didn't reply, just laid her on the bed.

"Sleep."

She closed her eyes, but did not go back to sleep. Primrose heard him move around the room, then the splash of water as he washed. Cracking her eyes open, she saw broad shoulders and arms corded with muscle. The candlelight cast him in a golden glow.

She should be shocked but wasn't. What she was, was intrigued. She'd never seen a naked man before. Not that she could see all of him, but what she saw was beautiful, sculpted muscle beneath golden expanses of skin.

He washed himself, then threw water over his head, and it cascaded down his body. Her mouth went dry. When he started to rise, she closed her eyes. She was only so brave.

"You can open your eyes now, I have my breeches on."

"How did you know I wasn't sleeping?"

"Your breathing."

Rolling onto her back, Primrose grabbed the blanket and sat upright against the headboard.

"Thank you for leaving me some food."

"I could not eat all that."

"I could have."

"Shall I call for more?"

He shook his head. "This will do for now."

The shirt was loose and too big on him. It billowed around his body, open at the throat. She thought he looked like a pirate.

"What happens now, Benjamin?"

"We need to get you back to Rossetter . I have sent word to my brothers, explaining what happened and that I have just found you now."

"Because otherwise people will think I have been in your company… alone?"

He placed the last of the meat into his mouth, then lowered the fork. Getting to his feet, he came to sit on the other side of the bed beside her.

"I wanted to save your reputation."

"Thank you."

"Primrose, what happened between us should not have. But no one will ever know."

I will know.

"Of course. I have no wish for you to in any way be forced to do something you do not wish."

"Meaning what?"

"Meaning that I know you are an honorable man, and should someone challenge my reputation I would not want you to have to step in."

Before he spoke, she hurried on.

"Besides, I am to go back to Pickford. If my reputation were ruined, it would be of no consequence."

His brows drew together. "It would be of consequence to me."

She didn't know how to answer that, so she ignored it. "Will we contact the authorities in the morning to help us retrieve the book?"

"The magistrate won't be back until tomorrow evening. Apparently he is visiting his first grandchild."

"What is to be done then?"

"I found where Sanders is staying, and he has the book with him. His henchmen are sleeping in the stables. I will sleep for a few hours, then try and relieve him of the book. If that doesn't work, there is little to be done, I'm afraid. I'm not risking either of us for a book about plants, no matter how important it is." The yawn that accompanied those words was wide enough to make his jaw crack.

"Do your eye and jaw hurt?"

"Only when I laugh." His smile was small. "How about your cheek?" The finger he ran down it was gentle.

"No. I can no longer feel it."

"I'm still going to make him pay for that."

"I don't want you to."

"I'll take the floor" was all he said, getting to his feet.

"No. There is enough room on this bed. You will be more comfortable there with all your aches and pain."

"That's not a good idea."

"Surely as we are both tired and no one will know, it is all right. Come." She patted the bed beside her. "It will be all right."

"It would be if I didn't want you as much as I do."

CHAPTER TWENTY-SIX

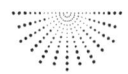

"Oh."

To Ben's exhausted eyes, Primrose looked like an angel.

"But that is silly. You are tired, as am I. You need to sleep."

An annoying angel who never knew when to stop talking.

Her dark blonde hair was damp, and she'd left it unbraided. It hung in tangles to her waist. He wanted to touch it. Rub it between his fingers. Fist his hands in it while he kissed her.

"I will take the floor," Ben said, looking at the curve of her shoulder. The blanket had slipped, as had whatever she wore underneath. The curve was alluring, as was the soft, pale skin beneath. He clamped his lips together at the thought of pressing them to it. "Good night."

He felt her eyes follow him as he walked away from the bed.

"No!"

He stopped in the act of lowering himself to the floor.

"I want you to sleep here beside me. We are adults, and… and…, well I'm sure we can refrain. Both of us."

He straightened, his muscles twinging from the movement. He hadn't looked forward to a night spent on the hard wood, but he would have done it if she'd wanted him to.

"Come, there is enough room, and we have much to do tomorrow, so you will need your strength."

"We," he said, retracing his steps, "do not have much to do. I have much to do." In this he was adamant. She would not be put in danger again.

"I am not letting you do it alone. If we are to get that book before it sets sail, then I am helping."

He braced a knee on the bed and leaned over her.

"No, you are not."

Primrose may have chattered a great deal, and usually had an opinion on most things, but she was nobody's fool. He was an angry, tired male, and obviously she'd had exposure to them in her lifetime, as she shut her mouth. To his surprise, she then turned on her side, presenting him with her back, and appeared to be ready for sleep.

He didn't move for a few seconds, letting his eyes run over her hair and down her back. The blanket was wrapped around her body, but he could still see her feet. Pale, the arches were delicate, as were her toes. Lust bolted through Ben just looking at them.

"Blow out the candle, please," she said in a prim little voice.

He did as she asked and began to walk away from the bed, sure that he couldn't resist her unless he slept on the floor. Something stopped him. Stupidity, exhaustion, need—he didn't know what. But seconds later he was lying beside her on the bed.

"You have beautiful hair." He touched a long, damp curl, rolling it between his thumb and forefinger.

She didn't reply.

"I don't think I can do this." He went for honesty.

She rolled onto her back, then over again until she was facing him. He rolled onto his side facing her. They were now inches apart.

This close, he could see her eyes in the dimness. There was no fear there. She lifted a hand and began to trace the contours of his face. Her touch was gentle, the lightest brush of a fingertip, and his entire body tensed.

"Primrose," he warned her.

"Benjamin." She sighed, closing the inches that separated them.

"I am tired and have little resistance. This is not wise." His voice sounded gruff.

"I know, but I cannot seem to help myself. Once, I did not believe in passion, but with you, and after those kisses we shared, I have changed that opinion."

Her honesty aroused him.

"Kiss me again, Benjamin. Please."

Her breath brushed his lips like a caress.

His hand went to her hair, fingers delving through the thick, damp locks.

"I'm not sure I can stop." His voice was hoarse with his need for this woman.

"Then don't."

"You don't know what you are saying, Primrose. This will change everything."

"Only we will know what happens in this room." She cut off his next words with her mouth, and Ben was lost.

Rising up on his elbow, he kissed her softly, tracing the contours of her lips with his, brushing the inside with his tongue. Tasting her.

"I want to feel it again. Those wonderful sensations you created inside me in the barn, Benjamin."

He gave up the fight then. Opening the blanket, he

skimmed his hand up her body, feeling the curve of her hips and slender strength in her limbs.

"I-I want to touch you also." Her voice was hesitant.

"You may do as you wish," he gritted out. His mouth went dry at the thought of her hands on his body.

She slid her hands under his shirt and skimmed her fingers up his body. The breath hissed from Ben's throat at her touch.

"You are beautiful."

"No, that description is reserved for you alone, Primrose."

"I disagree." Her fingers grazed over his nipples, making him twitch. She did it again.

Ben eased her shift up her body, his hand roaming silken flesh.

"Sit forward."

She did, and he removed it.

"Exquisite." He leaned closer and took her mouth again in a fierce kiss. "You're not afraid?"

"No. Not here with you."

"Primrose—"

"I don't want to speak of anything out there. Only now, and this." She arched up into him, wrapping her hands around his neck. "I know there can be nothing more."

"You deserve more."

"But you do not have it to give."

Before he could speak again, she kissed him softly. Ben took over, and their next kiss was bordering on savage. A desperate need drove him to take her, but she was an innocent, for all that she showed no fear. He would not frighten her.

He stroked the smooth skin over her ribs, then cupped the soft flesh of a breast. The weight settling perfectly in his palm. Her gasp as he ran the pad of his thumb over a taut nipple made him smile.

Of course she'd be responsive. His Miss Ainsley would not hide how she felt.

"Oh, Benjamin." She made a humming sound that went straight to his groin as he moved lower, kissing every inch of skin he could reach until he arrived at her chest.

"I could worship your breasts for hours." Ben licked one thoroughly. He then took her nipple into his mouth.

"I-I've never felt this way."

"I should hope not."

He stroked her thighs and moved into the soft hair between her legs. She stiffened, but then her thighs opened, allowing him to touch her again.

"God, you're beautiful." He looked up her body. Her eyes were slumberous, skin silken. Her lips were swollen from his kisses. He felt something heavy settle in his chest, but pushed it aside.

"Can I explore you, Ben, as you are me?"

"No." He couldn't cope if she did that. He'd promised himself to make this about her, and he would stop before it reached the point of no return.

"Why?" She looked down at him. "I want to explore your body too."

"I only have so much restraint, Primrose. Let me pleasure you."

"Oooh." She fell back as he stroked the curls between her thighs. He found the hard bud and ran his thumb over it, making her shudder.

Ben could feel her tension, feel that she was close to achieving something she'd never achieved before—and it would be at his hands. The thought shouldn't make him as happy as it did.

"That's it, sweetheart." He could hear the rasp in his voice as his body became so hard it was painful. If he touched himself he would explode.

Taking her breast again, he sucked on the nipple as he pushed a finger inside her wet heat.

She screamed, her body shuddering as he pushed in and out of the tight sheath. A second finger joining the first, he pushed her higher and closer to the climax.

"Let go."

"I can't.... Oh, bluebell and carnation!"

Her shriek was followed by a shuddering release that was beautiful to watch, but left him twitching with unfulfilled need.

He lay down beside her, pulling her close, holding her as she came back to reality.

"I-I never truly understood what could be between a man and woman." She turned her head to look at him. Those blue eyes were still smoldering with passion.

"Not just any man and woman," he felt the need to say.

"But you did not—"

"It matters not," he gritted out, easing his body away from hers. If she touched him, he'd ignite.

"It does matter."

She pushed herself upright, following him; she was soon braced above him. Her hands reached for his shirt.

"No!" He scrambled away, falling out of bed in his efforts. "We can't do that." Ben leaped to his feet, uncaring of the pain in his body, and lit the candle.

She followed him. Naked. Christ, her body was a work of art.

"P-put your shift on."

She did as he asked, bending to retrieve it, her movements graceful and making his mouth go dry. The effect was no better. He could see her nipples through the material.

"Why can we not do that?"

She advanced on him.

"Because you will go to your marriage bed with H-

Herbert a virgin." The thought made him sick. He wanted no other man to touch her, even if he could offer her nothing more than what they'd shared. "I will not do that with you. It is not right."

She kept stalking him.

"Yet it was right for you to touch me there and k-kiss my breasts?"

Even in his tense state, he noticed she was not quite as confident as she seemed. Her stutter gave her away.

"Primrose, I will not take advantage of you. Get back into bed."

She kept walking until she had him backed into a wall.

"But what if I t-take advantage of you?"

She stepped closer and pressed her body into his, and he moaned. It slipped out, long and deep. Ben wanted to grip her hips and press his groin into hers, but he was no animal. He could stop this.

Mother of God, her hands were on his buttons.

"Please, Primrose." His voice sounded tight and high.

"Benjamin," she whispered, sliding her hands inside his shirt. Her finger caught on the edge as the buttons didn't go the entire way down the front, and she had to untangle it. "I-I've never done something like this, but…."

"B-but?" Now he was stuttering.

"But I want to try, even though I am scared I'll get it wrong."

"There is no wrong," he said when what should have said was "back away." *Take charge, Ben.*

"Go back to bed, Primrose. Please." He felt no shame in begging.

Her eyes held his, wide, uncertain, and then she pushed his shirt up his body, leaned in, and kissed him.

Another moan was torn from his body. She continued to place kisses all over his chest. Ben clenched his hands into fists and thought about anything but her; then she licked him, and he gave up the fight.

Sinking his fingers into her hair, he lifted her head and kissed her hard. Her hands took over from her mouth in tormenting him. Ben wanted more.

"Be very sure, Primrose." He walked her backward until her thighs touched the bed, then picked her up and laid her on her back. "I have no more resistance." His whisper was ragged.

"I don't want you to resist."

"So be it."

He pushed up the shift, bent at the waist, and gave her the most intimate kiss of all.

"Ben!"

He didn't stop, just held her thighs open and tasted the woman who had been driving him slowly mad for days.

She moaned and cried, and every sound had him wanting to plunge deep inside her, but he didn't, instead concentrating on taking her to the edge of pleasure once more. Only when he felt the little tremors and her pants grew louder did he remove his breeches and step between her legs.

"Look at me now."

Her hands were fisted in the covers, body flushed with excitement.

"Primrose, this will hurt you, but I hope not for long."

"Y-you hope?"

He was so aroused it was painful.

"I can stop if that is your wish," he managed to rasp out.

"No! I want you now."

She reached for him as he eased closer, nudging at the dew-drenched folds. Moving forward slowly, he vowed to take it easy, vowed he would cause her as little pain as possible.

"I can feel you stretching me," she whispered.

He stopped.

"Don't stop!"

"Then shut up!" Ben thrust deep inside her. Bracing his hands on either side of her face, he leaned down and kissed her.

"Primrose, open your eyes and look at me."

She did, and he lost himself in the blue depths of her eyes.

"How is the pain?"

"Easing." Her hand cupped his cheek. "I have often wondered about this."

"Now you know." Ben pulled out, then gently thrust back in. He kept the pace steady, watching her the entire time while he fought with the need to drive into her again and again. Blood pounded through him as the tension climbed to an unbearable point.

Her first moan told him she was there with him, then she arched off the bed as he drove into her and shuddered her release. Ben followed one thrust later.

Dragging in a lungful of much-needed air, he picked her up and lowered her onto the bed the right way. Following, he just had enough strength to pull up the blankets. He pillowed her head on his shoulder and closed his eyes.

"Promise you won't leave the room without me, Benjamin."

"I promise that tomorrow we shall both leave for Rossetter together." He kissed her cheek.

She muttered something he didn't catch, and then she was asleep. Ben followed seconds later.

CHAPTER TWENTY-SEVEN

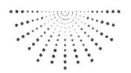

*P*rimrose opened her eyes as dawn light filtered through the curtains. Her head was resting on something. Looking to the right, she saw an expanse of skin. She was using Benjamin's arm as a pillow. Moving slowly so as not to wake him, she laid her cheek on his back, as he was lying on his front.

Closing her eyes briefly, she enjoyed the feel of his large, warm body pressed into hers. She let her mind remember every little detail of what they had shared last night. Felt her face heat with embarrassment as she pictured what he had done to her… and what she had let him do. Enjoyed, if she was being honest. Very much enjoyed. In fact, Primrose could say with clarity that she had never before felt the way she did last night, ever.

This man had transported her to places she had not known she was capable of reaching.

Looking around the small room, she tried to memorize everything. The faded blue curtains and simple furniture. The painting of a ship run aground on a sandbank, framed in dark-stained wood. The blue-and-white-striped wallpaper and door that hung on an angle so there was a small gap in the top left-hand corner.

Lifting a hand, she touched the curve of Benjamin's shoulder blade. He was so much warmer than her. Continuing her exploration, she stopped when she reached the covers at his waist. Lord, he was exquisite.

"If you wish to press a little deeper between my shoulder blades, there is a place there that is sore."

Primrose moved her hand quickly and rolled off his arm to the other side of the bed. Granted, it was not a huge bed, but she moved as far from him as she could. She didn't know how to deal with this situation. What did she say? How did she act?

"Good morning." Ben reached out an arm and hauled her back to where he lay, now on his side facing her. Rising on an elbow, he leaned over and placed a soft kiss on her lips.

"Good morning." Primrose wasn't sure where to look. "We need to get moving, otherwise Sanders will be on that ship and gone before we have retrieved the book."

He moved again, his body now half lying on hers. One hand touched her chin, forcing her to look at him.

"Why won't you look at me?"

"We need to get going."

"Primrose. What we did last night changes everything, surely you know that."

"It changes nothing. No one knows what happened." She saw the brief flash of relief in his eyes and knew she'd used the right words. Ignoring the arrow of pain in her chest, she continued. "Anyway, we cannot speak of that now, Benjamin; there is much to do."

"We must speak of it." Now it was he who wouldn't meet her eyes, and she could feel distance between them suddenly. He hadn't moved his body, but he'd withdrawn from her. "I need you to understand that when we return to Rossetter , I will be announcing our betrothal."

"No! You have no wish for that, and nor do I. I want to return to Pickford." Primrose wanted to press a fist to her chest to stop the pain. She knew he could never love her, but still, deep inside her, she longed for it. From anyone, she added silently.

"I had not planned on marrying, but—"

"Never?" Primrose felt her heart sink when he shook his head. "Your mother, is it—"

"I have no wish to discuss her." His tone was clipped and curt.

"And I have no wish for us to wed."

"I took your innocence last night, and so I will marry you." There was now steely determination in his tone.

It was almost as if just saying the words caused him pain. His jaw was clenched so tight, it looked ready to shatter.

"You are saying this only because you are honorable, Benjamin. I wanted what happened last night as much as you did. Please, I do not want it to change the course of your life. I am not like the other young ladies. I will return home and be happy. I do not have the expectations of others."

"What if there is a child?"

Dear Lord, she had not even contemplated that possibility.

"Then I will of course let you know instantly."

His eyes held hers. "We will continue this discussion on the return trip to Rossetter , Primrose."

"But—"

He put his hand over her mouth, lowering his head until their noses touched.

"Enough. We will speak of this later. Right now, I have to get that book back."

"I will help." Primrose scurried out of bed as he released

her. Dragging the blanket with her, she tried to wrap it around her body. He was holding the end.

"Release the blanket, please!"

"I've seen your body, Primrose, and you are an extremely beautiful woman."

His mood had changed to playful. The man was exhausting.

She tugged harder; he held on.

"I do not parade about naked in front of men!"

"I should hope not." He gave her that smile she was sure had annoyed his twin a time or two.

"Stop teasing me," she hissed. "We have no time for that."

"There's always time for teasing." He tugged, and she was soon off-balance. She landed on his chest, and he settled her along the length of his body. Primrose didn't know where to look.

"Last night you were not shy." The words were spoken into her neck.

"Release me, Benjamin."

His sigh carried enough force to lift her hair, but he did release her. She hurried to the water to wash, very aware that he was watching her.

"You are not coming, Primrose." He climbed out of bed to join her. She didn't look at him or that wonderful naked flesh she knew was on display.

"I am coming."

"Be reasonable. I want you to be safe, and to achieve that I need you to stay here."

"No."

She quickly finished washing and began to pull on the clothes the maid had left her. Was it only last night? She felt a different woman to the one who had entered this room several hours ago.

When she was finished wrestling her hair into a braid,

Primrose looked at him, sure that he too would have pulled on something. She was wrong.

"Wh-why are you not dressing?"

He gave her a knowing look that suggested he was amused by her discomfort—*fiend*—and then pulled on his breeches.

"Better?"

"Marginally," she muttered.

"I want you to stay here, Primrose," he tried again, his tone reasonable.

"No."

"Yes."

She tried to pull the bodice of the dress into place. It was tighter on her, but the rest fitted well.

"That's a nice fit."

"It's too small." She tugged again. Unlike the nightdress this was not loose at all.

"I think it looks very nice."

She stopped fussing to look at him.

"Because my chest is exposed?"

"Of course not," he lied. "This color suits you."

"It's the color of cow excrement."

"And yet it goes with your eyes."

"My eyes are blue."

"With cow excrement highlights."

"Idiot." She found her mouth forming a smile. "Now let us leave; we need to get that book."

"If I cannot stop you from coming, I can insist that you do exactly as I say."

Her hesitation was only brief, but he saw it.

"We are not leaving this room until you agree, Primrose."

He had pulled on his boots and now stood with his thighs braced beside the door.

"You have no necktie."

"Or jacket, and stop changing the subject."

"Oh, very well," she said ungraciously. "I will do exactly as you say."

"There now, that didn't hurt, did it?"

She didn't answer, simply sailed out the door before him.

"Sanders is staying up the other end of town, so I think we should be safe here, but even so we must have a care."

He pulled her to a stop, then forced her behind him.

"I am going first."

"Of course."

"I will hold you to that," he said, starting down the stairs. "First I want some food, but before that, I need to see what time the ship Sanders is sailing on is due to leave."

The thought of that book leaving England was not a happy one for Primrose. They had to get it back.

"We wish to eat, please," Ben said to a man hovering at the base of the stairs.

"We have a small parlor, sir, with a family in there. They will have no problem sharing."

Ben half-turned and murmured to Primrose, "Go in and smile, but don't speak. I know that will be difficult for you." He didn't wait to hear her protest, he simply strode to the door that would take him outside and disappeared. Primrose gave the man waiting for her to follow him a weak smile.

"Come this way then, ma'am."

What if the family knew her? How would she explain why she was there with Benjamin? But why would someone from society be here now, when most of them were in London or at house parties?

The man opened the door, and Primrose followed after a loud exhale, only to stop just inside the room as she looked at the people seated around a table.

Oh, bloody bothering hell.

Her feet suddenly lost the ability to move as she took in

the three people. They did not know her, but Primrose knew the Sinclair family… at least, she knew who they were. She'd never actually spoken a word to any of them.

The eldest, who was getting to his feet, was Lord Sinclair. The one seated next to him was Mr. Cambridge Sinclair, and lastly, the Duchess of Raven, their sister.

There were plenty more family members back in London, but these three were enough to have her tongue sticking to the roof of her mouth.

"Good morning." Lord Sinclair smiled. He was a handsome man—in fact, all of the siblings were handsome people, tall, dark, with stunning green eyes, all except the duchess, who had gray ones. Primrose knew these details because she spent a great deal of time observing while hiding in corners at society gatherings.

"Good morning." Primrose forced herself to speak and move her feet.

"The ship is still…." Benjamin's words fell away as he entered the small parlor. "Oh now, this could prove tricky."

"Benjamin?" Cambridge came around the table with his siblings. "What are you doing in Dover?" He didn't add, *with a woman, alone*, but it was implied.

"Cam," Lord Sinclair cautioned. "It is impolite to ask questions."

"I just asked what you and Eden were thinking, ordering those smelly kippers," the middle Sinclair said. "Questions help us ascertain things, brother."

"Yes, but some questions are better left inside your head. Now be quiet," Lord Sinclair added.

"This is Miss Primrose Ainsley," Ben said, not looking upset about finding three members of the ton seated in the same parlor they were about to have their morning meal in.

Primrose, however, was so tense that if someone touched her, she'd shatter.

The Duchess of Raven frowned, her eyes fixed on Primrose. Her brow lifted.

"I thought I recognized you. How do you do, Miss Ainsley?"

Primrose ducked into a curtsey.

"Mortified about now, actually," Ben added. "If you will share your table, I will attempt to explain what has happened and why we are here."

"Oh, B— Mr. Hetherington, we should leave."

"These are good people, Primrose, they will help us."

"You are in trouble?" Lord Sinclair frowned.

"Yes, we were, and are now in need of help to catch the fiend who stole something from the Duke of Rossetter ."

"Then of course we are at your service," Lord Sinclair said.

"Please, Miss Ainsley, come and share our table. We are, as Benjamin says, good people and friends of his and his family." The duchess took Primrose's hand and led her to a seat. "And I have been bored rigid by my brothers for the last few days. I will be grateful for anything to alleviate that."

"Harsh. You wanted to come with us to have a break from your children," Cambridge Sinclair said.

"Yes, but I'd hoped for some excitement. Instead we have discussed withers, hooves, and ship rigging. It has become tiring. I should have stayed in London."

"As we tried to tell you," Lord Sinclair reminded her.

The duchess didn't appear put out by her brother's words. "Sit, please, and tell us what has you here, alone and dressed in someone else's clothes."

"I doubt you'll believe the story," Ben said, appearing at ease while Primrose, still tense, tried to stay calm.

"I thought you were at the Rossetter house party?" Mr. Sinclair said. "We were invited but could not make it."

"We are... were."

"Miss Ainsley was abducted from Rossetter along with a valuable, rare copy of a book."

"*The History Of Plants* by Lucian Clipper," Primrose added so they understood the gravity of the situation.

"Our sister, Essie, made a trip to Rossetter specially to see that," Lord Sinclair said.

"Miss Ainsley likes things that grow," Ben added.

"Really. So does Essie; she's very good with herbs and can fix any number of ailments," Mr. Sinclair added. "I have this nasty spot on my—"

"Cam!" Lord Sinclair snapped at him. "Let Ben speak, and no one wishes to know about your ailments."

"That's not strictly speaking true; my wife was most solicitous."

Primrose bit back her smile as he winked at her.

"Idiot," Lord Sinclair muttered. "Please continue, Ben."

As a maid returned, they ordered food… an extraordinarily large quantity to Primrose's mind.

"My brothers eat more than a small pachyderm, Miss Ainsley," the duchess said.

Once the maid had left, Ben outlined what had happened. He seemed comfortable with these Sinclair siblings, so Primrose hoped his faith in them was warranted.

"It's my belief Finn and Alex should arrive tomorrow if they travel through the night."

"Good Lord, you must have been terrified, Miss Ainsley," Lord Sinclair said. "You are to be commended for your bravery."

"Or stupidity, whichever way you choose to look at it."

"I rescued you," she said slowly, refusing to behave any way but ladylike in front of the Sinclair family. "Had I not climbed on that carriage, they could even now be throwing you in the hold of that boat with the other lumps of meat!"

"She has a point," Cambridge Sinclair said. "She did save you, Ben."

"She should not have taken the risk," he gritted out. "But this is getting us nowhere. What we need is a plan to get the book back."

"But I did save you, as you saved me," Primrose felt she needed to add.

"So that makes us even? What about the times I've fished you out of the water?"

"And the one where I held you upright because you were too drunk to do so by yourself?" Primrose said sweetly.

"It sounds as if you have had some intriguing times together," Mr. Sinclair said with a look in his eyes that said he had added two and two and come up with a great deal more than four.

"We are friends," Benjamin said. And he was right, they were, but in a small part of her mind she'd hoped he thought that maybe they were more than that. "Nothing more," he added, which just confirmed to Primrose she was unlovable. Not that she needed confirmation.

Idiot. Stop dreaming of what you will never have. Unlovable, Primrose reminded herself.

She was pleased he did not mention to these people that he'd said they would marry. Primrose didn't think she wanted to marry a man who had vowed to never wed. It couldn't be conducive to a happy life.

"We want to get the book back," Primrose said. "It is very important to England that it stays here."

"You sound like Essie," Lord Sinclair said. "But if that is your wish, then of course we will help."

"Oh no—"

"Excellent," Ben cut Primrose off.

"But it could be dangerous," Primrose felt she needed to say.

"I have excellent hearing, and my brother can see many things. We shall be of great help to you," the duchess said.

Primrose thought that an odd thing to say—after all, she had good hearing and sight too—but she kept silent.

"Can I borrow a jacket and necktie, Cam?"

"Of course, I shall get them now," the man said, leaving the room.

"I shall get you a shawl, Miss Ainsley, and perhaps a bonnet?" the duchess said, rising also.

"If it would not be too much bother, I would be thankful."

"And gloves," the duchess muttered, hurrying from the room.

The food arrived, and Ben fell on it. Primrose nibbled, suddenly feeling nervous.

"Should we just leave, do you think, Benjamin? Those at Rossetter will be very worried over our disappearance."

"I wanted to do that earlier, and you said no. Why now?" His eyes settled on her face.

"I do not want anything happening to any of us."

His smile was genuine and made her stomach flutter, which annoyed her, as she had no time for fluttery stomachs or to be any more enamored by this man. A man who now knew her more intimately than any other.

"We will not put ourselves in danger, I promise, Primrose." He turned back to face Lord Sinclair. "I never asked why you Sinclairs were in Dover," Ben added.

"Cam and I are looking at purchasing a new ship. There is one here that will suit us perfectly. Plus, a matched set of grays that Cam has fallen in love with for his wife."

Primrose ate while they discussed ships and moved on to steam engines. Ben had extensive knowledge on the matter, as did Lord Sinclair, and Primrose enjoyed listening to them both.

When the others returned, they all ate and finished

outlining their plans to get the book back. They then donned the clothes and Primrose felt marginally better with her chest covered.

"No risks, Dev, Cam, and you, Duchess," Ben said, shaking hands and kissing the duchess's cheek.

"We shall be fine, Ben."

"Indeed, we will," the duchess said, looking far too excited considering what they were about to do, Primrose thought.

"You and Miss Ainsley must take care also," Mr. Sinclair said. He then gave Primrose a hug, much to her surprise, and the siblings left to take up their positions down by the ship Sanders was leaving on.

"It will be all right, Primrose. This is what you wanted, remember," Ben said, rising also.

"I feel a deep sense of foreboding, Benjamin."

"It's probably those kippers. Now come along, we have no time to waste."

He squeezed her fingers and led her from the room silently, and Primrose battled down the fear that something was about to happen—and not a good something.

CHAPTER TWENTY-EIGHT

"They are the best of people, Primrose, and I trust them, even if they are slightly odd," Ben said as he led Primrose outside and onto the street.

"Odd how?"

"Well, Dev's eyes, they're—"

"Green?"

"Yes, but a very bright green."

"A crime indeed," Primrose said, looking from left to right as they moved down the street. Danger could be lurking anywhere,.

"And Cam, he's always sniffing like a hound."

"I've noticed that, actually. He did it several times at the table. I had wondered if he had a head cold."

"He doesn't; it's something he's always done. I've also noticed the duchess has remarkable hearing, and their cousin, Wolf, is absurdly good with animals. He can get them to do anything."

"You're talking to me to keep me calm, aren't you, Benjamin?"

She was pale and worried, and he could do nothing to

ease that as he felt the same. But most of his tension came from the fact that she was at his side. He worried she'd fall into trouble again and he could do nothing to save her.

"Some, but also what I'm saying is the truth. They are unusual."

"But very nice people."

"Very much so. They all live on the same street in London. It's quite bizarre and provides a great deal of gossip fodder for society. But they don't seem to mind that, plus they have a duke and an earl in their family, which carries a great deal of weight."

"And also many friends."

"Yes, we like them, and they like steam engines." He smiled at Primrose, but she didn't respond.

He wondered if one day he'd forget what she smelled like. Forget the smile she gave him when she thought she'd got the better of him.

She'd turned down his offer of marriage, but he'd had to make it. Would need to make it again when they returned to Rossetter . She was right, honor told him he must do this, no matter how much he wanted the opposite.

"I liked them."

"I want you to stay here, Primrose." He grabbed her hand and squeezed it hard. "Will you let me do this? I will be back in no time to collect you."

"No. I am part of this now," she said quietly.

He knew her intimately now. Knew the body that walked at his side, and the noises she made when he made love to her. Surely he could marry her and not love her? Surely they could live a good life together?

I'm unlovable.

She deserved to be loved, Benjamin realized. Guilt sliced through him that he'd taken her innocence when he'd had no intention of giving her his heart. He needed her to understand that would never happen.

"Primrose—"

"I'm coming with you, Benjamin."

"Very well, but you must stay out of sight," Ben said, relieved he did not have to say what he'd been about to. "Come, we must get moving. The others will be in position."

Primrose followed him once more.

"Wait. It is Sanders."

"He is going to board," Primrose said, looking over Benjamin's shoulder at the man striding down the incline.

"I believe so."

They waited until he was out of sight, then hurried to follow, watching him take the gangway up and disappear aboard the ship.

"It is to leave shortly," the Duchess of Raven said as they reached the place Primrose was to wait with her. "As Sanders is now on board and has the book, I fear it may be hard to retrieve it."

"How do you know that he has the book?" Primrose asked the woman.

"I overheard two men talking."

She and Ben exchanged looks, both remembering the conversation they'd just had about the Sinclair siblings.

"Primrose, stay with the duchess."

"Where are you going?" She grabbed his hand.

"To retrieve the book."

"I'm going with you."

"No, you are not. Stay with the duchess, and I will return soon."

"You are going aboard, aren't you?"

Her pallor increased, but Ben had no time to comfort her; he needed to get on that ship, and fast, so he could retrieve the book and get off before it left.

"You can't, the ship is sailing. Look, they are removing ropes as we speak!" She grabbed his arm.

"Change of plans," Ben said, forcing her back a few paces. "Stay," he added.

Ben ran and hoped she wouldn't follow. Ducking behind several crates, he watched the men going through the preparations for departure.

You can do this, Ben.

A whistle had him looking left; he saw Lord Sinclair with his hand raised. His eyes were a vivid and almost unreal green as he focused on the deck of the boat. Ben waited, unable to see anything. Lord Sinclair lowered his hand and ran to where Ben crouched.

"Sanders is in a cabin to the left. The book, I suspect, is with him. He is alone."

"I'm not asking how you know that."

Lord Sinclair smiled. "It's best that you don't. There are plenty of sailors up there, and possibly men who will recognize you, so have a care, and at the first sign of trouble, call or run. Go now, and I will be watching. Cam is there." He pointed to several barrels. "Here." He handed Ben a pistol.

Taking it, he thrust it into his waistband.

"The ship is preparing to leave, Ben. There is no time to wait. You must grab the book and return."

Ben hurried to the gangway.

"Can't board, sir, the ship is leaving."

"And I'm supposed to be on it." Ben motioned the man to one side. He hesitated, but eventually moved, and Ben took the gangway in a hurry. Once on board, he walked slowly, appearing as if he was meant to be there. Around him was a hive of activity.

"Can I help you, sir?" One of the deck hands approached him.

"Where is Sanders?" Ben said, raising a brow.

"Are you to sail with us?"

Ben nodded.

"I was not aware of that. I will need to speak with the captain."

"Of course, but in the meantime, I wish to speak with Mr. Sanders. He is a friend."

The man studied his face but said nothing further. He pointed to a cabin below a set of stairs. Ben nodded and headed that way. Once there, he knocked on the door, took out the pistol, and entered.

"I believe you have something that belongs to a friend of mine," he said to Sanders. "I want it back… now."

"I should have shot you!" Sanders snarled from his position behind a desk. "You won't get off this ship alive."

"Give me the book now." Ben held out his other hand.

Sanders picked a wrapped parcel up off the small desk and thrust it at him. Ben tucked it under his arm.

"I should have just shot her. That idiot woman brought you here and caused all this trouble."

"Miss Ainsley is no idiot, and say another word about her and it will be to your detriment. My anger has not cooled over the mark you left on her face. Were it not important for me to leave, I would set about teaching you some manners."

"She deserved it, meddling bitch," Sanders snarled. "You have the book, now go!"

A jolt had both men stumbling. Ben managed to retain his grip on the pistol and the book, but fell to his knees.

"We are moving," Sanders said, laughing. "What now, Hetherington? Will you hold me captive all the way to France?"

Ben ran to the window. They were moving, although slowly.

"Open the door." He waved Sanders toward it. "Walk out and hold your hands high. I will follow."

The book was wrapped in a thick skin, which relieved him slightly. If Ben had to throw it, surely this would protect it from too much damage. It was strange how much it had come to mean to him suddenly.

"Stay back!" he ordered the men on deck. "Move to the railing, Sanders."

They walked slowly. Holding his pistol in Sanders back, he looked over the rail. He found Primrose running along the dock with the Sinclairs.

"Ben!" Her cry of desperation carried to him on the wind.

He couldn't jump yet; he would end up crushed between the dock and the ship's side.

"Catch!" He threw the book as hard as he could. Cambridge Sinclair ran backward several feet and caught it.

"No!" Sanders roared. But he could do nothing to stop the book staying in England.

"Ben!" Primrose screamed his name again. He could see the desperation on her face. Thank God she couldn't reach him. He knew she'd try if she could.

Foolish and brave, he thought.

"What now, Hetherington? You cannot travel the entire distance like this, and I will have you gutted and thrown overboard should you remain," Sanders snarled.

Ben nudged Sanders away from the rail. He had no wish for Primrose to see anything that happened on board the ship, especially if he took a bullet. He had one chance at this, and it was not something he could hesitate over.

Sanders moved to stand a few feet before Ben, facing him, the crew at his back.

"You're trapped. Say goodbye to your friends now, Hetherington. In fact, say goodbye to England and your life," the man said, looking far too happy with himself.

He could shoot one of the men, but it may not be fatal and would not stop all of them from grabbing him.

Lowering his pistol, Ben slumped his shoulders in apparent defeat and took several slow steps to where Sanders stood. Dropping the weapon, he drew back his fist and slammed it into the man's jaw.

"That was for Primrose!"

Running along the deck, he evaded the hands that reached for him, then leaped over the side.

CHAPTER TWENTY-NINE

*P*rimrose couldn't stop sobbing. She'd never felt such despair before. Seeing the ship leave with Ben on board, her heart had nearly stopped beating. If he left on there, he would not return, she was sure of it. Those men were Sanders accomplices and they would kill him.

And this is all my fault.

Dear Lord, the pain nearly doubled her over, but she kept her eyes on the ship. She'd seen Ben at the railing, looking down at her.

He had not answered her desperate cries, but he had seen her, she was sure of it.

"I have never felt so helpless," Mr. Sinclair said, wrapping an arm around Primrose's shoulders and holding her close. "We should not have let him board, but I thought there was time."

"Y-you could not h-have stopped him," Primrose whispered.

"What is being said?" Cambridge asked his sister.

"Just threats from Sanders— Wait!" the duchess held up a hand. "I just heard what sounded like a bone breaking."

"Benjamin, dear lord, don't let them hurt him!" Primrose cried.

"No, it is not Ben, I believe—"

"He's running," Lord Sinclair said, moving along the dock to the end. "I can see him running."

"Christ!" Cambridge Sinclair started tearing off his jacket. "He's diving overboard."

She watched, horrified, as Ben appeared. He leaped over the railing and was soon plummeting toward the water. He hit close to the stern of the ship.

"Can you see him?" Primrose ran to the edge. "Benjamin, dear God, tell me he is all right!"

"I'm going in." Cambridge Sinclair pulled off his boots.

"I can see him below the surface!" Lord Sinclair roared.

Primrose tore off her bonnet and shoes, then her shawl. Taking a huge breath, she then dived into the water. Using her arms to propel her deeper, she opened her eyes and tried to find Benjamin. It was an impossible task; there was only darkness wherever she looked, but she had to try. When her lungs threatened to explode, she felt hands pulling her up to the surface.

"What the hell are you doing, you idiot woman!"

"Benjamin!" Primrose lunged at him, sinking them both. They came up spluttering.

"Desist!" he roared, grabbing her around the waist. "God's blood, you couldn't have waited for me to surface?"

"I could not be sure you would."

His hair was flattened to his head, and he'd never looked more wonderful to Primrose.

"Primrose"—he pulled her close, almost cracking her ribs as they sank again—"I-I wasn't sure I'd see you again."

She kissed him. Right there in the water, in front of the Sinclair siblings and anyone else who cared to watch.

"Bloody hell, Hetherington, that was a spectacular dive." Mr. Sinclair appeared beside them.

"Come to the edge!" Lord Sinclair yelled from the dock.

Ben pushed Primrose upward so Lord Sinclair could pull her out, then he and Mr. Sinclair followed.

"Dear lord, how wonderful you were, Miss Ainsley," the duchess cried.

"Wonderful?" the three men roared.

Primrose did not say anything further. Ben was safe and on English soil, as was the book, and the boat carrying the perfidious Sanders was drawing further away. She was happy…, well, as happy as a person could be with three angry men glaring at her.

THINGS HAPPENED QUICKLY after they were all dry and clothed. They hired a carriage for Ben and Primrose. It was also arranged that the maid accompanying the duchess would travel with them.

"Mary will come back to London after you are safely back at Rossetter , Miss Ainsley," the duchess said. "It is best you arrive with another woman in the carriage," she whispered.

"Of course, thank you."

The duchess gave her a firm hug.

"We shall catch up again in London. I will introduce you to my family; they will love you."

Primrose nodded, then yawned. Everything had caught up with her, and all she could think about now was sleep. Hugging the book close, she waited for Ben. He may let her sleep using him as a pillow. She had to say the idea made her smile.

He ran out of the lodgings they had stayed in last night, worry etched in every line of his face. "Something is wrong."

"What?" Primrose tensed, looking around her.

THE LADY'S DANGEROUS LOVE

"Not here. Something has happened to Alex. Come, we must leave at once!"

"Twins," Lord Sinclair said, hurrying them to the carriage. "They know things about each other. My sisters are the same. God speed, my friends, and we hope whatever awaits you at Rossetter House is something minor."

Ben clasped his hand and nodded to the others, and then they were inside.

"I'm sorry, Ben."

He didn't reply. Face grim, he looked out the window.

The journey was fast. They stopped regularly to change horses, but said very little. They ate, stretched their legs, and then they were on the road once more.

He was solicitous to her needs, but his touch impersonal. Primrose reasoned this was because he was worried for his brother. But she wanted him to talk to her, wanted him to confide his fears so she could soothe them.

She slept off and on, and Ben sat silently, fists clenched on his thighs.

She tried to talk to him several more times, but he'd respond in curt one-syllable replies, so she gave up. Primrose knew he feared for his brother, but it felt like he was shutting her out.

"Ben, he will be all right," she said when Mary, the maid, slept. Not wishing her to overhear the conversation.

"You can't know that." The look he turned on her had Primrose pulling back. "I left him."

"You can't have known—"

"I left him to chase after you and that bloody book!"

"You're not being rational. You have no way of knowing—"

"My brothers have always been there for me. I should have been there for Alex. He is in pain, I can feel it."

"I-I'm sorry." Something cold and dark lodged inside her.

She knew it was fear and worry making him speak this way, but it hurt.

"THANK GOD!"

Primrose woke to Ben's words. Looking out into the early evening sky, she saw the silhouette of Rossetter.

"Please, dear God, let my brother be alive."

"He will be all right. We will watch over him and help him to heal."

His eyes passed over her briefly, and the look in them was cold and unemotional. Gone was the man who had shown her such infinite tenderness and care.

"I will care for my brother."

"Oh, of course. I just meant that I will be here—"

"I will need nothing from you. Return to London, and I will come when I can."

"Benjamin, please…." Her words fell away as he looked right through her.

"I told you I will never let a woman into my heart. Told you no woman will ever mean more to me than my brothers. Return to London and await me there."

"You have never spoken those words to me, nor I have not asked anything of you," Primrose felt she needed to say. In fact, he had told her nothing of a personal nature about himself, but she had guessed how he felt. "I have no wish for your love," pride had her adding.

"Good, then you will have no foolish notion that love will grow between us either, because it never will."

"I understand you are scared for your brother, but there is no need to be mean," Primrose said with what dignity she could muster. She would not let him see how much his words hurt her. "I had hoped we could at least be friends," she said as he reached for the door.

THE LADY'S DANGEROUS LOVE

He didn't reply, instead throwing open the door as the carriage stopped and leaping from it, leaving her to follow more slowly.

"Miss Ainsley, how pleased we are to have you back safely with us."

"Thank you, Alders." Primrose kept her chin up as she walked up the steps toward the Rossetter House front door. She would not show that inside, her heart was breaking.

Mother of God, she'd fallen in love with Benjamin Hetherington. Only that could explain the pain she was feeling.

"Primrose!"

"Heather." Primrose ran into the arms of her friend as she appeared on the top step.

"Are you all right? We have all been so worried for you."

"Tell me first how Mr. Alexander Hetherington is?"

Heather's face seemed to crumple in her distress.

"He fell from his horse—a deer startled it—as he galloped to help you and his brother. Viscount Levermarch brought him home. He has yet to regain consciousness. His wife is of course devastated."

Taking her hand, Heather led Primrose inside.

"What are the doctors saying?"

"They are doing what they can, but are saying it is possible he will not regain consciousness."

Dear Lord, Benjamin will be devastated.

The Duke and Duchess of Rossetter were in the entrance way waiting for Primrose.

"Miss Ainsley, we have been worried for you." The duchess hurried to greet her.

"I am well. Please, Duchess, could Mary, the maid who has accompanied me home, be cared for? She is then to return to London to the Sinclair family."

"Of course, she will be taken care of at once. Alders."

"I shall see to it immediately, your Grace."

"Thank you, Mary." Primrose squeezed the maid's hand. "I have your book, Duke." She held it out to him.

"You and Benjamin were more important, Miss Ainsley, but I am grateful to have it returned. I will ensure that this time it stays here. We are indebted to you for what you have done and endured on our behalf." His smile was genuine and made Primrose want to weep, which told her how exhausted she was.

"Come, you must be tired." Heather took her arm.

"I shall have a bath drawn and a tray sent to your room," the duchess added.

"Lady Jane?"

"Will be relieved, as she has been very worried for your welfare," Heather added.

Primrose did not miss the looks passing between the duchess, duke, and Heather.

"What are you not telling me? Is Mr. Hetherington worse?"

"No, he is still unconscious, but no worse," Heather said. "It is just that people are talking."

"About what?"

The duke excused himself with a pained look on his face, stating he was taking the book back to the library. The duchess hurried away to order food and have water heated for her bath.

"Heather?" Primrose looked at her friend.

"Everyone has tried to stop the rumors, but as the guests were all asked to leave after Mr. Alexander Hetherington's accident, and have done so, or will do by tomorrow, there is no way they can be snuffed out completely."

"What rumors, Heather?"

"Primrose, we know what happened to you was not your fault—"

"Just tell me, please."

"People are saying you have been compromised. That you were walking through the house late the night you were kidnapped to meet a man. Not just any man, but Mr. Benjamin Hetherington."

"What rubbish." Primrose felt her cheeks heat. *If only they knew.*

"Most of us know that you were taken against your will, but some are saying differently. Saying you ran away with Mr. Benjamin Hetherington. The duke has tried to squash the rumors, but he is only one man."

"Utter rot." Primrose opened the door to her room to find Lady Jane pacing the floor.

"Leave us, please, Miss Fullerton Smythe."

"I shall speak to you tomorrow." Primrose hugged her friend and urged her out the door.

"Are you well, Primrose?"

"Yes, thank you, Lady Jane."

"Excellent. We leave for London first thing in the morning. I know of a man who is desperate for a nubile young wife. He has children but no heirs. You will do perfectly."

"I... pardon?"

"You have been compromised. No man but a desperate one will have you now. Unless Mr. Hetherington has offered for you, we must take measures to secure your future now, before it is too late."

"H-he has not offered for me." Primrose made herself speak the lie. He had, but only because of his honor, and after the conversation she had just had with him, she would not marry him now if he was the last man standing!

"I had thought not. Mr. Hetherington will not marry you, his family will not allow it. My decision is made."

"I will go home, my lady. I have no wish to marry someone who sees me as a brood mare."

"Don't be foolish, girl. Such marriages are made every day! Besides, I have written to your parents. They will be aware by now of your disgrace."

"It was not my fault!" Primrose felt panic climb inside her. "Surely you cannot blame me for being taken from Rossetter against my will."

"It matters not the circumstances, only that your name is tarnished beyond repair."

"I came home in the company of a maid."

"But what about before that?"

The injustice of it all took her breath away.

"We are returning to London."

"And from there I am going home," Primrose vowed, ignoring the vicious tug of pain Lady Jane's words had caused her. "I want no part of a society that would treat a woman in such a way when she has done nothing wrong."

"You have constantly flouted social standards. Leaping into the water several times, and what were you doing walking about the halls the night Mr. Sanders grabbed you?"

"I was going to retrieve a book from the library as I could not sleep!"

"And what about the last few days? Where were you then?"

She could not say the truth. How did she tell Lady Jane that she had experienced more emotion in two days than she had in a lifetime? That she now had to change one of her long-held opinions. That actually, she did believe in love... even if it was for a man who would never marry her.

Instead Primrose told Lady Jane an abbreviated version while she washed and ate. She would not be appeased, and stood firm in her belief that Primrose's only chance for happiness was marriage to whoever would have her. They argued, but Lady Jane would not be moved, so Primrose gave up for now. Later, when exhaustion was not dogging her every move, she would discuss the matter once more and make her see reason.

When finally she was left alone, Primrose fell into a deep, dreamless sleep. Upon waking, she tidied her appearance, then went to see if there was any more news about Benjamin's brother.

"When are you leaving?"

Benjamin appeared before her. His face was lined with fatigue and worry, eyes narrowed and tight. He had yet to change his clothes, and he looked more beautiful than she'd ever seen him. Her dark, angry angel. She wanted to hold him and share his pain. Instead she stopped and clutched her hands together.

"How is your brother?"

"Still unconscious." His tone was clipped.

"Benjamin, we need to—"

"What? Discuss what happened? I have said I will marry you, there is no need to push the matter, Miss Ainsley. Now leave for London as I have already asked you to do. I will come when my brother wakes."

"No, I am not here for that. I am here to help in any—"

"We need none of your help. Everyone who is close to Alex is at present in the room with him. What possible use could you be?"

"You are punishing me for something I had no hand in, Benjamin. Why?"

"I am not discussing this any further with you. My brother needs me."

"Benjamin, please, I am your friend." She had to try to reach him again. Just once more. She loved him, and although he did not love her, surely they could be friends.

His eyes ran over her face.

"I need no friend. Now leave, and I will call on you when

my brother is well. Ours will be a marriage like so many others in society. Loveless."

She grabbed his arm as he tried to brush by her, but he shook it off and walked away, and Primrose then understood the meaning of a true broken heart. The pain nearly doubled her over.

She turned, wanting only to hurry back to her room. Tomorrow she would leave and then return to Pickford. She would get over this and be happy there.

"He is not himself, Primrose."

Lady Levermarch was standing in a doorway; she had no doubt heard every word.

Primrose's throat was clogged with tears; she could find nothing to say.

"Benjamin is not like the other brothers; he has a deep mistrust of women, which Finn believes is due to his mother's abandonment."

"It matters not."

"It sounded like it matters. It also sounded like Benjamin is to offer for you." Lady Levermarch looked tired, her beautiful face tight with worry.

"No. He would do so out of honor only, but I have no wish for that. I will be going home. Goodbye, Lady Levermarch. Please tell him I release him from any commitment to me."

"If you care for him, then fight for your happiness—and his, Primrose."

"But he does not care for me," Primrose said softly. "Goodbye."

CHAPTER THIRTY

"Hannah, please lie down for a while. Just rest, even if you don't sleep." Ben urged his sister-in-law out of her seat. "Alex will be furious with me when he wakes to find I have not looked after you."

"I-I just want him to open his eyes."

"I know." He held her briefly. "And he will, I believe that with everything inside me, Hannah. But you must take care of yourself and the babe now. When he wakes and starts roaring his displeasure, I have no wish to bear the brunt of it."

He found a smile as he handed her to Phoebe, who looked as exhausted as Hannah.

"Stay with her, please, Phoebe."

Her beautiful face was blotchy from weeping, but she sniffed, held her shoulders back, and led a broken Hannah from the room.

"The doctor is due to return," Finn said from his place at the end of the bed, where he had stood watching vigil over his little brother since Ben returned.

"Sit, Finn, for pity's sake, before you fall."

Ben pushed a chair into the back of his legs, and like a mighty oak, Finn fell into it.

Moving to the seat Hannah had just vacated, he took his brother's hand and held it tight.

"You need to wake up now, Alex." Ben had said that every few minutes over the last two days. He'd slept briefly, and usually in a chair in the room, and left only when necessary. One of those times he'd run into Primrose.

Fear had made him cruel to her, he'd known it just as she had, but he'd been unable to stop the words falling from his lips. Ben didn't know how to explain to her what was going on inside him, so he'd pushed her away. He'd make things right with her as soon as Alex woke, he promised himself. And he hoped she'd forgive him because she was Primrose. Open and honest, and yes, caring.

They'd tried to make him and Finn leave to get some sleep, but they had stood firm. Until Alex opened his eyes, this was where they would be.

His brother looked as he always did, lying there. As if he slept and would soon wake. His hair was pushed back from his forehead. He needed a shave, but Ben wouldn't let anyone touch him.

"Alex." Ben touched his jaw. This man was his other half; to comprehend life without him was too painful.

"I thought of you as my sons, you know? Even though the years between us are not great enough for it to be so, I still thought of you that way."

Ben looked to where Finn sat. His head was resting on his hands, his eyes on Alex.

"We know, and were it not for you, neither of us would have understood the meaning of the word family, Finn. You taught us to value life, when before we cared nothing for it."

"I sometimes think it was you who suffered more than he when Mother left."

"What? Why would you believe that?" Ben dragged his eyes from Finn; his heart was suddenly beating hard inside his chest.

"You never really let women get close to you."

"Rubbish. Your wife and Hannah are close to me."

"But they are married."

"You have it wrong," Ben rasped.

"I don't think so. It's also my belief that you have feelings for Miss Ainsley."

"No." Ben shook his head even as he heard the truth in his brother's words. For so long he'd vowed never to feel that emotion, that it had become natural to deny it.

"Yes, Ben. You cannot go through your life avoiding emotion; it will make you a lonely and bitter old man. I have never mentioned this before, but now, with Primrose, I think things are different."

"I have no wish to discuss this now." Ben's chest felt tight as he thought about Primrose.

"Very well, but we will, and soon," Finn said.

Ben did not reply, and they sat in silence watching their brother as another hour ticked by.

"I can't lose one of you now, Ben. Not after years of worry that you would do something reckless to endanger your l-life," Finn said, his voice thick with fatigue and tears.

"I-I don't know if I can live without him," Ben said. "He knows me better than anyone. What I'm thinking before I think it. He even knows where I am going before I've told him. My life would be nothing were he no longer in it."

The door to the room opened as Ben finished speaking, and the stranger who walked in had to have felt the desperation that hung in the air. "Good afternoon."

"Who are you?" Finn wiped his eyes as he got to his feet.

"I am Dr. Siblinguyer."

"I'm not attempting to say that," Finn said. "What is it you are doing here? Where is Dr. Crofter?"

"He said he can do no more for your brother, but I would like to try. I have been treating Lady Althea, and she wished for me to come and see your brother."

He was young, about Ben's age, and he looked more like a poet than any doctor he knew. Tall, slender, with longish hair and a gentle smile.

"Ben, move and let the doctor see Alex."

"How do we know he's any good?"

"Because Thea and Ace trust him, and surely that is enough for us?"

"You have a point. Go to the other side of the bed, Doctor. I am not moving."

"Of course," the doctor said. "And you are twins, I understand?"

Ben nodded. He watched as the man checked Alex over, lifting his eyelids and taking his pulse, all things the other doctor had done.

"He is a healthy man, and one who I believe will regain consciousness when he is ready."

"Which will be when?" Ben demanded.

"What I need you to do, Mr. Hetherington, is to start talking to him."

"I have been doing that."

"Also stimulating the senses. Touch, smell, and hearing. If he has a favorite flower or scent, you need to bring it into this room. Does he like the feel of a certain something against his skin? Find the things that will stimulate his senses."

The doctor talked to them for ten more minutes, explaining what he believed would rouse Alex. He then left with a promise he would return tomorrow morning.

"He said to open the curtains and windows to let air and

light in." Ben started to draw them back. "Go and get that waistcoat he has that he's always stroking, Finn. The one with the rose satin stripes, and then fetch that cologne he gave me."

"Ben—"

"Do it, Finn."

"Very well. I shall return shortly."

Ben opened the windows to let the breeze waft in, and then sat to wait his eldest brother's return.

"I have the things."

Ben took them from Finn and went back to his seat beside the bed. Opening the scent, he waved it under Alex's nose. Nothing.

"Run that waistcoat over his face," Finn suggested.

Picking up the waistcoat with its ridiculously decadent fabrics and feminine colors, he ran it down his brother's cheek.

"Did he just twitch?" Finn hurried to the other side of the bed. "I'm sure he twitched."

Ben picked up the scent again and waved it under Alex's nose.

"He twitched," Finn breathed.

"Open your eyes now, Alex," Ben said, bracing his hands on either side of his twin's head. "We love you and need you to open your eyes."

His heart thumped as Alex's eyelashes flickered.

"He's waking up." Finn grabbed his other hand. "Please God, tell me he is."

"Alex!" Ben touched his cheek.

The eyes opened, and he allowed himself to cry for the first time since he'd walked into the room.

When he was assured by Dr. Siblinguyer, who had now

become something of a hero in the household, that his brother would indeed make a full recovery, Ben allowed himself to leave his twin in the capable hands of his wife and seek his room. He thought about finding Primrose, but looking down at his clothing, he knew he needed to wash first. Sleep also was something he must have before he fell flat on his face—and food, he added to the list.

His valet stripped him, helped him bathe, then helped him stagger into bed. He was then forced to eat until finally his body gave up the fight and slept.

He woke twenty-three hours later with a raging fever. His throat was raw, and he could barely speak a word.

"My brother?" he rasped as Dr. Siblinguyer walked into the room, no doubt having been summoned by his valet.

"Is doing very well, sir. You, however, are not. I would suggest exhaustion and the last few days have caught up with you. Plus, you have an inflammation of the chest, and your throat is red and swollen. You will not be leaving this bed until you are better."

He tried to argue, tried to get out of bed, but he was suddenly as weak as a kitten. He felt a desperate need to seek out Primrose, but soon sleep was dragging him back down.

The next few days were spent in a daze of pain and sleep. Liquid laced with honey was forced down his throat, and the elixir made him sigh as it soothed his raw throat.

"You will see them soon, Ben. Rest easy now."

Finn was there every time he turned over with a cool hand that he pressed to Ben's forehead.

"Come, brother, you must take some broth."

Finn spoke, and Ben obeyed, and then he would slip into a deep, dreamless sleep once more.

Six days after he'd taken ill, Ben thought he may live. The last few days he'd been slowly recovering, even if he was still weak. He'd thought constantly about Primrose, but had no wish for her to see him in this state or contract whatever he'd had, so he'd not mentioned her name.

Today he would see her and apologize for the way he'd behaved. He would also need to bare his soul, which was not a comfortable thought. In fact it made him itch, but she deserved that from him.

"I wish to wash and get out of bed today, please, Heggley," he told his valet. "And shave," he added, running a hand over his whiskers.

"Perhaps your dressing gown, sir, and you could take your morning meal in the chair beside the window."

"I wish to see my brother, so I will take tea with him."

Whatever Heggley saw in his eyes had him consenting.

Ben allowed himself to smile. His brother would live.

He'd dreamed about Primrose. Hot, fevered dreams that had disturbed him as he couldn't talk to or touch her. Every time he got closer, she seemed to fade away.

Staggering out of bed to the bath, he sighed as the warm water soothed his aches.

He ate the food that was brought to him, then dressed, feeling a great deal better. The walk to his brother's rooms felt good, even if he was breathless after climbing the stairs.

"Enter!"

Smiling at the strength in his twin's voice, he let himself inside the room. Finn was there, as were Hannah and Phoebe.

"Good God, what are you doing out of bed?" Finn stormed across the room. "You look like death."

"Lovely to see you also. But I am fine, just a little weak."

"You could never let me do anything on my own," Alex said. He still looked pale, but the sparkle in his eyes made Ben's heart feel light. "I'm sorry I could not come to you, Ben."

"You could have done nothing but contract whatever I

had. Staying here was the best thing for you, Alex. How are you?"

"Much better, and I will leave this bed tomorrow if it kills me."

"If Dr. Siblinguyer says it is right to do so," Hannah said, hovering. "You boys must obey his wishes."

"Yes, Hannah," the twins said in unison, making everyone laugh.

"Right, now I want to hear this adventure you have been on, Ben," Alex said. "I have heard snippets, but I want to hear all about what happened to you and Miss Ainsley."

"It seems so long ago now," he said, dropping into the seat Finn pushed him toward.

Ben told them everything, starting with the night he saw Sanders grab Primrose.

"She climbed on the carriage as you did?" Finn shook his head. "That woman is either incredibly foolish or brave."

"Brave," Ben said before he could stop himself.

"Do you care for her, Ben?" Hannah asked in her no-nonsense way.

He remembered then how he'd treated Primrose in the carriage, then later here, when she'd wanted only to comfort him. The way he'd pushed her aside as his fear and guilt had overwhelmed him.

He'd struck out at her, and she'd done nothing to deserve that.

"Will you leave us, please, I have something I want to discuss with my brother," Alex said.

Before Ben could stop them, Finn, Phoebe, and Hannah had left the room.

"Why have you sent them away?"

"Because, Ben, we need to talk, you and I. A twin talk."

"I hate those when I'm the one being talked at." Ben knew he was not going to like what Alex said.

"Ben, do you like Miss Ainsley?"

"Yes, she seems a nice person." Even to his ears his words sounded weak.

"Nice person. Not a wonderful person, or someone you could spend your life with? Not someone who when they walk into the room your entire being lights from the inside? Not someone who smiles and that place inside you that was cold for so long, warms?"

He forced out a laugh, but it was high-pitched and shaky. "Have you been reading poetry?"

"Ben, you cannot live your life believing women will turn against you. Finn and I have discussed this, and we now realize that you suffered after our mother left, even if you say otherwise."

"I loved her." Ben decided the time for honesty had come. "I was heartbroken when she left. I begged her to stay, and she laughed at me." He still felt the pain of that day.

"You never told me that." Alex looked shocked, because they usually shared everything.

"I know, and I should have."

"And because of her, our mother, you made the choice not to care for a woman?"

Ben nodded.

"You must know that not all women are like our mother."

"It just seemed easier to live my life avoiding love." Ben shrugged.

"But you do care for a woman now, don't you?"

The silence that settled over the room was so thick it nearly choked Ben.

"I don't want what you have," he said, as he always did when someone questioned him like this.

"But you may not be able to stop it happening, Ben. I believe you already know that. That you are fighting what you feel for Primrose."

"I won't be hurt." The words were a low growl.

"And what of her? Could you hurt her? I know nothing of her family life, only that Lady Jane alluded to me once it was not a very comfortable one for Primrose."

Ben knew that. She'd not moaned about her fate. In fact, she'd only let a few things slip, but he'd added them together to form a bigger picture. Primrose had been a burden to her family.

"She believes she's unlovable," he said, remembering her words and how foolish he'd thought they were. "Her family see her as a burden. Can you imagine that, Alex? A woman like her, a burden. She is everything that is good and sweet."

"And you love her?"

"God." Ben slumped into his chair. "I don't know if I do or not. But I do know that I owe her an apology. I was rude to her when I realized you were hurt. I deliberately pushed her away."

"You're scared to admit your feelings for her."

Ben got out of the chair and walked around the room.

"I was scared that you would die, and I was not coping with that so I pushed her away."

Could he take a chance on Primrose? If she hurt him, could he stand the pain? Because Ben knew that with her it would be different. He'd never recover if she walked away from him.

"Imagine just for a moment that in fact you could live happily with Primrose, Ben. Imagine the children you would have, and light and laughter in your life. You cannot know what it is like to wake with the woman in your arms who carries your heart."

He looked at his brother lying there, and the quip he'd wanted to fire back at him died on his lips.

"I'm scared."

"I know, but you are strong, and you must do this because you deserve happiness like your brothers have."

He didn't speak again, simply gripped his twin's hand hard.

"Now go and open the door, they will be out there listening."

They were.

"Did you talk some sense into him?" Finn asked.

"Yes, and now I must go and see Primrose," Ben said. Poking around inside his chest, he thought that perhaps he felt different somehow. Acceptance, he realized. He'd accepted that in fact Primrose did mean something to him.

"She's gone, Ben."

"What?"

"The guests have all gone," Phoebe added. "No one is here now. It is many days since you arrived home. She has gone back to London with Lady Jane, and in any case, I imagine she doesn't wish to see you after how you spoke with her in the hall."

"You heard that?"

"I did, and she was devastated."

"I didn't know what I was saying. I was out of my head with exhaustion and fear for Alex."

"I know, but she was adamant you would not marry her out of honor and told me she was going home to Pickford. She wanted me to tell you she released you from any commitment you felt you may have to her."

"I'm a bloody fool!" Ben prowled the room again. He had to get to her and tell her he'd been wrong to say what he had. "I don't want to be released, I want Primrose."

"Lady Jane insisted they left immediately, considering," Hannah said, brushing the hair back from Alex's forehead.

"Considering?" Ben looked around him at the faces of his family. "What are you not telling me?"

They were clearly uncomfortable, and silent signals were swirling around the room. Eventually, Phoebe was designated speaker.

"The rumors after you both left were rife, Ben. Suggestions that she had been going to meet up with her lover... you. That she ran away to be with you. You know what people are like. Facts have never been terribly important in the face of a scandal."

"They are untrue!" He felt his entire body fill with heat at the thought of Primrose being victimized in any way. And yet, he knew what society was capable of. Knew how she had been treated already by those who saw her as beneath them.

"You spent several days alone with her, Ben," Phoebe said gently. "This was bound to happen."

"Not alone! She was abducted, and then I was. When we did manage to free ourselves, the Sinclairs were there."

"Yes, you said as much, and for that I'm grateful, as the duchess's word will hold a great deal of weight if she stands by Primrose."

Ben pinched the bridge of his nose.

"There is more," Finn said, and the look on his face was grave.

"What?"

"The duchess overheard Lady Jane discussing Primrose with one of her friends on the day they left. She said that the Ainsley family did not want her to return to their home; they wanted her married at all costs," Phoebe said.

"How could they treat her so callously?" Hannah demanded.

"God's blood, that family!" Ben stalked across the room. "They've made her believe she is unlovable. Can you believe it? The woman is eminently lovable."

"Yes, she is." Alex was smiling at him.

"Tell me what else you know, Phoebe," Ben urged her.

"Lady Jane then said that after what had happened between you and Primrose, and the fact her reputation was now less than pristine, she would have to resort to widening her net for a husband, as it was clear you would not marry her."

Ben felt the color drain from his face. "What did she mean?"

"She has decided that Lord Formby will make Primrose the ideal husband. He has no need of her dowry but wants more children, and due to her age she will give them to him."

"Lord Formby is sixty-five years old!"

CHAPTER THIRTY-ONE

"You are sad, Primrose?"

"No, I am just deep in thought. Forgive me, Heather, what was it you were saying?"

Her friend had come to visit, and the two women were seated on the sofa together in Lady Jane's parlor.

"Primrose, I know our friendship is new, but I feel I have known you my entire life, and that we have an unbreakable bond."

"Yes, I agree. I have never felt as close to someone as I do you, Heather." *Except maybe Benjamin.* "I do not have many friends."

"I'm sorry for that, but now you have me." Her friend smiled.

"Yes, I do." She forced a smile of her own onto her lips.

"I know you are to go visiting with Lady Jane soon, but I have something I wanted to discuss with you, Primrose. Two somethings, actually."

Primrose nodded. Ten days had passed since they had left Rossetter House. Ten painful days where she'd tried not to think about Benjamin and what a fool she'd been to give him her heart.

She tried to forgive him for the way he'd spoken to her. He'd been mean, and Primrose had not deserved that. Yes, she knew he'd been worried for his brother, but now that time had passed she realized that his behavior was because he could never love her… or any woman, for that matter.

Benjamin had unresolved concerns from this childhood, and she knew they were a result of his mother's treatment of him. Unless he acknowledged and dealt with them, he would never let a woman close.

She didn't like to think of him with another woman. It made her feel irrationally angry.

The real problem was that he, like everyone else in her life, had not been able to love her. But with him it hurt a lot more.

"Primrose, do you love Benjamin Hetherington?"

Shock held her silent. There Heather sat, as she had several times since their return to London, a pretty picture in cream muslin with tiny sprigs of lavender embroidered all over it.

"I know that you do, Primrose, because you have deflated since leaving him at Rossetter ."

"I beg your pardon?"

"You are flat, dear. As if the life has suddenly been sucked out of you."

"I-I…." No other words were forthcoming. She felt the humiliating burn of tears stinging her eyes. Blinking rapidly, she tried to hold them at bay.

"I know that you do, Primrose, so you may as well tell me everything."

"I am a f-fool, Heather."

"I doubt that. I have yet to meet a more sensible person than you. Now be honest. You love him, don't you?"

"I do, but he does not feel the same. I will come around to accepting that fact, but it is just taking time."

"But how do you know that he does not love you?"

"He told me he has no wish to ever love a woman. Plus, he has not come to London to find me, Heather, and he must know about the scandal surrounding my sudden departure from Rossetter when I was abducted."

But fool that you are, you released him from his commitment to you.

Pride had made her speak those words to Lady Levermach, and while she knew they had been the right thing to say, a small part of her thought that perhaps she would have been happy to be his wife without love. Because one thing Primrose did know was that she'd love him until she drew her last breath.

"Lady Jane told me his brother has recovered, as the Duchess of Rossetter wrote informing her of that. But still he has not come, Heather."

"He is staying at his brother's side, Primrose. Surely you are not so selfish you think he should leave?"

"Heather, are you being deliberately rude?"

"Yes. It is something new I am trying. Honesty, instead of agreeing with everyone and everything."

"It's working," Primrose said flatly. "Well."

"Excellent." Heather beamed. "But I am right, surely? Benjamin Hetherington would not wish to leave his brother yet?"

"There is more. It is suggested by Lady Lindle and Lady Rosewater, who called yesterday, that he would never consider someone such as I now, and that was reinforced when I went to the soirée three nights ago. No one spoke to me, and the whispers and titters were horrible. Why would a man wish to be saddled with a wife who is a p-pariah?"

But had he loved me, he would care nothing for that.

Dear lord, she missed him. She had once decided naively that love was not for her; then she'd fallen helplessly for Benjamin Hetherington. Now she knew why she'd taken the original stance. The pain was excruciating. She was obviously a person destined to have no lasting relationship… with anyone. Except maybe Heather.

"Rubbish! Why are you listening to such rot now, Primrose? Those women are conniving gossipmongers and simply called here to humiliate you. I have no idea why Lady Jane allows such behavior."

"To be fair, she had little choice, Heather."

"Well, I would not put up with it," her friend said with spirit. "Now, back to Benjamin Hetherington."

"Must we?"

"He was with you through that terrifying ordeal, Primrose. He knows you are not a trollop—"

"Heather!"

"Sorry, no other word fitted the moment."

"Well, I have no wish to continue this discussion. Had Benjamin Hetherington cared anything for my reputation, *or me*, he would have returned to London by now. He has not, therefore we will not speak of it again."

"But that suggests he is callous and heartless and has no honor. I do not believe he is such a man."

He had honor, to be sure. It had made him offer to marry her in a cold, heartless manner. Primrose would not wed a man under those circumstances. She would rather live her life alone than like that.

"I'm not someone who inspires love, Heather. I have come to understand this and will likely live alone."

Heather laughed, but it stopped when she saw Primrose had not joined her.

"Oh, you are serious."

"It is not something I'd make a joke of."

"But it is ridiculous. You are a wonderful woman. Intelligent, funny, and beautiful. I love you."

"I don't wish to discuss this further, Heather, and thank you, that means a great deal to me, but I still stand by what I said."

"But—"

"Enough, please." Primrose battled the despairing sob she felt well up inside her. She would not weep for him… at least not outwardly. "What else did you wish to discuss with me?"

"Very well, we will not discuss it again, but I think you are wrong, and that one day you will find true love."

Primrose said nothing.

"I have seen Jeremy several times," Heather said.

"Who is Jeremy?"

"Mr. Caton."

"Ahh."

"My parents saw us together one night, talking. The next day they forbade me to ever see him again. They then told me they had received an offer from the Marquess of Heam. He wishes to marry me."

"On no, Heather. I am so sorry." Primrose grabbed her friend's hand, her own worries suddenly pushed aside.

"Jeremy and I are going to elope tonight."

Her mouth fell open.

"Something will fly in there if you do not shut it."

"Are you serious?"

"Extremely. Jeremy has tried to dissuade me, but I am adamant. We have everything planned." Heather looked calm; Primrose felt anything but.

"Well," Primrose said, to give herself time to think. "Good Lord." For once she was speechless.

"I wanted to come and say goodbye to you."

"I-I don't know what to say." She felt desperately sorry for herself that she was to lose her friend. It was selfish, but in light of everything else going on, she felt it anyway.

"I am leaving the house after my parents retire. Jeremy will be outside, and we shall make for Gretna Green."

"Bluebell and carnation," Primrose whispered. "Are you sure, Heather? It seems such a drastic step."

"Yes. I have tried to reason with them, even told them I care for another, but they will not listen to me and are adamant I marry Lord Heam."

"I am so sorry, Heather. What will you do?"

"Jeremy says he has money and that his brothers are good men who will stand by us."

"But surely then—"

"No. Mother has her heart set on a title. Nothing will change that."

"Why is it that our parents care nothing for our wishes?" Primrose wondered out loud.

"I don't know, but I will ensure I listen to what my children say," Heather vowed, getting to her feet. "And now I must go, as there is still much to do. But I shall send word as soon as we are settled."

"I shall miss you, my dear new friend."

"And I you, Primrose."

They hugged each other tight.

"You will come and visit me as soon as I am settled."

Primrose nodded. Her throat felt choked with tears again. She had only just found Heather and now she was to lose her.

They parted as the door behind them opened and Lady Jane entered.

"We are to leave now, Primrose, to visit Lady Gray."

"Of course. I shall see Heather to the door, then collect my bonnet." Primrose often accompanied Lady Jane when she paid morning calls on her friends.

After hugging her friend again and whispering that she hoped with all her heart Heather was happy, she ran upstairs with her head still reeling.

"That bonnet is fetching on you, dear." Lady Jane came forward and pinched Primrose's cheeks when she returned. "But you are pale still. I hope you are not coming down with something."

Primrose let Lady Jane chatter as the carriage rolled through London. She smiled and answered when required to do so, but her mind was on Heather and what she was about to do, and of course him. Benjamin bloody Hetherington.

"Lord Formby is a well-respected, wealthy man with many estates, Primrose. I want you to be especially nice to him today."

"Lord Formby? I thought we were visiting Lady Gray?"

"Indeed we are, but she is his sister you see, so there is every chance he may be there also."

Searching her memory, Primrose remembered hearing that he had six children, and his third wife had died three years ago.

"Lady Gray and I entered society together but do not see each other often."

"How nice that you are still friends then."

"Try and smile today, Primrose. Lately I have not seen you do so often. In fact, since your return you have been quite morose. Are your nerves still suffering after your adventure?"

"I'm sorry, have I been a dull companion?"

"Not dull, no, but I am worried about you. Especially after the disaster at the soirée. You have not been back into society since."

"I think it is time I went home, Lady Jane."

Primrose had thought about this a great deal and believed it was for the best. At home she could live a simple life, and when her family was there, she'd at least have some company.

"Your family left for India five days ago, Primrose. You cannot go home."

"The Putts are there, as they always have been. We rub along well together. I shall return to them."

"No, they are not. They were dismissed, and the house has been let for the year."

"I beg your pardon? I knew nothing of this."

"Your father wrote to me a week after you came to London to inform me of these plans." Lady Jane spoke calmly. Primrose was anything but. How could her family have left without speaking to her? How could they have dismissed the Putts?

"B-but where am I to go?"

"You will live with me until you are married. I enjoy your company, Primrose."

"B-but I am not going to marry! Who will wed me now, with my reputation in ruins?"

Primrose didn't like Lady Jane's smile; in fact, it made the hairs on the back of her neck stand.

"We will speak of it no more for now, dear. All I ask is that you be polite to Lord Formby if he should be there today."

"I am always polite," Primrose said as something began to take root inside her head. *Surely not?* She had to be wrong. Lady Jane would not want her wed to a man old enough to be her grandfather. She remembered then the conversation they'd had at Rossetter the day she'd returned after the abduction. *I know of a man who is desperate for a nubile young wife.*

Primrose studied the woman across from her, but Lady Jane's gaze flitted away out the carriage window.

"Is there something you are not telling me, my lady?"

"Of course not, just that Lord Formby is a good man, and it would not do to annoy him."

Unease traversed her spine.

"Are you—"

"Excellent, we are here!" Lady Jane cut off her words. Minutes later they had stepped from the carriage.

"Lady Jane, I really must insist you tell me—"

"Come along, Primrose, Lord Formby and his sister are waiting."

The trickle of unease turned into a torrent.

The entrance way was austere and dark inside. It was a huge mansion that no doubt had many rooms that servants were forced to clean and heat from sunrise to sunset during the colder months.

They followed the butler to where she now knew Lord Formby and his sister awaited them. In fact, Primrose doubted this visit was ever simply about a reunion between old friends. She felt betrayed by yet another person.

The room they entered had burgundy walls and rugs, matching brocade curtains, and dark furniture. It was gloomy and depressing, and no way did Primrose ever want to be mistress of such a place.

"Good day to you both! It is wonderful to see you again, Lady Jane," Lord Formby boomed as they were announced.

Tall, elegant, with gray hair and a face that wore the lines of his years, Primrose thought Lord Formby looked pleasant enough. However, she did not want to look at him across the breakfast table for years to come, if that was Lady Jane's intention—which she now believed it was.

"Virginia, how wonderful to meet with you again." Lord Formby's sister came to take Lady Jane's hands. Younger than her brother the woman was elegantly dressed.

"Cynthia, it is wonderful to see you also. And this is Miss Ainsley." Lady Jane introduced Primrose.

She dropped into a curtsey, then looked about for a chair that was far enough away from Lord Formby to make her comfortable.

"Come and sit, my dear." Lord Formby held out a hand toward a sofa.

"Oh no—"

"Sit, Primrose." Lady Jane took her arm and propelled her forward. To her horror, Lord Formby took the seat to her right.

"I understand you like children, Miss Ainsley. I have six."

"Yes, I do. How lovely for you."

"I want more," he said, which had Primrose stiffening. "Ring for tea, Cynthia," Lord Formby instructed his sister.

What followed was a gentle, if persistent inquisition, and by the end of it, Primrose was left in no doubt that her suspicions were correct. She was being paraded as a prospective wife to this man. The thought made her angry. Like Heather, she was about to be forced into something she had no wish to be part of. Unlike Heather, she had no money, and nowhere to run.

Primrose embraced the anger, as it took the hollowness inside her away. It gave her something to focus on other than her pathetic love for Benjamin Hetherington.

She ate, smiled, and talked, and felt her anger grow with every second she sat next to Lord Formby. The injustice of her situation stoked the rage growing inside her.

Her family had turned their backs on her and also taken away her home. She had no doubt they had hopes she would marry well and fund their next adventure. Society was shunning her through no fault of her own. Then there was Benjamin. If she didn't love him so much, she'd hate him. Which made no sense to anyone but her. *Fiend.*

When it was time to leave, Primrose made her farewells

and let Lord Formby hold her hands longer than propriety dictated. She even smiled, but inside she raged.

"Well, that went well." Lady Jane sat back on the carriage seat looking satisfied as they rolled away from Lord Formby's house.

"You had no right to do that," Primrose said calmly. No good would come from allowing the anger that she felt to show.

"To do what, Primrose?"

"You took me there with the express purpose that Lord Formby look me over as his future wife... or should I say breeding mare!" Some of her anger slipped out.

"Formby is a good man, and as no other has stepped forward, he will make you a wonderful husband." Lady Jane dropped the pretense. "You should be grateful. Good Lord, Primrose, you have to marry, and he is a wonderful prospect. Many young women would be pleased to wed such a man."

"He is old enough to be my grandfather!"

She flicked her wrist, dismissing Primrose's words, and the anger and frustration inside her climbed.

"Girls wed such men every day. He will care for you and provide you with a home of your own, and likely children. You will want for nothing in your future."

"And I am to have no say in the matter?"

"Your father has made me your guardian in his absence, and in this matter I am to make the decisions."

"I do not need a guardian."

She understood somewhere deep inside herself that Lady Jane was doing what she believed was best for Primrose.

"I will guide you through this and help you make the correct decision."

"I understand that you have done so much for me," Primrose said as calmly as the raging torrent of emotion inside her would allow. "But I will not marry unless it is my wish to do so. I will not marry a man for his money and the life he can give me. Will not... cannot," Primrose clarified.

"Don't be foolish, girl," Lady Jane snapped, no longer calm. Her voice had risen, just as it did when she was scolding a servant. "It is the only option for you, and one I insist you take!"

"No."

Lady Jane slapped the seat beside her with considerable force, in a gesture so unlike the woman, Primrose could only stare. She was not given to such displays of emotion. Lady Jane, as her mother had once said, was a woman who understood her standing in society and never deviated from what was expected from her.

"You will do this because I wish it. I have promised your family I will see you wed, therefore I insist you accept Lord Formby's proposal."

The mention of her family made Primrose's insides clench tight.

Why am I so hard to love?

"My family may not care about me, Lady Jane, but I do. I'm sorry if this upsets you, and I am of course grateful to you for all you have done for me, but I will not marry Lord Formby."

"Don't be a foolish girl, of course you will!"

"There is nothing else to be said on the matter then," Primrose said as calmly as she could. "I will find alternative arrangements."

"Where? There is nowhere else for you to go! You have no prospects and no money."

She didn't speak again as Lady Jane proceeded to talk at her for the rest of the journey, an extremely long ten minutes.

"Good day, Lady Jane," Primrose said after they'd left the carriage.

"Where are you going?"

"I need some air. I shall see you later."

"Primrose, you cannot walk about London unescorted!" Lady Jane tried to grab her arm, but Primrose evaded her. "As your mother's friend, I insist you stay!"

"I shall return to the house later. Good day." She walked swiftly along the street without looking back.

She had no destination in mind; she just needed to walk. The anger inside her did not ease as she'd hoped as she put some distance between herself and Lady Jane.

Sadness, rage, it was all there. She had no idea what to do or where to go now. But one thing she was certain of was that she would not marry Lord Formby.

Surely she could find her own way in the world? She was no fool, there must be work for her somewhere. But where would she live? Thoughts ran through her head as she struggled to come up with a plan.

Primrose had no idea how long she walked for or who or what she passed along the way. Only that she needed to keep walking before the grief caught up with her.

Keep it inside, she said over and over to herself. Because if it escaped, surely it would consume her, and how would she cope?

She hadn't realized she'd been walking to Heather's house until she stood outside the front door. She knocked and was admitted to a small parlor; her friend joined her minutes later.

"Primrose, what has happened?"

She couldn't answer as the tears finally began to fall.

CHAPTER THIRTY-TWO

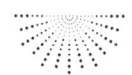

Ben travelled to London by coach, as the journey was a long one and he needed to regain his strength. Reaching his small townhouse, he greeted his staff, then fell into a chair and slept.

Upon waking he felt a great deal better. After a meal, he called for his horse and headed to where Lady Jane lived, anticipation building inside him.

He was to see her. Primrose, the woman who he now acknowledged meant a great deal to him. The woman he loved.

The words did not scare him as they once would have. Now they sounded right inside this head.

He wasn't sure what had changed inside him but something had. Perhaps because he'd nearly lost Alex? Or was it because he realized he didn't want to live without Primrose? Whatever the reason, he had to see her and make her forgive him for the way he'd behaved.

His family had given him their blessings, telling Ben they liked Primrose very much and that they would return to London soon to hopefully meet his betrothed.

He smiled at the future he foresaw for them. Lots of laughter and debates. She would listen as he spoke about steam engines, and he would listen to her discussions about plants and spend time in the gardens with her.

His heart felt fuller since acknowledging how he felt about her. He missed her desperately, and the dark places inside him were now light.

His love.

For the first time in forever, he felt a ridiculous sense of hope, and yes, freedom. He was no longer shackled by the fear that a woman would hurt him if he let her too close.

Primrose would never willingly hurt him. Her nature was too sweet for that.

Rapping on the front door, he acknowledged the stately butler.

"I wish to speak with Miss Ainsley, please."

The butler looked agitated by his request.

"Is there a problem?"

"Who is it, Perks?"

"Mr. Benjamin Hetherington, my lady."

"Send him away!"

Ben wasn't having that; he stuck his boot in the door and pushed it open, gaining entry.

"How dare you force your way inside my house, Mr. Hetherington!"

Lady Jane was standing in the entrance hall looking agitated like her butler. Something was not right. Unease crept over him.

"Where is Primrose?" Ben said with a calm he was far from feeling.

"Not here," Lady Jane said.

"I understand that, but where is she?"

The shoulders that had been rigid slumped.

"In truth, I do not know. Dear lord, I wish I did."

THE LADY'S DANGEROUS LOVE

"Care to explain what the hell you are talking about?"

She didn't flinch at his language, instead walking toward a door.

"If you will come this way I will tell you all the details. Perhaps you can find her, as I cannot."

"I don't understand what you are saying, Lady Jane."

"She has run away, Hetherington, and I don't know where to!"

"Good God," Ben slumped into a chair.

He didn't drink the tea she poured, instead sitting on the edge of his seat as she talked.

"I thought I was doing right by her. Her family do not want her and see her as a burden. You did not offer for her after she was abducted and therefore shamed in the eyes of society. So, I thought marriage to Formby would see her comfortably set up for the future. But she is not like other young ladies."

"No, she is not. Primrose has spirit," Ben said slowly. "She would never be happy with a man like Formby." He wanted to feel sympathy for this woman; she had simply done what she thought was best, but in doing so she had forced Primrose to flee. "And I do want her, but I was unable to come to London until now."

Where have you run to?

"They all turned their backs on her, as is the way when a young lady is compromised. Not that she was very popular to begin with, but it was far worse when we returned from Rossetter ."

"And yet I, the man who compromised her, am free to walk anywhere I choose without censure." Saying the words disgusted him.

"It has always been so." Lady Jane looked at him, and to Ben's mind she'd aged since she'd left Rossetter . "Do you care for Primrose, Mr. Hetherington? Was I wrong to suggest otherwise?"

"You were."

"When we received word your brother had recovered, I thought you would come to London if you cared for her. When you didn't, like her, I believed otherwise."

"I became sick with a fever myself. I was not fit to travel."

"Oh dear." She pressed a hand to her lips. "I thought you had turned your back on her."

Ben got out of his chair and began to pace. "When I returned to Rossetter House I did treat her badly, pushing her aside in my fear over my brother. But once I regained my senses I realized that Primrose is one of the most amazing women I have ever met. Where is she, Lady Jane?"

"I don't know. We went to visit Lord Formby, and during the return journey she grew agitated, saying she would not marry a man for his money and title. She then said she was going for a walk. When she finally came home, we did not speak. She went straight to her room and had her evening meal on a tray."

Ben could see Lady Jane was genuinely upset, but all he could think about was Primrose and how desperate she must have felt when she learned that Formby was to be her future husband. She must also believe he had deserted her, just as Lady Jane did.

"Did you tell her that her family did not want her?"

"To my shame, yes, I did. I told her the family home had been let and servants dismissed, and she was to stay with me until she wed."

Christ.

"I am happy to have her with me, she is excellent company, but I wanted to see her married and secure also. Surely you can see my motives were pure."

THE LADY'S DANGEROUS LOVE

He nodded, not trusting himself to speak. "Continue with your story."

"When her maid went to rouse her this morning, she was gone. Her bed had not been slept in."

The thought of Primrose walking about at night on her own in London was not a happy one for Ben.

"Where could she have gone?"

"I have sent word to her friend, Miss Fullerton Smythe, as she visited Primrose yesterday and is really the only acquaintance she has in London. I have received no reply."

"That is where I will start, then. Please furnish me with her address."

Once he had it, Ben bowed to Lady Jane.

"Find her, Hetherington, and this time don't let her go."

"I will send word when I have done so."

Once again on his horse, he rode through London a great deal faster than on the journey to Lady Jane's, his mood vastly different also. He wished Alex or Finn were here; they would help him in any way they could. But his brother was still recovering, and Finn had stayed at Rossetter to watch over him.

The Fullerton Smythes lived in a large brick townhouse in the right part of town. It had an imposing façade with grand white columns and white front steps. Many windows decorated the side facing the street, and he knew the gardens at the rear would be manicured to perfection. Appearances were everything to the Fullerton Smythes.

Lifting the brass knocker, he rapped it hard three times.

"Good day." The butler who opened the door had just the right amount of haughtiness in his expression to please his mistress.

"Here is my card." Ben handed it over. "I have come to call upon Miss Fullerton Smythe."

"She is not accepting callers today, sir."

"Then I shall call on Lord Fullerton Smythe. Please tell him I am here."

"I am afraid Lord Fullerton Smythe is from home."

"Lady Fullerton Smythe?" Ben raised a brow.

"Not accepting visitors today."

To his credit, the butler kept his face calm, but the eyes had a tight look to them that suggested he was under a great deal of strain. Ben wasn't sure what prompted him to say what he next did. Call it instinct.

"I have information about Miss Fullerton Smythe."

"One moment, please." The door was shut in his face. Not terribly polite, but he was sure the drama unfolding behind said door was the reason for that.

Something was off here also, he just wasn't sure what. But what he did know was that it involved Miss Fullerton Smythe and very likely Primrose. Dear Lord, let it involve her; let the Fullerton Smythes be able to tell him where she was.

Worry gnawed at his gut as he waited.

Where is she?

The problem was that she was impetuous, and he worried she'd stumble into something and he wouldn't be there to extract her from it.

Guilt over his treatment of her sat heavily on his shoulders. Had he been kinder, had he told her how he felt, none of this would have happened.

"If you will come this way, Lady Fullerton Smythe will speak with you."

Ben followed, admiring the pristine halls and polished floors. Was everyone forced to go about in their stockings in here?

"Mr. Benjamin Hetherington, my lady."

Lady Fullerton Smythe was seated in a high-backed chair that resembled a throne. Immaculate as always, she looked as she had every time Ben had seen her… although she did have the same tight expression on her face the butler had, and now he was closer he could see her eyes were red, very likely from crying.

"My lady." Ben bowed.

"Please, sit down, and tell me what has brought you to our humble doorstep on this day?"

He'd never liked this woman. Her every move was for effect, and she never hesitated to flaunt her status and wealth in the faces of those she saw as less worthy.

Ben already knew Primrose had been the recipient of her ill-will.

"I shall be honest with you, my lady. I am trying to locate Miss Ainsley, and as she is your daughter's friend—"

"My daughter would never befriend such a woman! The scandal surrounding that… that person is unpardonable, and I will not allow it to taint a child of mine!"

Stay calm.

"Be very careful what you say about Miss Ainsley, Lady Fullerton Smythe. She is a very dear friend to me and my family, and a particular favorite of the Duke and Duchess of Rossetter . I would not want word to get back to them that you have been speaking in derogatory terms about her."

"Everyone is speaking of her behavior!" She didn't look quite so confident now.

"Which was not her fault. She was abducted, and I saw that happen."

"She was alone with men!"

"Which, again, was not her fault." *Patience, Ben.*

She made a huffing sound but said nothing further.

"Lady Fullerton Smythe, where is your daughter? I would like to question her about Miss Ainsley."

"Sh-she is unwell!"

"I hope it's nothing serious?"

She wouldn't meet his eyes.

"No indeed, we h-hope she will be herself again in a matter of d-days."

"Are you sure I cannot speak with her?"

"Absolutely not. Heather needs her rest!"

Ben knew he wasn't about to get any more information out of the woman, so he rose to leave.

"Good day, my lady. Please pass my best wishes on to your daughter."

Ben stood out on the street minutes later and wondered what the hell he was to do next. Primrose had run away from Lady Jane's house last night, but where had she gone?

"Psst!"

Looking to the left, he saw a footman lurking behind a pillar. The man nodded to the right, which suggested to Ben he needed to move in that direction, so he started walking.

"Left," a voice behind him directed.

Ben found himself in a garden and hoped he was not about to be jumped from behind and robbed.

"Were you asking about Miss Fullerton Smythe?"

Ben turned to look at the footman.

"I was. What can you tell me about her?"

The man said nothing. Ben pulled some money out of his pocket and handed it to him.

"I would rather the lord and lady did not hear of this." The footman looked suddenly nervous.

"Of course, I will say nothing."

"They're not the easiest people to work for, you understand."

Ben didn't say anything to that, but he knew some nobility were notoriously mean-spirited to their staff.

"Please continue with the information you have about Miss Fullerton Smythe."

"A young woman called late yesterday afternoon to see the young Miss. I've not seen her here before."

"Did you hear what they said?"

"Only that she was upset, and the two young ladies hugged. Lord and Lady Fullerton Smythe were from home, so the ladies went up to Miss Fullerton Smythe's room. They stayed there for two hours. The second carriage was then called, and the young lady taken home."

"To where?"

The address was Lady Jane's residence, which told Ben it was Primrose. He had a feeling there was more, so he remained silent.

"The staff aren't meant to know, but she wasn't in her rooms this morning when the household rose, and has not been seen since."

"Miss Fullerton Smythe?"

The footman nodded. "Bill, one of the drivers, said that a young lad named Milky told him he saw Miss Fullerton Smythe leave the house in the early hours of the morning. A carriage had stopped outside, and she got in."

"Did she now," Ben said slowly, his mind whirling.

"The carriage was a hired one. Milky followed it up the street until it stopped again. Another lady was waiting there. From the boy's description it sounded like the one who visited Miss Fullerton Smythe. She got inside, and it drove away."

"Do you know where it was hired from?" Ben held out more money.

"Jessop Street stables, sir."

"Thank you, you have been very informative. I will pay for any further information you have, and you can send it here." Ben gave him his card.

He made for the stables. After handing over more money, Ben learned that a man who matched Mr. Caton's description had hired that carriage. The driver was to take them to Gretna Green.

Why the hell was Primrose accompanying Mr. Caton and Miss Fullerton Smythe to Gretna Green? He didn't have time to think about that answer. This was Primrose; she did not think like other women.

"Ben?"

"Will?" He turned to find his friend approaching.

"I had not realized you'd returned to London. I hope you left Alex well?"

"I did."

"What has you here? Are you looking at a horse?"

"No."

"Carriage?"

"No again."

Will frowned. "Have you recovered from your own illness?"

"I have, and now I must go."

Will moved left, blocking his exit. "What's going on, Ben? I can see something is bothering you."

"I have to leave, Will."

"Why?"

"Must you know the reason?" Ben needed to get moving if he had any hope of catching Primrose.

"Your brothers are not here, but I consider myself an admirable stand-in."

He stood before Ben as unmoving as a large tree trunk. He could possibly outrun Will, and likely win in a fight, but the man would not give up, that much Ben knew.

"The story is a long one."

"As you see, I have nothing pressing. The horse I came to see was not worth my time. I am also very discreet. Whatever you tell me will go no further."

"That's a lie, you're a shocking gossip."

"Well, yes, but not about anything serious," Will defended himself.

"I sometimes think it would be quite nice to be unloved. You could get about without anyone knowing in which direction you placed a foot."

"No, you don't." Will laughed. "Now tell me what is going on, Ben."

"In brief, Primrose's reputation was shredded after that incident."

"This I know."

"Lady Jane wants her to marry Lord Formby. She does not fancy the idea, and it appears she has run away with Miss Fullerton Smythe, who in turn is eloping to Gretna Green with Mr. Caton."

It took a great deal to silence William Ryder. Ben had just achieved it.

"I am now going to get on my horse and go after them, just as I suspect Lord Fullerton Smythe is doing as we speak."

"As you should, because you love Miss Ainsley." Will found his tongue. "And as I am at a loss to know what next to do, I shall accompany you."

"I could be gone for days!"

"I have two weeks before my family return. That's plenty of time to get your woman and bring her back to London."

Ben didn't argue; in fact, he may need Will's help. Shaking his head, he left the stables with Will on his heels and hoped that Primrose kept out of trouble until he reached her.

He didn't hold out much hope.

CHAPTER THIRTY-THREE

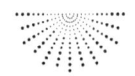

"You must simply drop me at the first village," Primrose insisted, and not for the first time.

"We will not be doing that, Miss Ainsley. Heather and I have the rest of our lives together. We can share some of it with you."

"Primrose, please. As I am involved in your elopement, I feel we must be less formal."

Heather giggled, looking extremely happy with herself. She showed none of the fear Mr. Caton wore all over his face. She seemed almost lighthearted in her relief at leaving behind London and her parents.

"And my name is Jeremy."

After Primrose had appeared on Heather's doorstep distraught over what had transpired yesterday, her friend had smuggled her up to her rooms without the servants' knowledge. Primrose had serious doubts about this. Servants knew everything.

"Mama will not be happy, you understand, Primrose. Apparently, you are unworthy of me. We both know, of course, that is utter rubbish."

Lord and Lady Fullerton Smythe were from home visiting someone. Heather had faked an illness to stay and prepare for her elopement.

It had taken her precisely fifty-two minutes to convince Primrose to run away with her and Jeremy. She'd argued, of course. It was a ridiculous thing to contemplate. But Heather would not be deterred. She had even written a hasty note that she'd summoned a footman to send to her beloved. His reply had arrived thirty minutes later.

Of course, we must take her with us!

"I do hope Father doesn't do anything foolish and take it into his head to follow us," Heather said, looking out the window. "Although we do have a good head start on him."

"We are going to marry," Jeremy said, with more force than Primrose had ever heard him use. "I will not let him take you back to London without me, my love."

"Oh, Jeremy." Heather fell into his arms.

Primrose looked out the window to let them have some privacy. The fact that she would never have what Heather and Jeremy did was a bitter pill to swallow now she knew what could be between two people who loved each other. Not that Benjamin loved her, but she loved him.

She was, however, also a realist. She knew how to be happy with her plants and would take steps to make sure she secured a future for herself… whatever those steps may be. Perhaps she could find work as a nanny; that would suit her, as she liked children. Or maybe in a shop? She had excellent handwriting and could read. Could she find work as a companion? References could be a problem, but Primrose was sure she could work around that somehow. Perhaps Heather would write her one?

"I want you to drop me at the next village we pass through." Primrose put some strength into her voice. "I have enough money to secure a room. I will then see if there is any work available."

"No," Jeremy said. "You are staying with us, and I want nothing more said on the matter, Primrose."

"Jeremy is right, we want you with us," Heather added.

"But I cannot," Primrose said. "You will be newlyweds, it is not right."

"Newlyweds with their dear friend living with them," Jeremy added.

The thought was not a happy one for Primrose. Again she was to be a burden.

They both looked determined, so for now she kept quiet.

"The trip will take four days, during which time we shall need to stop and change horses," Jeremy said.

"But the cost will be great," Heather said, opening her reticule.

"I am not without funds, Heather. Just because I am the third son does not mean I am perpetually short in the pockets. My brother is a generous man, and I have invested wisely. You will not go without."

"I have this." She handed him a necklace. "It will be worth something."

He folded her hand inside his and pushed it back toward the reticule.

"No, love. We will not need that. Now rest as much as you can. The journey will be tiring, but we must reach Gretna Green as fast as we can, or your father may catch us."

"We will not be parted," Heather said with determination on her face.

THEY CHANGED horses and ate food with haste, then took to the road again over the next four days. As the miles passed,

Primrose thought that perhaps Scotland may suit her as a place to live. It was far enough away from London that she need not run into Benjamin, and her family would not bother to come after her… or indeed care where she had gone. They would merely be pleased she was no longer a burden on them.

Primrose had come to the conclusion that she did not like her family very much anymore. She may love them, but that was another matter entirely.

"We are to stop once again soon," Jeremy said, looking at Primrose and Heather. They were all tired and needed to sleep, but knew they must press on.

"We will take some time here, just an hour or two, and I shall see if there is a room for you both to rest."

"No! Jeremy, we cannot." Heather clutched his arm.

"We can, my love. Your father will not catch us now."

They didn't put up too much of a fight, but staggered into the small posting house, and fell into the bed they were shown by the maid.

"I cannot remember a time when I was this tired," Heather said, smothering a yawn as she pulled the blankets over them. "I am so very glad you are here with me, Primrose. I have the man I love, and the only friend I truly adore."

"He is a very good man, Heather." This time it was Primrose who yawned. "I am glad you are to marry him."

"As am I." Heather's words were slurred now. "I love you, Primrose."

The words gave her a jolt as she'd never heard them before. Turning her head on the pillow, Primrose looked into the tired eyes of her friend.

"Really?"

"Really." Heather's lashes then fluttered downward.

Primrose's did the same, but this time she slept with the

knowledge that at least one person loved her. The thought warmed her to her toes.

Primrose woke first. Heather still slept deeply, so she slipped out of bed. Washing in the water provided, she changed her dress and brushed out her hair. Braiding it, she tied a ribbon around the ends, then left to find Jeremy and some food.

Dusk had fallen as she stepped outside after searching the interior of the posting house and not finding him.

"You!"

"Mr. Sanders!" Primrose tried to retreat back inside, but he grabbed her arm.

"You and that Hetherington have cost me a great deal of money, Miss Ainsley."

His face was twisted in an angry mask. He looked nothing like the immaculately presented gentleman she'd once known. His hair stood off his head, and his clothes were creased. His nose seemed to be slightly crooked now too, and bigger.

"What happened to your nose?"

"Mr. Hetherington did this, and one day I will make him pay."

Primrose opened her mouth to scream, but he slapped his hand over it. She then felt the stab of a blade in her stomach.

"Scream and I will stab you."

"How did you get off the boat?" Primrose mumbled.

"I was lowered over the side in a rowboat," he snarled, removing his hand. "I could not go to France, as the man who commissioned me to steal that book paid me a large sum of money in advance. He would have been most displeased."

Her luck had not improved, it seemed. She was now in the hands of this man again.

"So you are going to Scotland?"

"I have another commission there, and this time no one will stop me from achieving it and receiving the money."

"Commission," Primrose scoffed. "You are a common thief, Mr. Sanders, and nothing more."

"Why are you here? Don't tell me you and Hetherington are making a run for Gretna Green?" The smug look on his face had her wanting to smack it, but as the knife was still pressed into her she did not. If she could keep him talking long enough surely someone would see her talking to him?

"No. I am alone and making my way there for work."

She did not want him to know about Heather or Jeremy, and hoped they would simply appear and the distraction would help her escape the clutches of Sanders again.

"Let me go and you will never see me again, I promise," she said.

"No. I'm not sure what to do with you, but someone needs to pay for what happened to me."

"You will not get away with kidnapping me like you did last time," Primrose said, attempting to sound brave.

"As you have said, you are alone, Miss Ainsley, and at my mercy. I fail to see who will stop me. So it would be in your best interests to do exactly as I say."

Alone, as I always am. The thought was a depressing one, but still she did not want to let this man win. She had a life to live, and perhaps it would not be with Benjamin or anyone she loved, but she still wanted to live it. It was strange how she suddenly realized that.

"But you have no need of me. I can give you nothing, and no one will pay you for my return. It is foolish to take me with you on a whim, Mr. Sanders. We loathe each other."

His eyes suddenly changed, and Primrose felt unease slither down her spine.

"I had not realized quite how pretty you are, Miss Ainsley. Perhaps I will have a use for you after all."

"No!" She tried to get free, but the knife dug into her skin.

"Now we are going to walk to my carriage. Make one wrong move and I will kill you where you stand."

Primrose walked to the carriage that awaited Mr. Sanders. Benjamin was not here to save her this time, so she would have to save herself.

"I won't let you hurt me," she said. "I'll kill you before I allow that."

He opened the carriage door and pushed her inside, issuing orders to the driver.

"Sit and be quiet," he said, joining her.

"You do realize how foolish this is, don't you?" Primrose tried again to get him to release her.

They were now rolling out of the courtyard and onto the main road. A horse and rider galloped past them, but they were moving too fast for her to alert them that she was being abducted... again.

"What possible reason could you have to take me with you other than vengeance?"

"It's as good a reason as any, but I have other uses for you."

"I will not let you touch me!"

Primrose didn't like the calculating look in his eyes. "I have no wish to touch you, but I think you are going to make me some money, Miss Ainsley. In fact, I think I may have found a way to recoup my losses after losing the Clipper book."

Primrose battled down her fear.

"A word of advice, Mr. Sanders. It would not pay you to close your eyes, as you will not like the consequences if you do."

He barked out a laugh. "You're an entertaining woman,

Miss Ainsley, even if an infuriating one. But I will tie you up if I need to sleep. For now, I will contemplate how happy my friends are going to be when I present them with you. They own a brothel in Edinburgh, you see. Its specialty is providing clients with young innocent women."

CHAPTER THIRTY-FOUR

Ben and Will had been following the trail of Primrose, Jeremy Caton, and Miss Fullerton Smythe for three days.

"Strangely, we have yet to encounter Lord Fullerton Smythe," Will said, standing in his stirrups to ease his aching muscles. "And yet we know by the descriptions matching him that he is ahead of us. I am amazed at his stamina. I would have thought he'd have given up by now."

"Perhaps he has caught his daughter?"

"But not returned, or we would have seen the carriage as this is the main road back to London."

They were only a day's ride from Scotland now, and he hoped Primrose was still with her friends and hadn't decided to leave them somewhere on the way.

Moving to one side of the road as a carriage approached at speed, Ben tried to look in the window. A pale face appeared.

"Primrose!"

She opened her mouth and screamed something, and then someone pulled her back. Ben thought it was Sanders.

What the hell is that man doing here? How did he get his hands on her again? This time Ben was killing him.

"Sanders has her!"

He turned his horse and set off after the carriage, that had picked up speed, at a gallop. He and Will quickly drew alongside, but it was about to pass over a narrow bridge, so he had to pull in behind it.

Horrified, he watched the door open, and then Primrose was being thrown out. He couldn't reach her as she flew through the air and then plummeted down toward the water.

"Christ. Primrose!" Ben roared her name as he galloped over the bridge and down the bank. Dismounting, he ran to the water's edge, ripping off his jacket as he prepared to jump in.

"St-stop!" She surfaced, spluttering. "You don't need to get w-wet!"

Ignoring her, he waded in and grabbed her, hauling her into his arms.

"Primrose, tell me you are all right?"

"I am." She pushed against his chest. "Release me, please."

"Never."

She pushed against him harder, forcing him to stumble backward, then walked around him and out of the water. "Good day."

"Where in God's name are you going?" Ben followed.

"Back to the inn."

"Primrose." He grabbed her arm and turned her to face him. "Sanders just threw you out of a carriage. Stop and let me take care of you. You could be injured."

"I am quite well. Good day."

"Will you just stop and listen to me!"

She wouldn't look at him. Her hair had come loose and was a wet tangle of curls. She was shivering, as the weather was cooler here, and her clothes clung to her lovely body. He felt the tension that had gripped him when he'd been in London ease.

Primrose was here with him and unhurt. He bent to grab his jacket and wrapped it around her shoulders.

"We have n-nothing to say to each other."

"Look at me."

"I d-don't want to look at you."

"Please look at me."

"You can carry on with your journey now."

"I am not here by chance, Primrose."

"Why are you here, Mr. Hetherington?" Her eyes were on his left shoulder.

"I came to find you."

She looked at him then, and he saw the utter devastation in her lovely eyes.

"Why?"

"Because I was wrong to speak to you as I did."

"You c-came all this way to apologize?" she scoffed, and it was a brittle sound. Benjamin realized just how much pain had been inflicted on this woman by him, her family, society, and Lady Jane.

"I'm sorry I hurt you, Primrose." He cupped her cheeks. They were ice cold.

"V-very well, you have apologized, although why you had to c-come all this way to do it I have no idea. Now I must leave, as it is g-getting cold."

"It is, but before we do leave, I want to tell you something else."

"What?" She tried to pull out of his arms again, but Ben gave her a little shake.

"Stop fighting me and listen."

"Say it then!"

"I love you."

If he'd thought that would make her happy, he was sadly mistaken. She was furious.

"Don't you dare lie to me!" Her blue eyes fired to life.

"I'm not. I love you."

"No, you d-don't! I told you, people don't love me… well that's actually not true. Heather does, but no one else." She wrenched out of his arms and stomped away. "It is wrong of you t-to make fun of me with your lies."

She sounded like she was going to cry.

Ben looked to where Will stood with Ben's horse a few feet away. He was listening unashamedly. His friend made a shooing motion that had Ben following Primrose.

"Primrose." He caught her. "You are loveable, and I know this because I love you."

She wouldn't look at him, just kept walking, her shoes squelching, as were his boots. The wind was cold, and soon she'd be frozen.

"Is this your idea of f-fun, Mr. Hetherington? Because I had once thought better of you."

"Damn it, will you just stop, woman!" Ben was starting to get angry. "I love you!"

She stopped before him suddenly, and he had to wrap his arms around her so he didn't flatten her.

"Benjamin?" She turned, pressing her hands into this chest. "I-I h-have had a challenging few d-days… weeks actually."

"I know you have, sweetheart." He cupped her cheeks, tilting her face so their eyes met.

"I d-don't think I will cope if you are lying to me."

"I'm not. I love you. It took what happened to Alex, and then me falling ill—"

"You've been ill? Are you all right? What happened?"

It humbled him that she was so concerned.

"I'm fine now. But what I'm trying to say is that it took

those things happening to make me realize I was a fool to deny my feelings for you."

"Oh." Her mouth formed a perfect O, so he kissed her chilled lips.

He saw the hope in her blue eyes when he pulled back, and it made his chest ache.

"Miss Primrose Ainsley, I love you and desperately want to marry you. I don't want to live a day without you. Please put me out of my misery and say yes."

"You said horrible things to me. Mean things, Benjamin, and I did not deserve them."

"I know, forgive me. I was scared for Alex, but more importantly scared of my growing feelings for you."

She looked at him then, reading his expression.

"Why did you take so long to come for me?"

"I was ill, and when I was well again you'd gone. I came to London as soon as I could, love, I promise."

"Oh… I, well, it's just that I…. Do you really love me?"

"Yes, I really love you."

"Oh, Benjamin." She threw herself at him, and of course Ben caught her. "I love you, too."

"I had hoped that was the case. And now we've sorted that out, can we go somewhere and get warm?"

"I believe I can help with that." Will arrived. "Hello, Miss Ainsley."

"Lord Ryder." She attempted to bob a curtsey, but Ben wouldn't let her go.

"There is a posting house not far from here," she said when she was seated on his horse.

"Excellent, let's go." Ben climbed on behind her and pulled her back into his arms. "And just so you know, you are completely loveable."

Her little sigh made him smile.

"But I need to tell you both something."

"Mr. Caton and Miss Fullerton Smythe are in the posting house, as they are eloping to Gretna Green?" Ben said.

"Yes. How did you know that?" She looked up at him.

"How is it you think I am here? I was told by a footman of the Fullerton Smythes' that Miss Fullerton Smythe had eloped and that you were accompanying her."

"Servants really do know everything, don't they, Benjamin?"

"Yes. Now tell me if I'm right, and that was Sanders who threw you from that carriage, Primrose?"

"Yes. He's going to Scotland to steal something else. I was to be sold to his friends who own a brothel as punishment for foiling his last commission."

Ben tightened his arms around her at the thought of what could have awaited her in Scotland.

"That man needs to be dealt with," Will said, and Ben agreed. They would see it done with a little help from Ace, who had many contacts.

They pulled in to a small posting house and stabled the horses a few minutes later. It was as they approached the building that they heard raised voices.

"I think Lord Fullerton Smythe has arrived," Ben said as they entered.

"Oh dear, that's not good," Primrose said, clutching his hand tight.

"Go up those stairs and change, love, and we will see what's happening," Ben said to her.

To his surprise, she nodded. He kissed her before she left.

"I like her," Will said.

"Me too."

They found Jeremy Caton, Miss Fullerton Smythe, and her father in a parlor.

"You'll come home with me now!" Lord Fullerton Smythe was roaring.

"No, Father, I will not. I am to marry Jeremy."

The runaway couple were standing together holding hands.

"Good day to you all," Will said.

"Ryder! Hetherington!" Lord Fullerton Smythe looked ill at seeing them.

"Good lord, what has Mr. Caton and Miss Fullerton Smythe here, and her without a maid?" Ben said, pretending to look shocked. "Surely this is not what it appears?" He winked at Jeremy.

"My daughter has been with me the entire time, Hetherington. Mr. Caton has just arrived," Lord Fullerton Smythe bluffed.

"Oh now, you don't expect us to believe that, do you, my lord?" Ben said.

"Why are you wet?" Miss Fullerton Smythe asked. "Have you found Primrose?"

"I have. She is at present getting changed."

"Thank God." She slumped into Caton. He held her close. "I was so worried she'd run off, as she had a silly notion we should be alone."

"Release her!"

"Lord Fullerton Smythe, if you do not let these young people wed, I will return to London and tell everyone who will listen that your daughter has been compromised," Will said in a conversational tone. "If you do consent, then we will all go back, they can have the grand wedding your wife wishes, and no one will know she has even left London."

"I spoke with your wife, and she told me Miss Fullerton Smythe is unwell, so I'm sure that as long as she is not seen, your daughter's reputation will remain pristine," Ben added.

It took a bit more convincing, but eventually Lord Fullerton Smythe gave in.

"You must travel with the Fullerton Smythes, my love,

and I will follow." Ben intercepted Primrose as she came back down the stairs.

"But I don't want to leave you." She wore a simple cream day dress, and her hair was in a long braid. She looked so beautiful that his chest ached.

"You're not. I'll follow, I promise."

She looked worried.

"Primrose, I love you, and I will always love you. Nothing will ever change that. Put your faith in me."

"I want to."

"But no one has ever given you reason to trust them?" Ben took her into his arms. "But I will, if you'll give me a chance to."

"I do trust you."

"Excellent. Now, all you have to do is stay out of trouble, and the water, until we reach London and all will go well."

That made her smile.

"I have never loved anyone like I do you, Benjamin."

"I feel the same way, my sweet. When we are married you can tell me that every day, at least twice… possibly more."

Her smile would have melted even the most hardened of hearts.

CHAPTER THIRTY-FIVE

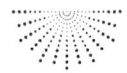

Primrose refrained from pinching herself as she and Heather stood outside the church. Looking up at the imposing façade she could hardly believe that Benjamin awaited her inside. Today they were to be married, and at her friend's insistence they were to do so together.

"You looked beautiful, Miss Ainsley."

She turned and saw the Duke of Rossetter. He was dressed immaculately and looked every inch his title.

"Thank you, your Grace."

"Will you call me Joseph?"

"Thank you, it would be my honor."

"And it would be my honor to walk you down the aisle, Primrose."

She didn't know what to say. Tears filled her eyes and choked her throat, and she had a terrible feeling she would be sobbing loudly soon.

"I don't understand?"

"As your father is out of the country and Lord Fullerton Smythe already has one beautiful lady on his arm, I thought

I'd stand in and take your father's place. If you will accept, of course?"

"Take his arm, Primrose," Heather ordered her.

"I don't know what to say," Primrose whispered.

He simply took her hand and placed it on his arm, patting it with one big gloved hand.

"Lead on, Lord Fullerton Smythe," the duke said in his deep voice.

They walked into the church and a hush fell over the guests. Some gasped as they saw her on the arm of the duke; others sighed.

Mrs. Fletcher, Lady Ryder, and their husbands smiled. Lady Althea and Mr. Dillinger did the same. Her soon-to-be sisters-in-law waved. Looking down the aisle, she found Benjamin flanked by his brothers.

"Oh Lord, he loves me."

"Yes, he does, and isn't that a splendid thing," the duke said calmly.

"It really is," she whispered, smiling. "I never thought that would happen."

"Being loved?"

"Yes," Primrose whispered as she smiled at the Sinclair and Raven families. She was so happy they had come, as they had visited her regularly at Lady Jane's house.

"Everyone is loveable, Primrose, it just takes that special someone to see it."

Primrose didn't reply, she simply nodded. Ben had turned to look at her, and the words remained lodged in her throat.

BEN HAD NEVER SEEN anyone as beautiful as Primrose at that moment. She looked like an angel on the arm of the Duke of Rossetter . His angel. Feisty, confrontational, and every inch the woman he loved.

Her dress was lemon satin, the skirts swirled around her legs as she walked. Her hair was pinned in a mass of curls, and on her head was a simple circlet of flowers. Every inch of her was exquisite.

"Hello," he said as she arrived at his side.

"Benjamin, are you—"

"We are standing at the altar, Primrose, in front of hundreds of guests. Yes, I am sure I want to marry you, there is no need to keep asking me."

She had done so every day since he'd told her he loved her. Ben understood why. Primrose had never been loved before and was just getting used to the concept. He would keep reassuring her until she was.

The minister cleared his throat, but Ben ignored him. He took her hands in his and looked deep into her eyes.

"You are my life now, Primrose. My heart is yours to break, my sweet. Tend it with care."

"Oh, Benjamin, I do love you."

"Then if you are sure, shall we let the minister begin the service?"

"Yes, please." She turned and smiled at the man who was waiting patiently. Faced with so much beauty, he smiled back.

"Dearly beloved, we are gathered here today…."

THE END